Elena's Conquest

Elena's Conquest

LISETTE ALLEN

BLACK
lace

Black Lace novels are sexual fantasies.
In real life, make sure you practise safe sex.

First published in 1994 by
Black Lace
332 Ladbroke Grove
London
W10 5AH

Typeset by CentraCet Limited, Cambridge
Printed and bound by Cox & Wyman Ltd, Reading,
Berks

ISBN 0 352 32950 5

Summer, 1070 AD

Chapter One

With a rebellious little sigh, Elena put down her basket on the dusty flagstones. It was still only half-full. But the day was so hot; far too hot to be gathering herbs for old Sister Winifred's medicinal salves!

Overhead, the sun burned down from a cloudless blue summer sky, its heat trapped within the mellow stone walls of the little herb garden. Elena heard the chapel bell tolling noon, its silvery chimes hanging heavy in the still air. White doves murmured sleepily in the eaves. The dark, thick forest that surrounded the convent was silent, as if waiting for something to happen.

But nothing ever did happen here at this remote little convent of Linby, lost in the northern wilds between the hills and the sea – this place where Elena had spent nearly all her life. And their very remoteness, Sister Winifred would remind her severely, was why they were safe – why their impoverished, tiny community had survived, when all around them the king's soldiers were wreaking savage punishment for the great Saxon uprising last winter. Elena had heard murmurs of terrible happenings, rumours of harsh bloodshed, like

3

the rustling of the leaves in the forest before a storm. She'd heard that at Thoresfield, the great Norman stronghold to the south, the king had installed the notorious Aimery le Sabrenn as commander of the garrison. At the very mention of his name, the nuns crossed themselves, as if to ward off evil.

But nothing had changed here at Linby, except that perhaps food was harder to come by than ever, and people were more fearful, more wary of strangers. Just occasionally, they had visitors; travellers who stopped for a night or two with the old priest, Father Wulfstan; mysterious, hungry-looking men who rested and moved on quickly. Otherwise, here in the little convent, they were shut off from the world. And this, thought Elena, with a sudden pang, was to be her life, for ever.

There were some travellers staying with the priest at the moment. Elena knew, because yesterday she'd been ordered to take some of the nuns' meagre rye loaves over to the priest's little cottage. She'd not gone inside; the priest's slatternly housekeeper had taken the bread from her quickly, then given her a bundle of tallow candles that the priest wanted taking to the chapel, and bade her be gone.

Elena had turned slowly back along the path to the convent – and then, through the trees, she'd seen the man. He was coming towards her, heading purposefully for the priest's house; tall and fair-haired, holding himself proudly in spite of his shabby clothes. Elena's heart skipped a beat; Sister Winifred had told her sternly that she must never, ever talk to Father Wulfstan's visitors. But this man, who was perhaps not much older than herself, was blocking her path! Catching her breath, she dipped clumsily to one side to avoid him; the tallow candles slipped from her basket and scattered on the ground.

The man bent swiftly to gather them up, while Elena stood by helplessly, her face burning with confusion. He placed the candles carefully in her basket, and said,

'They are undamaged. I'm sorry if I startled you – you are from the convent?'

'Yes – I must take these candles to the chapel.'

He still barred her way, assessing her carefully, taking in the long white veil that had slipped askew as usual over her thick blonde hair, and the shabby grey gown that concealed her slender figure. 'So,' the tall man said, 'they've shut you up here? With only those old nuns for company? What have you done to deserve such punishment?'

Elena, startled by his direct question, couldn't bear to be disloyal to the kindly nuns. 'The sisters have been good to me! My parents died of the fever when I was but a child – I was left with nothing, so they took me in, gave me a home.'

She was uneasily aware all the time of his eyes burning into her. Vivid blue eyes, that burned with fire in his tanned, masculine face. Her heart thudded uncomfortably. How different he was to the men she was used to; the worn, kindly old priest, the haggard peasants who scraped a living from the forest clearing. Something stirred restlessly within her as she gazed helplessly up at this tall, golden-haired Saxon. She caught a glimpse of smooth, sunburned skin at the base of his throat, where his tunic lay open, and she felt her mouth go dry.

'You are too beautiful,' he was saying softly, 'to be locked away here. Yes, beautiful. Don't you realise it? Has no-one ever told you?'

'I – I know that it is wicked to be vain,' stammered Elena.

'Vain?' smiled the disturbing man. 'It is not vain to know that you are beautiful, it is God's gift!' He lifted one hand and softly touched her blushing cheek. 'You should not let them shut you away. Those nuns are like old carrion crows, preying on your youth and innocence.'

In the distance, through the trees, Elena caught sight

of Sister Winifred looking out anxiously for her. 'I must go!' she blurted out desperately.

The golden-haired man had shrugged, and watched her with narrowed, thoughtful eyes as she hurried back to the convent in confusion.

That encounter had made Elena strangely restless. Locked away here, he said. Yes, she was! And he had told her she was beautiful; but surely, he himself was beautiful, with his vibrant, masculine features, and his strong body so tautly muscled beneath his shabby clothing! Last night, she had dreamed strange, disturbing dreams that were shadowy and dark. She often had dreams, but the nuns told her that it was wrong, and she must forget them.

This time, she dreamed that she was lost, alone in the forest, and a man riding by saw her and came slowly towards her. She knew it was sinful of her; but instead of running away she found herself drawn towards him, as if under a spell. He held out his arms, and she felt her heart fill with happiness. But as she ran into his embrace and looked up into his face, expecting to see the tanned Saxon features of Father Wulfstan's nameless guest, she felt a terrible, deadly chill strike into her heart. *The man who held her was one of the king's soldiers* . . .

Even now, here in the familiar safety of the little walled garden, she felt a strange tightening in her stomach as she remembered the alien horseman of her dream. Her rough linen shift chafed suddenly at her breasts; her hand moved instinctively to adjust her gown, and she discovered, with a little, juddering shock, that her nipples were swollen and hard. She snatched away her fingers as if they had been burned, aware that her breathing had become shallow and ragged.

The nuns had always instructed her that it was the work of the devil himself to even think about – let alone touch – your own flesh. Elena always tried to accept

6

their rulings without question. But her dream had unsettled her, and she knew, without a doubt, that it would return.

Her lips felt full and slightly swollen; she moistened them and tried hard to fight down the strange yearning that filled her tender body. It was the heat, she told herself desperately, that made her feel so restless. Oh, but she was wicked. Perhaps too wicked to become a nun! She must do penance for her sinfulness, for feeling this aching dissatisfaction with her fate when all around her people were suffering so much as a result of King William's punishment of the rebels.

But even as she resolved to make her confession to Father Wulfstan, she knew, with a quiet feeling of despair, that she would never forget the dark, unknown stranger in her dream.

The familiar, everyday sound of the chapel bell broke into her anguished thoughts. Elena jumped from the stone bench and picked up her wicker-basket hastily. She would be late for the service! How quickly this last hour had gone!

Then she realised that something was wrong. The chapel bell was not tolling the hour steadily and calmly, as usual. Instead, it was being pealed in panic, almost desperation, over and over. A cracked, uneven sound. Elena froze to the spot, suddenly cold in the sunlight. In disbelief, she heard the sound of horses' hooves; of people running; people shouting; doors slamming.

'The Normans! God help us, the Normans are upon us – ,The hoarse cry broke off, and somewhere a woman's high-pitched voice lifted in a scream. The doves rose clamouring from beneath the eaves. Iron-shod hooves clattered on the cobbles of the courtyard; harsh foreign voices cursed aloud. Elena heard the sound of steel being drawn, and smelled the stink of burning thatch. Trapped by fire or slaughtered by Norman steel – how many others had died like this?

Her heart hammering wildly, Elena ran out of the

little walled garden and stopped, transfixed by terror. There were mounted soldiers in the courtyard – rough men-at-arms in stained leather jerkins. Aimery le Sabrenn's soldiers had found them at last! And one of them had his swordpoint at the old priest's throat. Poor Father Wulfstan, who'd herded the terrified nuns indoors, and run out of the little chapel to face *this* . . .

The soldier was threatening the priest in a low, menacing voice. 'The rebels, old priest – the Saxon rebels. We know you harbour them on their travels, give them shelter. Where have you hidden them? Tell us, or it will be the worse for you, you old fool!'

Elena listened in anguish. *The rebels.* Father Wulfstan's mysterious visitors, who came and went with such secrecy – the tall Saxon who had spoken to her yesterday . . .

In a flash Elena understood it all. The soldiers from the great stronghold of Thoresfield had come here because Father Wulfstan was sheltering Saxon rebels! She let out a little cry of despair and one of the horsemen, on hearing her voice, wheeled round to face her. His horse, startled, reared up, and its great forequarters plunged down towards her.

A sudden blinding pain seared Elena's senses as a flailing hoof caught her on the side of her head. She called out in terror, and then the blackness engulfed her.

Darkness fell early in the forest that night. It was still hot and sultry, with the threat of thunder hanging in the air. The light of burning torches, held on high by the men who rode slowly on horseback, cast grotesque shadows on the wavering line of figures that tramped with bowed heads southwards along the forest track. Now and then, someone slipped or stumbled, jerking at the line of coarse rope that bound each one tautly by the wrists. Whenever this happened, the lash of a horseman's whip would hiss through the air, and everyone would tense involuntarily as they waited for the scream. Afterwards, the silence would be strangely intense.

Back at the rear of the roped line, someone missed a step, slipping on the sodden leaf mould. A mounted guard, his flaming torch held high, cursed and moved his big horse back towards the offender.

'God damn these Saxon rebels,' he muttered. 'More trouble than they're worth . . .' Then he saw who had fallen, and smiled slowly.

The prisoner, who was desperately scrambling up before he could reach her, was female. The flickering light from his torch danced mockingly over the tangled fair curls that tumbled to her shoulders. The plain grey gown, that clung to her slender figure, was stained with mud from her fall. She was one of the little prisoners they'd taken from the convent – the convent that sheltered those cursed Saxon rebels.

His thin lips curled suddenly, and he leaned across the high pommel of his saddle, his dark Norman face keen with sudden anticipation.

'Pick your feet up, convent brat!' His voice was silky and slow as he fingered the leather whip in his belt. 'Or I'll give you reason enough to move . . .'

The Saxon prisoner looked up in sharp fear as she was dragged along by the thick hemp rope. Already, he could see, her fragile wrists had been rubbed raw.

Blood of Christ, he breathed to himself, but this one was a little beauty. Her features were delicate and regular, her wide, terrified eyes a dark, sultry blue such as he'd never seen before, and her small pink mouth was full and ripe. Even the drab grey of the hideous convent gown couldn't conceal the high swell of those rounded little breasts. He moistened his lips. A nun? A disguise, most like. Yet more evidence of the rebels' cunning ways.

She said, in a low, broken French, 'I pray your forgiveness, sire. There was a branch across the path.'

9

The Norman gave a harsh laugh. So she knew their language! An educated bitch! 'Save your prayers, little sister,' he jeered, his white teeth gleaming in his coarsely handsome face. 'You'll need all the prayers you can think of where you're going – to the stronghold of Aimery le Sabrenn, lord of Thoresfield!'

He saw how the wench shuddered and briefly touched the crude wooden cross that hung on a thong of leather at her breasts. So, she'd heard of the Breton lord Aimery. The devil himself. She knew what she was in for.

He felt a sudden, urgent need for this fair-haired Saxon maid. His eyes narrowed as he rode alongside her, and he licked his dry mouth, feeling the familiar ache in his loins, the tightening. Damn le Sabrenn, he thought suddenly. Hadn't their fine lord started out as a Breton mercenary, no better than the rest of them? Would he miss one of these Saxon sluts that they'd picked up along with the rebels? Why, with a bit of luck, he wouldn't even know she was missing! Surreptitiously he adjusted his constricting breeches, stroking himself briefly as he did so, like a secret promise. Later, perhaps. Later, he would show this little slut what a real man was made of.

He rode back to his place at the front of the procession, his smoking torch held high. The image of the blonde wench from the convent inflamed his blood.

Elena watched him ride off with a strange, sick feeling in the pit of her stomach. She couldn't forget the way he'd looked at her, with that hungry light in his dark eyes. She swallowed down the nausea that suddenly shook her, and struggled to keep walking, though she didn't know how much longer she could go on. The rope had rubbed the skin from her wrists. Her thin leather shoes were almost worn through, and her tender feet were cut and bruised.

Was it worth going on? Shouldn't she just refuse, and lie there? If she did, they would cut her free of the rope, and then they'd flog her. Already on this nightmare journey she'd seen strong men quail at the floggings. Yet could it be worse than where they were going? To the vile stronghold of the Breton lord Aimery le Sabrenn, William the Conqueror's notorious commander.

Even at their remote little convent, she'd heard of him. The nuns whispered of unspeakable happenings, of some strange, dark evil that Elena could only guess at. They said that he had personal reason to hate all Saxons with a hard, relentless fury.

The twisted black branches of the forest reached out to grip her, like fingers tearing at her face. An owl cried and swooped low in front of her. Elena whimpered softly in her fear.

Her head still throbbed dully from where the plunging horse's hoof had struck her. When she had at last recovered consciousness, she had found herself lying in a cart, on filthy, soiled straw, along with other prisoners who were too weak to walk. The jogging motion of the cart along the rutted forest track had made her feel sick; the stench of the other prisoners, all sick or badly wounded, made her senses swim. When the man who was guarding them sloped off into the bushes to relieve himself, she had slipped from the back of the cart and tried to run.

She hadn't got far. Sneeringly, they had told her that if she was well enough to run, she was well enough to walk. Roped into line with the rest of the prisoners, she began her long walk into captivity, south to the stronghold of Thoresfield. They told her that she was a serf now, the property of Aimery le Sabrenn, great lord and friend of the king, persecutor of Saxons. This surely was her punishment for her rebellious, restless thoughts. 'Oh, sweet Mary, blessed Mother of God,' Elena muttered in despair. 'Help me in my hour of need . . .' A sob broke in her throat. 'Help me. *Please* . . .'

* * *

11

It was almost midnight when at last the commander of the guards ordered them to halt in a small, grassy clearing near a half-ruined hovel. As soon as the ropes were untied a man tried to run off into the trees. The other captives watched in despairing apathy as a guard on horseback quickly pursued him and dealt him such a vicious blow with the heel of his whip that he slumped unconscious to the ground. He lay where he fell in the darkness beyond the circle of torchlight, because nobody dared to go and help him. Elena watched it all in horror, her tender heart torn with pity for the poor man.

After that, the guards moved round on foot, tossing out hunks of coarse dry bread and passing round leather skins of brackish water.

The water went quickly, because the night was still oppressively hot; and by the time the waterskin reached Elena, it was almost empty. She took a small sip to wash the dust from her throat, and then, looking round quickly to make sure no-one was looking, she hid it beneath the folds of her grey dress. Then she moved silently towards the edge of the clearing, searching in the darkness of the overhanging trees for the fallen man.

She found him. He was conscious now, but his face was almost grey in the shadows, and a trickle of blood ran from his forehead, darkening his long fair hair. With a gasp of horror, Elena recognised him as the man who had spoken to her only yesterday as she hurried back from the priest's house. One of Father Wulfstan's guests – one of the rebels! She swallowed down her sudden, sharp distress at seeing him here, like this.

He looked up, dazed, at the slim, beautiful girl in the grey dress who knelt beside him. 'It's you . . . the girl from the convent . . .'

'Here is some water,' Elena whispered. 'Please drink it.'

The Saxon managed to raise himself carefully on one

elbow, though he grimaced with the pain. She held the waterskin to his parched lips and he swallowed feebly. Then he lay back on the ground.

'I have brought this upon you,' he muttered. 'And now you're going to the devil's lair. God help you, sweet maid.'

Again, Elena felt that tight constriction round her heart at the mention of Aimery le Sabrenn. The devil's lair? 'W . . . what do you mean?' she faltered.

The man's head twisted round in alarm. 'Hush! Be silent – ' Too late, Elena heard the crunching of boots through the undergrowth behind her. As she whirled round, a cry on her lips, a rough hand caught at her shoulder.

The Saxon man struggled to raise himself from the ground. 'Let her go, damn you! Vile Norman scum—'

The guard silenced him with a swift blow to the stomach that had him doubled up. Then he turned to the girl; and Elena realised, with a shudder of fear, that he was the mounted guard who'd spoken to her earlier and watched her in such a disturbing way.

'Well, well,' he said softly. 'The little convent brat. Like to explain what you were doing here, would you? With *him*?'

Elena struggled to free herself, but his strong hands dug into her shoulders. He was big and muscular, with a dark, floridly handsome face, and she could smell the wine he'd been drinking.

'I brought him water!' she retorted defiantly, hoping he wouldn't notice how her voice shook in secret fear. 'Poor man – he was injured! I couldn't just leave him there!'

His calloused thumbs were fondling her shoulders through the thin material of her gown. He seemed to be breathing strangely, and something in his hot, dark gaze really frightened her. 'A soft little heart, eh?' he said, grinning slowly. 'By Christ, but I've heard all about you convent brats. Desperate for it, are you,

13

sweetheart? Well, I've got good news for you – no need to make do with a filthy Saxon rebel – '

'I don't know what you're talking about! Let me go, please, you're hurting me . . .' But before she could even scream, the soldier's eager mouth had come down thickly on hers, his hot, rasping tongue capturing the inner tenderness of her lips. In desperation she struggled to push him off, but her anguished efforts seemed to excite him all the more. He clutched her helpless body hard against his; she whimpered beneath his fierce kiss and struggled again, but his hands pinioned her already sore wrists with iron strength.

'Here's one juicy little prize our fine lord Aimery won't get to first!' the soldier muttered thickly. Then he reached for the neck of her dress, and ripped at the coarse grey wool; it parted easily, as did her white linen shift beneath it. He went very still then, and his grip slackened involuntarily as he gazed with hungry avid eyes at Elena's small white breasts.

With a cry of alarm, Elena tried to turn and run, but he caught her and threw her roughly to the ground, pinning her down with the weight of his heavily-muscled body even as she kicked and struggled wildly beneath him.

'Oh, my little beauty,' he muttered as he gazed at her soft nakedness. 'My little dove . . .' And he moistened his thin, curling lips as he kneeled in homage over her prostrate form.

He bent low over her, to kiss her again; she jerked her head to one side in an effort to escape, but he'd got her pinned down, his hands holding her wrists against the ground on either side of her head, while his leather-clad thighs straddled hers. He gazed with lascivious eyes at the blue-veined whiteness of her innocent breasts; then, with a sudden groan, he plunged his head down and started to lick at her tender nipples with his hot, wet mouth.

Elena felt her body arch in spasm. She was fighting

him wildly, wrenching herself from side to side beneath him. 'Get off me! You brute – '

'You can stop pretending now, wench,' the soldier chuckled. 'The women back at the camp beg me for this, just as you would if I stopped now! Such lovely little breasts; so perfect, so white, my sweetheart . . .'

Still Elena fought on, though she was all but over-powered by the maleness of him, by the harsh threat of his powerfully muscled shoulders, his demanding mouth. Sweet heaven . . .'

She tried to kick him. With a harsh oath, the man swiftly pushed both her hands together on the ground behind her head, so that he had one hand free. As Elena felt her strength failing, she watched with wide, horror-stricken eyes as he fumbled with his leather tunic, pulling it up somehow and reaching under it. He seemed to be stroking and rubbing feverishly at himself, while his eyes began to glaze over with satisfaction.

'Ah, my little Saxon,' he sighed, 'I've been longing for this since first I laid eyes on you.'

Elena squeezed her eyes shut tightly and prayed for this nightmare to end. It must be a nightmare, mustn't it? With this hateful man, muttering and trembling above her.

She opened her eyes again to make one last, desper-ate plea. 'You must let me go. You must!'

The words died on her lips. Because what met her eyes was a rigid, swollen shaft of flesh. The soldier gripped it in his hand, seeming to stroke it in some private ecstasy as he gazed adoringly at her naked breasts. Seeing how her eyes opened in horror, he went very still, watching her, letting her get the full impact of his swollen penis. 'Not seen one of these before, my little nun?' he whispered softly, cajolingly. 'There's many a fine lady like yourself begged me for a sight of this, I can tell you, so take a good look . . .' He rubbed his hand slowly, luxuriantly, along the rigid shaft and a drop of clear moisture gleamed and dropped, glistening, on to her tender breast. He bent, adoringly, to lick it off her skin.

Elena screamed, but the sound was choked in her dry throat as the man lunged forwards and covered her mouth with a hot, devouring kiss. Darkness engulfed her. And then, in the stifling stillness of that forest clearing, there was a sudden, alien sound – a harsh, whistling crack – and the man above her let out a sharp cry of pain.

For a second, he arched rigid above Elena. Then he slumped to the ground, moaning and whimpering, while Elena hugged her arms round her bruised body, numb with shame and despair. Dear God, what was happening now?

Then she saw. In the shadows was a group of men, and the one at the front carried a whip. Even as she watched, he raised his hand in a cold, calculating gesture, and the whip cracked out again, cutting with deadly accuracy into the man at her side. The soldier let out a thin sob and doubled up.

The man with the whip stroked the lash softly, as if it were a friend. Elena, dragging herself to her feet, gazed at her rescuer in helpless fascination. Tall and wide-shouldered, he wore a leather gambeson, with soft deerskin boots encasing his strong legs, and a grey woollen cloak slung across his shoulders. As she watched, he turned and spoke to the men in the shadows.

'Take him back to the camp. Tie him up, and wait there for me.'

The men did his bidding silently, dragging the whimpering guard away towards the fires of the soldiers' camp. Elena was alone with the man who stroked the whip.

Chapter Two

*H*er heart thudding sickly, her dark blue eyes wide with despairing defiance, Elena gazed silently up at this new threat. Then, she almost stopped breathing.

Something happened to her when she met this man's scrutiny – she felt a shock of recognition, as if she knew him already. Yet how could she? Certainly, she would never have forgotten him – no one could. His eyes were a pale silver-grey, like ice. Cold, and yet they burned into her. With a little gasp, she felt his face imprint itself for ever on her mind; the thick, tawny hair, so unlike the severely-cropped cuts of his fellow soldiers; the high-bridged, arrogant nose; the harsh jutting cheekbones. And down one lean cheek ran a terrible scar. White and ridged, it drew up the corner of his thin mouth and gave him a perpetual, menacing smile. The most chilling smile she had ever seen. Elena shivered, and bit into her soft lower lip to stop herself from crying out when she saw it.

He studied her with cold scorn. 'I thought,' he said, in a low cool voice that sent tremors through her exhausted body, 'that you Saxon vermin would be too weary tonight for such entertainments. Obviously I was wrong. You must be truly desperate to degrade yourself with a common soldier like Mauger there.'

Elena pulled her torn gown across her breasts, and lifted her small head proudly.

'You think,' she breathed in quiet defiance, 'that I *wanted* him to do what he did? My lord, I would rather he had killed me!'

The scarred man's eyes narrowed. Why, Elena wondered desperately, had she called him 'my lord'? The words had slipped out by mistake; yet there was something about this man that commanded obedience and respect, even from her. She suddenly realised that he was staring at the little wooden crucifix on its leather thong, a pathetic reminder of her former status.

Abruptly, he reached out with the handle of his whip and touched the cross, playing with it. 'Such sweet defiance,' he mocked silkily, 'from a Saxon rebel. No wonder poor Mauger was inflamed. You tried to tell him you were in holy orders, did you, wench? I hope he considers you worth it.'

Elena almost cried out at the injustice of his words. 'He knew!' she choked out. 'He knew that I was from the convent!'

'The convent that was a nest of rebels?'

'I am no rebel!' Elena's voice broke. 'Though if this is the kind of treatment I can expect, then I wish I had fought along with them! I would rather be killed than treated like this!'

She gazed up at him, quivering with anguish. His eyes were as cold as the harsh steel of the sword he wore thrust in his belt. His face was hard and impassive. With an idle gesture, he moved the handle of his whip away from the crucifix, and jerked it at the torn material of her gown. It fell apart, exposing her breasts. He flicked lightly at one nipple; it stiffened involuntarily, tugging at the soft flesh of her breast, and Elena caught her breath, her hands helpless at her sides at this fresh humiliation.

'So you are still claiming to be a nun?' He sounded almost bored. Elena felt the blood rise in her cheeks as

18

he made light, circling motions on her tender skin with his whip.

'A novice, sire,' she faltered out. 'I was destined to take my vows next month.'

'And how old are you, little novice?'

'They tell me I was born in the sixth year of King Edward's reign – oh!'

He was thoughtfully feathering her nipple with the tip of his whip. She gasped, and felt a hot, churning sensation in her stomach. Her rosy flesh jutted out with a strange yearning and she felt weak and dizzy. What refined game was this? What was wrong with her? Her breasts swelled and throbbed as he toyed with them so casually. The blood rushed to her face. She wanted to feel his hand there. She wanted him to hold her. *His hands looked strong and firm, and cool* . . .

She shuddered, and he dropped the whip, bored. She clutched the material high to her throat, and tried desperately to regain control of her body.

The man was speaking to her, saying, 'Then you are two and twenty, and according to your account, which I take leave to doubt, a complete innocent. That man Mauger – did he violate you?'

Elena's face flamed. 'His very touch was violation, my lord!'

His face twisted mockingly. 'I can see I shall have to be more precise. Are you still the virgin you claim to be?'

'I am! How dare you doubt it?'

His mouth twisted cynically. 'Well, we shall see. And in the meantime, Mauger will get a flogging he won't forget.'

Elena's head jerked up at that. A man – a Norman – was being punished because he'd dared to assault her, a Saxon prisoner?

Seeing her surprise, the man went on silkily, 'You misunderstand, little Saxon. He is not being punished out of deference to your feelings but because he dared

19

to defile my personal property.' He paused; a sudden shaft of moonlight through the trees caught at his strong, hard profile and glinted on the tawny streaks in his thick dark hair. 'You see, I am Aimery le Sabrenn, lord of Thoresfield, the man who owns you. Ah, I see from your face that you are acquainted with my name. Learn the rules well, little nun, many don't get a second chance. No-one tampers with my personal property. No-one.'

Elena gazed up at him with despairing eyes. She'd known. Somehow, she'd known as she set eyes on him who he was. It was as if the last of her breath had been knocked from her body.

Meanwhile, the Breton's hypnotic silver eyes narrowed almost to blackness as he inspected his young captive's anguished face. It was a face of delicate, almost breathtaking fragility. Her skin was so pure and pale that it looked as if it would bruise at the lightest touch. Her deep blue eyes, fringed by thick, soft lashes, gazed helplessly up at him, still wide with despairing defiance. Her long blonde curls, totally disordered in her struggle with the arrogant fool Mauger, shimmered like a silver halo in the moonlight. He remembered her small, perfect breasts, and how she'd trembled as his whip brushed their rosy, nubile tips.

This Saxon maid was beautiful, and spirited. Isobel would like her.

At the thought of this new acquisition in Isobel's power, some distant, half-forgotten emotion stirred within him, as he considered how Isobel would make her suffer. His face hardened, and he pushed the thought away without any difficulty. She was a Saxon – a rebel, in spite of her denials. She deserved what she was about to get. They all did. And if she was determined to keep up this pretence of innocence, then she would serve the lady Isobel's purpose very well.

He smiled and Elena, on seeing that chilling smile, felt her greatest fear yet.

Aimery le Sabrenn took the Saxon girl by the wrist. She felt fragile, like some helpless bird. She didn't struggle. It was almost as if she'd given up as she followed helplessly in his shadow, back towards the firelit circle where his men were gathered. He'd unpinned his grey cloak and given it to her, to hide her shame; he didn't want any more trouble from his men tonight. She'd kept her eyes lowered as he fastened it around her. She looked dazed with weariness and despair; yet there was still defiance there, he knew, even in her silence.

Aimery wondered briefly to himself what would have happened if he hadn't been with his men that night. No doubt the girl would have suffered badly at the hands of Mauger and his friends. He knew, because he'd seen it happen before. She was Saxon, she deserved her fate. Nevertheless, he was angry with his men for attacking the tiny convent, even if it had been harbouring rebels. And, strangely, he was glad he'd been in time to save the Saxon girl from Mauger's crude attentions.

He glanced down at the girl's white face. Her pretence of being a nun was quite disarming. Whatever her story, he knew, from cold experience, that she would be sweet when he finally took her, sweet and tantalising, with that slender figure and beguiling though feigned innocence. Also, if Aimery's judgement was not at fault, her responses would be more than satisfactory once he and Isobel had trained her properly. There was no denying how her dark blue eyes had flown open, and her soft lips parted in a gasp, as he teased her tender little breasts with his whip. She had a lot to learn but he would teach her with care, and then would wait patiently, even indifferently, until she was ready.

His men-at-arms, lolling around the fire with their wineskins, jumped to their feet when he suddenly appeared at the edge of the clearing with the Saxon girl stumbling at his heels. Aimery le Sabrenn smiled to himself, feeling the taut scar pulling at his cheek. They were afraid of him. Good. That was how it should be.

One solitary figure moved slowly out of the shadows towards him. A man not quite as tall as Aimery, but burlier and more thickset, with a face and arms as dark as night, and a gleaming, curved sword at his belt. Elena stifled a little sob of fear as Aimery thrust her towards the man; he saw how she trembled but still held herself straight and proud. He was pleased to see this fresh evidence of her courage; she would need it.

'I want this girl put in chains, away from the rest of the serfs, Hamet,' Aimery said softly to the Saracen, his servant. 'For her own safekeeping. I will see to the punishment of the guard, Mauger. Keep the men away from her.'

The big Saracen looked at the trembling Elena keenly. 'She is beautiful, lord,' he said, in a foreign, sing-song voice. 'She is for you?'

'For the lady Isobel,' said Aimery. A wintry smile twisted his mouth. 'Do you think she will like her present?'

Hamet's black eyes gleamed. 'Oh, yes, lord,' he said softly. 'The girl is a Saxon – and untried?'

'So she claims. Whatever the case, we will soon teach her – Isobel especially.'

The black servant nodded, his eyes devouring Aimery's captive. He swallowed hard. Aimery saw it, and laughed shortly. 'You will have your turn, Hamet. But remember, Isobel as ever, is the tutor.'

Hamet nodded eagerly and went for the chains. When he came back with them, the girl cried out in protest but Aimery just nodded to his servant, who began to fasten the cold shackles around her wrists and ankles with powerful yet strangely gentle fingers. As he fastened her arms, the borrowed grey cloak slipped by accident from her shoulders, revealing her small, creamy breasts. The Saracen froze in his task, and Elena gave a low moan of protest as his hungry black eyes fastened on her vulnerable flesh. His big hand jerked slowly towards her tempting breasts, but his master's voice stopped him like a sword in the back.

'Lay one finger on her before I give the word,' said Aimery, watching impassively with folded arms, 'and, friend though you are, you will die. Very slowly, I assure you. Now, fasten the cloak around her, and get on with your task.'

As Hamet worked on her chains, the thunderstorm that had threatened for so long rolled down from the hills. Lightning played on the horizon; low rumbles of distant thunder menaced the still air. Heavy drops of rain were already pattering on the thick canopy of leaves overhead as Hamet fastened the last of Elena's shackles. Then he swung her easily up in his strong arms and, at his lord's command, carried her to the shelter of the half-ruined woodcutter's cottage that lay at the edge of the clearing, where he had already placed his master's things for the night. Aimery followed, and indicated that Hamet should take the girl into a small thatched outhouse that leaned against the main building. As Hamet lowered her to her feet inside the crude hovel, Elena struggled to hold herself upright, with a last burst of desperate defiance.

'I beg you, sire, if you have any justice in you at all, then you will let me go! I was not one of the rebels, I swear. What possible use can I be to you? Let me go back to the convent where I belong!'

The Breton watched her oddly, his hands on his hips. His harsh face, twisted by the scar, was suddenly lit up by a gleam of lightning. She shivered at the look in his cold, glittering eyes.

'The convent is no more,' he said softly. Elena cried out in anguish. He went on quickly, 'The nuns were spared, they will find refuge elsewhere. But you are no nun, Elena, and contrary to your own belief, you will learn to be a good deal of use to me, I think. You see, at my stronghold of Thoresfield you will have a new mistress – the lady Isobel. She will train you in your new tasks and Hamet, my faithful servant, will help you to learn. There is much you need to know.'

Elena's face jerked wildly from one to the other. They were smiling at each other as if they shared some dark secret. Wild with sudden fear, she twisted in her chains, but the shackles cut into her soft skin. She stumbled to the ground, and the Breton's grey cloak twisted around her body. Aimery knelt to restrain her struggles. She trembled at his touch, feeling a sudden wild heat blaze through her as his palms grazed her shoulders. His hands were almost gentle . . .

'Lie still,' he said in his low, compelling voice, 'and learn to accept what you cannot change. That will be your first lesson for tonight.' He stood up and said abruptly to his servant, 'Guard her well, Hamet. I'll be back soon, when I've arranged Mauger's punishment.' Then he was gone. Elena lay still, her heart thudding, because for one wild moment, a moment of utter madness, she had wanted the Breton to hold her in his arms.

Hamet sat cross-legged with his broad back against the turf walls of the half-ruined outhouse, watching the helpless girl. A tear glistened on her pale cheek, but she glared at him defiantly. Hamet was sorry for her; she must be so frightened, yet she was full of courage; few people spoke up against the lord Aimery. He wanted to help her, but Aimery had told him not to touch her, and Aimery was his master, the person who had rescued him years ago from a stinking dungeon in Messina, where the Normans were fighting the Moors. Hamet had sworn to devote the rest of his life to the Breton. Le Sabrenn, they had called him then, even his enemies, when he was a lowly mercenary living by his sword – Aimery the swordsman.

'Don't touch her,' Aimery had said. Hamet didn't. But the aching in his loins intensified as he drank in those soft curves wrapped in his master's cloak. He remembered that glimpse of beautiful white flesh, and softly stroked himself beneath his tunic, his dark face intent. 'It's all right, little Saxon girl,' he murmured in his own language. 'It's all right. I won't touch you. I won't harm you.'

The rain thudded on the thatched roof and the thunder rumbled across the forest. He watched until she was asleep, her slight body released at last from fear and tension. The storm had moved on. Hamet got up quietly and went across to where she was lying. He moved the cloak, just a little, and then adjusted her torn dress so that one small breast was revealed, its pink tip soft and innocent in sleep. Then he sat down again at her side and reached beneath his clothing for his already stiff penis. Slowly, ecstatically, he began to bring himself towards orgasm, whispering endearments as he gazed at the sleeping girl.

She was so sweet, so pretty, with her curling fair hair and her creamy skin. Once, he stopped what he was doing to reach out and touch her tender little nipple, but she shuddered in her sleep and he stopped, in case she woke. He sighed and thought of what the lady Isobel would do with her, what she would let him, Hamet, do with her if he was patient. His member jerked and stiffened anew at the thought. He closed his eyes, rocking softly and crooning to himself, as his feverish hands brought his erect penis to a shuddering climax at last.

When the throes of his ejaculation were over, he still stroked his dark flesh gently, lovingly. He was happy now. And so would this gentle girl be. He, Hamet, would make her happy.

Carefully he rearranged the sleeping girl's cloak. Then he sat by the door to wait patiently for his master.

Back at the stronghold of Thoresfield, in one of the candlelit upper chambers, Isobel de Morency also waited for Aimery le Sabrenn, only with rather less patience than Hamet the Saracen. Weary with pacing up and down her room, she moved yet again to the window and pushed aside the piece of oiled hide that curtained the narrow embrasure. Then she looked out into the courtyard below, drinking in the warm evening air, as if it could settle the restless craving in her blood.

There was the usual activity for this time of night. Sentries, sullen in the sultry night air, were posted around the palisade that surrounded the stronghold and its outbuildings; smoking torches fixed into iron holders gave a shadowy light for some late travellers arriving from the south. Grooms rushed to hold their dusty horses, and two off-duty young soldiers lounging against the armoury wall looked up with idle curiosity from their game of dice. Then one of the soldiers saw Isobel, up at her window, and his gaze, frankly admiring, warmed her. She watched him appraisingly for a moment, then turned away petulantly. No. Too coarse, too common. Oh, when would Aimery be back?

Isobel was wrenched by a sudden, hungry longing. He'd only left yesterday, riding into the wild country to the north, because there had been reports of rebel activity again. Only yesterday, but already it seemed too long! What did other women do during these long, hot summer evenings when their menfolk were away? Embroidery, she supposed, or some insipid music-making on their shrill lutes. Isobel's full, ripe lips curled in scorn. She smoothed her beautiful silk gown round her hips, and fingered the circlet of pearls round her neck. Aimery had bought them for her in France, from a merchant who travelled regularly to Constantinople for silks and spices and precious stones.

It was so hot, even at this late hour! Perhaps there would be a thunderstorm soon, and she would be able to watch the lightning playing above the dark line of the forest that surrounded them – anything to relieve the monotony of this place without Aimery. Sighing fretfully, Isobel flung herself across the white linen sheets of her wide bed and reached for the jug of white wine that her maid had left for her. She poured a refreshing draught into her silver goblet and remembered when she had first met Aimery.

It was nearly five years ago now. Her old, nearly impotent husband, the Baron de Morency, had hired a band of Breton mercenaries to fight in some petty skirmish on the borders of his land. Aimery le Sabrenn, illegitimate son of a poor Breton knight and a French serving maid, was the leader of those mercenaries. As soon as she saw him, Isobel wanted him, badly.

She sipped luxuriously at her wine, still cool from the dark cellars beneath the hall. Aimery had it imported specially from France for her, knowing how she couldn't bear the sour English ale. She stretched languourously and leaned back against the soft pillows that were filled with goose down. Aimery le Sabrenn, the swordsman, his own men had called him admiringly. She remembered how the Breton had first looked at her, cool and challenging, as she sat beside her husband at the high table. Her ripe breasts tingled pleasantly beneath the silk of her green gown at the memory. Thoughtfully she unlaced the fastening of her bodice and slipped her hand inside her white chemise, coaxing both her darkening nipples into a pleasurable stiffness with her fingertips. Already, the sweet wine was starting to course warmly through her blood.

There was a knock at the door, and her maid came in. 'Was there anything else you wanted, my lady?'

Isobel's slanting green eyes spat venom at the interruption. 'Nothing. Go away! And, Alys, if you disturb me once more – ' Alys beat a hasty retreat as Isobel sank back onto her bed. The candle flame, disturbed by the draught from the door, flickered crazily on the tapestries that adorned the bare stone walls. Isobel closed her eyes.

If she couldn't be with Aimery, she resolved silently,

she'd rather be alone with her desire on this hot, sultry night.

Her jewelled fingers fluttered slightly on the soft swell of her breasts. Oh, Aimery. She remembered their first night together, and parted her warm thighs softly beneath the rustling folds of her silk gown.

It had been hot, then, too; a velvety night in late summer. Isobel had found out from her maid that Aimery was alone in one of the guard rooms, attending to his armour. Isobel had pulled a hooded mantle over her thin chemise and run from her chamber under cover of darkness. The Breton was there, as her maid had said. As she entered the dark little room, he'd had his back to her, but she could see that he was polishing his long sword by the light of a guttering tallow candle. Isobel had stood very still, enchanted by the sight of him. He'd removed his soldier's leather tunic because the night was so hot and was wearing only his cloth leggings and deerskin boots. Isobel felt her heart thudding painfully as she drank in the wide-shouldered beauty of his body in the candlelight; the tanned, heavily-muscled yet graceful torso laced with silver sword scars; the lean hips, the long, powerful thighs. She wanted to run her fingertips over every inch of his warm, exciting flesh.

Even now, at the memory of that first night, her lips parted in a soft little groan. Her fingers trailed along her open thighs, gently caressing the smooth flesh above her silken hose, reaching up carefully to touch those tender, private parts that she knew would be swollen and moist already. She ran her small, pointed tongue over her lips.

When Aimery had turned round to see who his visitor was, Isobel had thrown back her hood, so that a mass of glossy black hair spilled out over her shoulders. The Breton had smiled, his strange grey eyes glittering, and Isobel had stopped breathing, because he was so beautiful. He'd said nothing – that smile had been enough.

He'd walked slowly towards her and removed her cloak. Slipping her white chmise from her shoulders, he let it fall unheeded to the floor. Then he bent his head to take each of her ripe breasts in his mouth, feasting on their luxuriance, laving and suckling with his tongue as she thrust them more and more urgently towards him.

Her breasts tingled anew at the memory. As she sprawled on the bed, her fingers stroked her tender clitoris with increasing urgency. Suddenly, she cupped the pulsing mound of her femininity with her cool palm, feeling how engorged the flesh was. It wasn't enough – oh, it wasn't enough! She needed something thick, and firm, and satisfying . . .

Her eyes heavy with desire, Isobel slid impatiently from her lonely bed and searched purposefully in the carved wooden coffer that contained her robes. At last, with a little sigh of satisfaction, she drew out an object wrapped in soft chamois skin. Slowly she unwrapped it, and drew out a long, coiled whip. Smiling, Isobel poured some scented oil from a small glass phial into her hand, then ran her palm up and down the long leather handle until it was slick and moist. Then she curled herself back on the bed, resting her shoulders against the pillows. Her tongue glistened between her white teeth as she parted her legs and began to slowly and sensuously stroke her pouting vaginal lips with the firm leather shaft. It glided sweetly across her already-moist flesh; her cheeks became softly flushed and she uttered a little sigh of contentment.

She remembered, then, how Aimery had barricaded the wooden door of the guardhouse. How he had spread her discarded cloak over the straw-covered floor, and lowered her naked body upon it. Isobel, already quivering with uncontrollable desire, had reached out desperately for him as he crouched over her in the candlelight. She'd covered the rippling muscles of his chest with kisses, run her hands wonderingly over the iron hardness of his forearms; and when he released his manhood from the constriction of his clothes, she'd gasped and felt the blood burn in her cheeks. She'd let out a little cry, and rubbed her soft thighs against the coarse silk of his body, begging wordlessly for his embrace.

At first he'd teased her, rubbing tantalisingly at her yearning entrance with his throbbing phallus, until she'd pleaded with him for mercy. Then, her pleas had become little guttural cries of delight as he at last impaled her, slowly easing the whole of that wonderful length into her quivering, juicy hips, only pausing to let her feel it properly and grip it deep within her hungry loins. He toyed with her then, sliding the pulsing shaft slowly out again so that Isobel had cried out with loss; only to thrust it back in, oh so deeply, as she clutched at his shoulders and gasped out as the approaching ecstasy built up inside her like an unstoppable flood.

She'd climaxed quickly, too quickly that first time, because she found the merest touch of him so exciting. She still did.

Now, alone on her bed, her breath coming in short, agonised gasps, she guided the thick leather handle of the whip longingly into her yearning vulva. Her inner muscles clutched with relief at the slick, hard shaft; the trailing lash tickled tantalisingly along the soft flesh of her inner thigh. Her straying fingers coaxed her sweetly engorged clitoris, as she imagined Aimery plunging himself deep within her, filling her, satisfying her . . .

Isobel rolled convulsively onto her side, her hips thrusting desperately against the long, solid shaft, as her whole body went into spasm. With furious fingers she slid the leather whip hungrily into herself, over and over again, as waves of pleasure engulfed her shuddering body. Aimery, oh Aimery.

She lay back exhausted on the damp linen sheets, her legs splayed, the smooth leather disappointingly cold and unresponsive within her still pulsing vagina. Frowning, she soothed her aching breasts.

It wasn't enough. Nothing was enough, without him.

When Aimery had left France for England with William of Normandy's motley, land-hungry army, Isobel had decided to leave her husband and follow him. Society had disowned her, but she cared nothing for that, as long as she could have Aimery.

Then, at Hastings, when the battle hung in the balance, Aimery had caught Duke William's attention by rallying the mercenary cavalry on the left flank as they hovered on the brink of retreat. When the duke was unhorsed, and the cry went up that he was dead, it was Aimery and his men who swung to surround him, standing firm against the wild onslaught of the Saxon shire-levies as they thundered down the hill towards the French army.

Duke William, now King of England, had not forgotten him.

Was it really only yesterday that Aimery had left the castle? Already it seemed so long. He'd taken his troop of soldiers northwards, after the Saxon rebels who were rumoured to be still in league with the Danish fleet that hovered off the English coast. Isobel had known better than to protest at his absence. After all, hadn't her lover been rewarded with lands and wealth in order to defend this northern outpost for his king, this isolated stronghold, Thoresfield, that guarded the ever-dangerous route between London and York? Isobel understood that Aimery was first and foremost a soldier, who had sworn allegiance to King William of England. But how would she survive without him? No-one compared, as a lover or a man, with Aimery le Sabrenn.

At least she had his return to look forward to. Rearranging her sadly crumpled gown, Isobel stretched lazily across the bed to pour herself some more wine, cheering up at the prospect. Perhaps her lord would bring back some captives, some young Saxon women, for his own pleasure. And for his own bitter, secret revenge, which only Isobel knew about.

She moistened her lips, freshly aroused at the prospect of training new prisoners. As she moved she felt the whip handle, still satisfyingly firm, nudging at her yielding thighs. What she needed was warm, hard flesh.

Isobel gave a rueful sigh and creased her smooth forehead in a frown.

It was no good. She would have to find someone else for her pleasure tonight. Her eyes half-closed, she began to make plans.

Chapter Three

*I*n the woodcutter's cottage in the heart of the forest,
Elena, utterly exhausted, slept. As she slept, she
dreamed her dream again; only now it was vivid, almost
real. The tall man on horseback dismounted, and came
slowly, purposefully towards her; she ran gladly towards
him, longing for his embrace, but she could not see his
shadowed face, and she wanted to, so much . . .

She woke an hour later with an instinctive cry of fear
as she glimpsed the big Saracen still watching her from
his place by the door. He had fixed a smoking torch into
the hard earth, and it cast grotesque shadows around
the little hovel. With his dark skin and exotic features,
he frightened her almost as much as his cold, scarred
master. She tried to move her limbs, and bit her lip as
the iron fetters reminded her of her captivity. The
Saracen, seeing her awake, slid softly to his feet and
padded across the damp earthen floor towards her.

She shrank back from him instinctively, but he held
out his hand in a soothing gesture. 'The lord Aimery
says that the chains can be removed now. If you
promise not to run.' His voice was soft and curiously
rhythmic, almost – kind. Kind? She must be losing her
mind – how could these men, her enemies, be kind?

She said, in a low voice devoid of emotion, 'I promise not to run.'

What was the point in trying to escape? Even if she managed to get away from here, the forest was not her friend. These wild northern wastes of England were full of starving outlaws, fleeing from the recent destruction wrought by King William and his commanders on the northern rebels. If she tried to flee, she would starve, or suffer an unknown fate at the hands of desperate Saxon runaways.

And, Aimery le Sabrenn had promised that she wouldn't be hurt. Elena knew it was madness, but somehow, she trusted him.

The big Saracen was surprisingly gentle as he released her from the chains. The huge, sinewy muscles of his forearms glistened, and he frowned in concentration as he undid the locks. He smelled musky and masculine; Elena had never seen a man with skin of such a dark, sunburned hue, though she had heard of such people. She blushed to think of his flesh being such a strange colour, every part of him.

'You must not be afraid, Saxon girl,' he said suddenly. 'But you must do as my master bids. In every way –'

Then he broke off, as a tall, forbidding shadow filled the doorway and Aimery le Sabrenn himself entered the little hovel.

Elena looked up at the man who held her captive, and felt strangely weak. He was tall and powerful in the knee-length leather tunic that emphasized his broad shoulders and was drawn tight over lean hips by a wide, buckled belt. In the sombre shadows cast by the torch, his face looked bleaker, harder than ever, with those strange light eyes a startling contrast to his dark, rain-streaked hair. In his cold gaze, there was a weariness, a hint of harshness that made Elena shiver uncontrollably. He was not so much older than her – he could not be more than thirty – yet somehow he looked so experienced, so bitter. Elena felt the muscles of her taut stomach contract painfully as his eyes raked her.

'Well, my little Saxon,' he said, almost lazily. 'You'll be pleased to learn that the guard who assaulted you is about to be punished. Naturally, you are to witness his punishment.'

'No!' gasped Elena. 'No – I could not bear to—'

The man's face twisted, and the pale scar lifted his cruel mouth in a mocking smile. 'It was not a question,' he said softly. 'Hamet, bring her to the clearing.'

The rain had stopped, though the forest still dripped damply around them. The man, Mauger, was already roped to a tree, his back laid bare for the whip. The Breton's men stood in a silent circle round him, waiting. Aimery took his position, and nodded to the sergeant, chief of his men-at-arms, who stepped forward. In his hand the sergeant held a thickly plaited leather quirt. Aimery reached for Elena, and held her wrist so that she had no choice but to watch. His lean, strong fingers burned into her delicate veined skin.

At first, Mauger was silent, though his sturdy, muscular body shook each time the whip seared his taut flesh. Elena turned her head away, revolted, as the leather quirt continued to mark its red weals on the soldier's broad back. Aimery saw her turn and gripped her small chin between his finger and thumb.

'You will look,' he commanded. 'This man is being punished for you.'

'No! You can't make me! I – I'll shut my eyes – '

'Every time you do that,' said the Breton softly, 'I'll add ten strokes to the man's punishment. Now – look.'

Elena thought she would faint. Aimery held her by the shoulders now, forcing her to witness the punishment. When at last he called out, 'Stop – it is enough,' she turned to swallow dryly, her throat agonised.

He waited one moment, then turned her tear-stained face up to meet his.

'You did not like that, little Saxon?'

'No!' she choked out. 'It – it was vile.'

He stroked one lean finger down her white cheek. 'Then you will have to be more careful about your complaints in future, won't you? You will have to grow up, little Elena. We are soldiers, in hostile territory, and discipline must be maintained at all times. The man's punishment was not severe. He is a good soldier, and we need him. But he has learned his lesson. As for you – you must learn to enjoy these little games we play . . .'

Games? Elena was dumbstruck. Meanwhile Hamet, at his master's shoulder, was watching avidly. 'Shall we begin now, lord, with her training? I have put your things under shelter, in the woodcutter's hut – it is quite private there – '

The Breton still held Elena by her shoulders, and was watching her carefully, his grey eyes narrowed in speculation. Elena felt herself tremble beneath his gaze. 'No, Hamet,' Aimery said at last. 'We will savour her education properly. Once we are at the castle, the lady Isobel will prepare her most thoroughly. It will be worth the wait, I assure you.'

Hamet's shoulders drooped with disappointment; Aimery said dryly, 'I see you have little patience tonight, my friend. Why not fetch a willing girl from among the captives?'

Hamet nodded eagerly. 'Yes, lord. And the Saxon girl – she will watch?'

Aimery frowned impatiently. 'No, I told you before. She will begin her education at the castle. Put her back in her chains and fetch yourself a girl.'

Elena, barely understanding their exchanged words but sensing the threat in them, began to struggle as the cold fetters were fastened carefully round her tender limbs once more. Aimery le Sabrenn said, 'You are foolish, little Saxon. Unless you submit to my orders, I cannot guarantee your safety. Would you rather be out

36

there alone with the other slaves, at the mercy of men such as Mauger?'

Elena sagged in Hamet's arms, forced to acknowledge the truth of his cold words. Aimery watched as Hamet carried the girl gently back to her shelter, and his lip curled in scorn. His heart was filled with renewed bitterness against the Saxons.

The girl, Elena, with her pretence of fragility and innocence, disturbed him. He told himself that her facade was all a cunning mask. She'd probably incited that fool Mauger, and no doubt she would cause yet more trouble before he was finished with her.

Hamet came back promptly, his teeth gleaming whitely in the darkness. He was trailing a Saxon redhead behind him, one of the rebels they'd swept in from the woods, who somehow managed to look voluptuous in spite of her ragged gown. Her eyes widened when she saw to whom she had been brought; she moistened her ripe lips as she assessed Aimery's strong, handsome figure.

'You wanted me, my lord?' she whispered.

Aimery let a cold smile twist his features. 'Of that I'm not sure,' he replied. 'But perhaps you can persuade me.' And he led the way purposefully across the clearing to the woodcutter's cottage, where Hamet had placed his things in the main room. A dim lantern flared shakily in one corner, casting flickering shadows on the sagging roof and earthen floor. Aimery leaned his back against the coarse flint wall, and folded his arms across his chest. On the other side of that wall lay the chained Saxon girl, in the little outhouse. Pushing the image of her frightened yet defiant face from his mind, he turned his cold gaze on the voluptuous redhead.

'Amuse me,' he said.

The redhead, gazing after him hungrily, nodded. Then she turned to Hamet.

She swayed sinuously towards the Saracen, pouting her mouth provocatively at the open delight in his face.

With one swift movement she slipped her ragged dress from her shoulders, to reveal full, luscious breasts with a dusting of freckles across the creamy skin. Hamet caught his breath. 'Oh, yes,' he sighed.

He lunged towards her, but with one finger at her mouth she stopped him, and indicated that he should lower himself to the ground. He did so, lying on his back on the uneven floor, with his big hands pillowing his head. Already his eyes were glazed in anticipation, and his white smile showed his pleasure.

The girl, breathing heavily, dropped to one side and bent over his hips. With nimble fingers she pushed back his tunic and felt for the ties of his leggings, eagerly pulling them away. When the Saracen's fully erect penis sprang into freedom, quivering with tension, she let out a little moan at the sight and stroked it with feverish fingers. Then she let her full breasts hang over it and teased the glistening dark knob with her nipples, each in turn, sighing at the pleasure it was giving her. Hamet moaned aloud, and the redhead glanced across at the Breton provocatively. Aimery, still leaning against the wall, watched the interplay of black and white flesh in the light of the lantern with a kind of languid detachment and made no move to join them.

Then the redhead bobbed down, her flickering pink tongue darting snake-like at the dark, swollen glans. She licked the bead of moisture from its tip, and swirled the tip of her tongue round its sensitive ridge. Hamet jerked convulsively. He reached out to grab at her breasts, his fingers clutching at the sweet, creamy flesh, and his hips arched to thrust his rigid penis full into her mouth.

She flinched at first, but forced herself to relax, and took as much as she could into herself, using her tongue to suck and caress as the big Saracen jerked and moaned beneath her. She was aware, all the time, of the Breton lord watching her. Now, there was the one she really wanted. She felt her own juices flowing, her flesh tightening in anticipation at what she hoped would come next. Meanwhile, she used all her skill on the Saracen, cupping his balls gently in her hand, feeling the wrinkled skin tauten and quiver until at last, with a great cry of release, he pumped himself into her soft, moist mouth. She did her best to hold him in there while he bucked, but it was hard, because he was so big. She sucked him and swallowed, hard, until at last his violent spasms began to subside.

Then he lay back with a groan, the satisfaction glazing his face, and the redhead turned with a coy smile to Aimery. 'Your turn, my lord?'

He was already unbuckling his belt. She watched, her small pink tongue flickering between her lips in hot anticipation as she appreciated his wide-shouldered, sinewy body. She knew, somehow, that this man would be the very essence of cool, powerful masculinity.

'Turn round,' he bit out curtly.

Disappointed, she dragged her gaze from his gauntly handsome face. Then she felt his hands pushing her roughly into place, on all fours. So *this* was how he liked it. She was sorry, because she would like to have seen that chillingly scarred face in the throes of sexual ecstasy. Perhaps, if she performed to his satisfaction, the Breton lord would summon her again. This was better than living as a runaway in the forest, scratching for food and shelter!

He was pushing her full skirts up round her waist. His cool, sensitive hands were on her flaring buttocks, feeling for the cleft; stroking, probing. She shuddered and involuntarily arched herself towards him, still wet and excited from the Saracen's attentions. The Saracen was watching her avidly from the shadows; she heard his master snap a sharp command to him, and the servant slid beneath the girl to suckle with his full lips at her tender nipples, making her quiver with delight.

Then she gasped aloud, as the Breton parted the wet lips of her swollen vulva with skilful fingers and thrust

39

his manhood in to the hilt. Once sheathed in her moist softness, he stopped moving, and held himself very still.

'Oh!' The redhead could not stop herself from crying out at the pleasure of it. The shaft of his penis seemed exquisitely long and smooth, and it filled her to the point of delirium. His refusal to move drove her wild; she waited as long as she could, raptly drinking in the pleasure of feeling him deep inside her; then, with a groan, she started to writhe along the hard, wonderful length that filled her, while the Saracen licked at her dangling breasts with hot, darting strokes of his stiffened tongue.

'Stop.' Aimery's low, masterful voice whispered in her ear. She couldn't stop, but continued to massage herself along his shaft, quivering in her mounting ecstasy.

Aimery's fingers clasped her buttocks, stilling her. 'I told you to stop. You were ordered not to move,' he repeated, in a calm voice that nevertheless chilled her heated blood. 'You will not move again until I give you permission – do you understand me?'

She swallowed hard, and nodded. Her left breast was on fire where the Saracen was licking her with his big, agile tongue, softly rasping at her burning nipple, sending dark, fiery pleasures arrowing down to her abdomen.

Aimery started to withdraw his penis very, very slowly. She wanted to cry out loud to him to thrust it within her aching flesh again; her hips quivered threateningly with her need.

'I said – *don't move . . .*'

She nodded dumbly and bit her lips hard as he slid himself slowly into her clutching vagina again. So beautiful, so firm, so strong . . .

It was no good. She gave a harsh cry of need and worked herself feverishly against him, the black man's hungry lips at her nipple driving her on into a delirious vortex of pleasure that was conscious only of his thrusting manhood deep within her. She writhed her hips in desperate abandon, and rubbed her swollen, aching breasts against the Saracen's face.

The Breton withdrew, leaving her cold and empty. She was still.

Then, coldly and deliberately, he re-entered her and began to drive himself to his own orgasm within her, his thrusts increasing with devastating impulsion, while she struggled to restrain her own pleasure. The Breton said nothing; all she could hear was the harshness of his breathing as he gripped her by the waist and drove his engorged manhood into her soft flesh. At last he gave a final fierce lunge, and she quivered involuntarily, unable to reject the wild pleasure as his long penis quivered and spasmed in the very heart of her body. With a high-pitched cry, she writhed against him, gripping at him, rubbing herself up and down the delicious shaft as her own inevitable orgasm convulsed her feverish body.

He withdrew, and began to adjust his clothing, watching impassively as the voluptuous redhead lay in damp exhaustion on the floor. Hamet, excited by the scene he had just witnessed, was erect again and straddling her prone body, he began to slide his throbbing member into her open mouth once more. The girl quailed momentarily, but the Saracen circled her damp lips with the glans of his penis, and the feel of his silken skin excited her so much that she willingly took him in. Hamet, throwing back his head in triumph, pumped himself with long, deep strokes into her mouth, spurting into her. The girl rolled over onto her side, sated and exhausted.

Aimery touched her disdainfully with his foot. 'You can go now,' he said, barely troubling to mask the scorn in his voice.

She sat up, clutching her torn clothing to her body. She gazed up at him lasciviously. Damn him, with that

41

fascinating scar and long, lithe body. In spite of his coldness, she still ached for him.

'My lord.' She reached out a beseeching hand. 'If you wish, I will warm your bed for the full night – '

He gestured her hand away. The hunger in her face disappointed him. There was no pleasure in it when they were so eager. 'She can go now, Hamet,' he said shortly.

She called back over her shoulder as the Saracen led her out of the hut. 'Send for me, my lord! My name is Morwith . . .'

The Saracen escorted her without a word back to the slave lines. She lay down to sleep with the rest of the serfs, and quivered with reawakened desire as she remembered the sweet feel of the Breton's manhood deep within her heated body.

She'd heard that Aimery le Sabrenn was like no other man, and now she knew it was true. Stirring feverishly, she reached down between her legs and stroked herself, moaning his name in the darkness as she shuddered towards climax once more.

Perhaps, thought Morwith longingly, her chance would come again – at the castle.

Elena lay awake in the outhouse, restless and disturbed. The chains were only a light restraint but, however hard she tried, she couldn't get comfortable. She could still hear the occasional rumble of thunder in the distance; the night was hot and oppressive.

Then, she heard the sounds, muffled by the dense stone wall. A woman's voice, first; then she recognised the Saracen's deep, velvety chuckle, and his master's harsh voice giving orders. Then silence; she thought they had gone, or perhaps slept.

Elena felt the breath catch in her throat when the woman started to moan. Little animal noises; a man's harsh grunt; then the woman's voice, crying out, over and over again, small, thin, high-pitched – as though she was somewhere beyond pain, beyond pleasure. Oh, what was happening? More punishments? More – *games*?

The muffled noises seemed to go on forever. Elena listened, fascinated in spite of herself, the blood burning in her cheeks, until the last sounds died away. Her pulse still beating wildly, she huddled up in her corner against the crude turf walls. Then she stopped breathing, as the rickety wooden door was pulled open from the outside and a gaunt shadow filled the entrance.

It was Aimery le Sabrenn. Elena stared speechlessly up at him, her heart thudding wildly as he stood there gazing down at her. She felt her throat go dry, not with fear, but with something else; some emotion she didn't recognise.

He watched her for a moment then said, 'I have brought you bread and wine. You must be hungry. Afterwards, you must sleep. We have a long journey tomorrow.'

As Elena watched, her blue eyes wide with unspoken questions, he put the wineskin down beside her, along with a manchet loaf wrapped in a white linen napkin. Then he was gone once more, like a shadow, and Elena lay trembling in the darkness, his lean, scarred face imprinted forever on her mind.

She knew now why she thought she had recognised him, why he had seemed so familiar; the way he walked, the way he moved, everything about his lithe, muscular figure. Aimery le Sabrenn, Breton lord of Thoresfield, was just like the man in her dream!

Elena squeezed her eyes shut against the sudden, dizzying sensation that swept through her body.

And she had wanted him to stay . . .

Chapter Four

*I*sobel said scornfully, 'I saw her from the window as you rode into the courtyard. She looks too young. And, my dear, so innocent!'

Aimery, who had been pacing the private chamber that Isobel had furnished as her bower, turned suddenly. 'She is twenty-two. And as for innocence – I thought, Isobel, that was what you wanted.'

Isobel stepped softly across the rush matting towards him and stroked his cheek where the thin scar split it, the hard ridge of tissue almost silver in the flickering light of the candles fixed to the walls. 'I thought that was what *you* wanted, Aimery my love. For your revenge.'

She pressed her supple body against him, running her hands up his brown, sinewed forearms, and pressing little, nibbling kisses against the smooth muscle of his chest, where she'd parted his tunic. That wicked Saxon blade had scarred his beautiful face, but he was still as exciting, as dangerous as ever, especially now that he was as rich and powerful as any woman could desire, basking as he did in the king's favour. As she caressed him, her coiled tongue was hot and enticing; Aimery pushed her away before his own desire should flare too openly. Isobel was worried at this hint of rejection, though she was too clever to show it. She wondered if perhaps he had heard about her visitor last night.

'She's ideal for our purpose,' he said curtly. 'She claims she was a novice in a convent – a convent that was harbouring rebels. She's yours to train, Isobel.'

'And yours to reward, my lord,' murmured Isobel de Morency. A hungry green light gleamed in her eyes. 'Shall I go to her now?'

Aimery nodded curtly. 'Yes. And send Hamet to me.'

He didn't need Isobel to remind him about revenge. The bleak anger rose in his throat as he remembered.

Last year, while garrisoned in York, Aimery's younger brother Hugh had taken a beautiful Saxon woman as his mistress. A golden witch. She'd ensnared Aimery too, persuading him to keep their mutual passion a secret from his unsuspecting brother. Aimery had despised himself, and worshipped her, even forgetting Isobel for a while.

The woman had led them into a trap – both of them. She'd been working for the Saxon rebels, all the time. When York was taken by the Saxon army, Hugh had died in captivity, while Aimery had escaped, scarred for life by the cruel sword that had split his cheek in two.

Since then, Aimery had vowed that the Saxons would pay for the death of his brother. It was his own personal mission of revenge; of which King William, who had entrusted him with this northern outpost, knew nothing.

Elena lay back, dazed, in the warm, scented water of the bath tub they'd brought for her. Her freshly washed hair, spread like damp silk around her white shoulders, gleamed in the soft candlelight. She didn't understand any of it.

She had spent the remainder of the journey to the

castle on the back of a horse; a quiet palfrey, roped to one of the guards, who'd been so respectful that he'd scarcely even dared to look at her.

They'd reached Aimery's stronghold of Thoresfield at dusk. Originally a wealthy thane's stone manor house, it had been strengthened in haste by the Normans last year in order to guard the dangerous route north, and to protect its garrison from the rebels and bands of outlaws who haunted the vast forest. It had become notorious. As the convoy of captives was led through the wide gates, Elena heard the ragged line of slaves whisper in fear; then the roped wretches were driven into the torchlit courtyard of the castle by burly guards, and driven off to the thatched hovels that lay clustered within the palisade.

Once, she caught sight of the Saxon man, whom she'd tried to help in the forest – the man who'd stayed with Father Wulfstan. She felt her heart give a little lurch as the blond Saxon man turned to smile at her, and she was glad he'd survived.

Then Elena waited breathlessly in the courtyard, deafened by the shouts of the soldiers and the jangling of horses' harness, her heart beating wildly. This was to be her home.

She'd expected to be lined up with the other serfs, but instead they'd brought her in here, into the very heart of the stronghold. Through the huge, raftered hall they led her, with its great fire forever burning at one end; up the stairs, along the gallery past the Breton's living quarters into this room, which she was told would be hers.

After the bare meanness of the little convent, even this tiny chamber was luxury. The maidservant who awaited her had helped her off with her ragged clothes, exclaiming with pity over her torn, bruised feet and her chafed wrists where the chains had been. Then she helped her to step into the wooden tub.

Elena, still dazed by everything that had happened,

lay back when the maid had gone, and revelled in the sweetly-scented soap and the delicious sensation of warm water lapping at her skin. She had never had a hot bath before. At the convent they washed every morning using buckets of cold water from the spring, and harsh soap made from wood-ash and lye. This was bliss. The small but private room was hung with tapestries, had a fire burning in one corner, and a hide curtain to the window. There was a narrow bed, covered with wolfskins as blankets, and real wax candles on the walls, not the crude, foul-smelling tallow they used at the convent.

She frowned and bit her lip. Perhaps everyone was wrong. Perhaps Aimery le Sabrenn was truly a kind man, who intended to help her. After all, hadn't he punished that evil man, Mauger, for attacking her?

She shuddered suddenly, remembering how they'd left his limp, beaten body roped to the tree. Aimery le Sabrenn – kind? She must be in danger of losing her wits! She swallowed hard, thrusting the Breton lord's disturbing image from her mind, and began to soap herself, luxuriating in the warm water. Her body was bruised and aching from the long ride. Exploratively she ran her fingers along her calves and up along her smooth, slender thighs. Her small breasts lay buoyantly just above the surface of the water; she soaped them carefully, and lapped the soothing water over their tender tips.

Suddenly, she remembered the puzzling noises that the unseen woman had made last night in the darkness, and frowned. At the same time, strangely, her nipples tingled and darkened, and as she touched one inquisitively, a pleasurable little shock arrowed down towards her flat stomach. She caught her breath and did it again. A vague, yearning ache flooded slowly through her relaxed limbs, and the warm blood rose in her cheeks.

She bit at her lower lip thoughtfully, and stroked her swelling breast. The Breton's low, compelling voice

47

echoed in her brain: 'You have much to learn, little Saxon . . .' With a blush of shame, she snatched her hand away.

At the convent, they'd been told it was a sin to touch their bodies. The younger ones slept in dormitories with older nuns to keep an eye on them, and they had to sleep with their hands above the coarse blankets or they were beaten.

Closing her eyes, Elena lay back, and her hands wandered down to her inner thigh. They were so bruised from the long ride. Perhaps if she stroked them a little, it would soothe them. Her palm, by accident, grazed the soft mound between her legs. Her body quivered and jumped. She did it again, her eyes wide open with surprise. Her little triangle of womanly hair was light golden, like soft down; she fingered it, and her hand slipped lower, exploring the strange, folded flesh in that secret place. She caught something with the tip of her finger – it felt like a tiny, sensitive bud – and a sudden, delicious sensation flared, spreading a melting heat into her stomach. She snatched her hand away quickly, but her cheeks flamed, and a little pulse beat wildly in her soft throat.

She jumped with shock, sending ripples of water over the edge of the tub, as the door that divided her room from the gallery was pushed aside and a woman glided in.

Elena thought that she was the most beautiful woman she had ever seen in her life. She was small and slender, with glossy dark hair and perfect, creamy skin, and a kind smile. She wore a green silk gown that matched her wonderful, dark-lashed eyes; it was girdled to fit her body tightly, pushing up her small, rounded breasts, while the skirt flared out in rich swathes from her hips to brush the ground.

She was carrying a silver goblet in her hands. On seeing Elena's blush of surprise, she came softly

48

towards her and knelt at he side, with a rustle of silk and perfume.

'My dear,' she said, in a low voice, 'don't be afraid of me, I beg you! My name is Isobel, and I've come to look after you. You poor thing, what a dreadful ordeal you must have suffered! How I feel for you . . .'

Elena tried to sit up, but the lady put out one exquisite jewelled hand, restraining her. 'There is no cause for alarm! Lie back – relax.' By accident, it seemed, her little fingers brushed Elena's exposed breasts. Elena let out a tiny gasp; the woman heard it, and smiled to herself.

'Here,' she said, holding out the goblet. 'Drink this. It has medicinal properties. You will find it soothes you, relaxes you.'

Elena, forgetting to be ashamed of her nakedness at those soothing words, gazed hypnotised into the woman's spellbinding green eyes, took the goblet and drank deeply. It was delicious, tasting of honey and sunshine, and strange, exotic fruits. Almost immediately her body was filled with a flooding sensation of languor. She gave a blissful little sigh and leaned back against the side of the tub, her eyes closed.

A smile flickered round Isobel's mouth as she studied her carefully by the light of the glimmering candles. Aimery was right. The girl was astonishingly beautiful for a Saxon peasant, with that sweet, heart-shaped face, and the full, curved lips, and the glorious golden hair that cascaded round her shoulders and curled into little tendrils where it was damp.

And her breasts! High and firm, they darkened deliciously into tiny rosebud crests. She was young, surely untouched. Isobel licked her lips and drew in her breath sharply. The girl stirred and her eyes flew open.

'Let me take the goblet,' Isobel said soothingly, taking the vessel from the girl's nerveless hands. 'And then let me finish washing you, my dear. You must be so tired – '

And, before the girl could protest, she picked up the

scented soap and the washing cloth, and began, with light, circling strokes, to lave at her shoulders.

Elena felt light, as if she were floating. She felt exquisitely calm and carefree after that wonderful healing drink. This woman, so beautiful and kind, was truly her friend.

Isobel's busy hands worked carefully at first, so as not to disturb her. She washed her shoulders and arms with gentle thoroughness, as a maid would have done.

But then, her white hands soft with soap, she slid her fingers round Elena's ribcage, and slipped them upwards to caress her soft, virginal breasts.

Elena gasped, and went rigid. Her eyes, which had been slowly closing with the heady effect of the wine, flew open in alarm.

Isobel said softly, 'Relax, my dear. Let me bathe you properly. You have no need to be ashamed of your beautiful body. After all, you are a lady of the castle, are you not? And this is what fine ladies do to one another.'

Elena nodded dumbly, because she couldn't speak. Isobel was kneading her nipples so slowly and exquisitely that the pleasure melted her and set up hot, churning sensations in her belly. She felt her breasts swelling and tugging, aching for some nameless release. Oh, what was happening to her? Her breath was coming rapidly and she could feel her cheeks burning with shame. She had to escape, and yet she didn't want this beautiful lady to stop. Her jutting nipples danced beneath Isobel's soapy caresses, and she felt a sweet, blissful ache in the soft, secret flesh between her legs. She suddenly thought of Aimery the Breton and quivered, as if his scornful eyes were watching her coldly. Her mouth went dry, and she felt herself ache for Isobel's cool hands to continue their work, to soothe her throbbing breasts, to –

Isobel stopped. She had watched the young Saxon slave's sweet, tormented little face, watched as her lips parted tremulously and her thighs rubbed against one another in an effort to sooth the exquisite need. She was thrusting her breasts involuntarily towards Isobel, trying to find those cool palms again. Definitely time to stop, decided Isobel, before she took her beyond the brink. Aimery would be angry if she went any further.

Isobel sighed. It was quite obvious that this stupid, naive girl was totally ignorant about her own body – had never even pleasured herself, brought herself to a feeble, solitary orgasm. How angry Aimery would be if he missed her first one.

Isobel was aware that she had probably overdone the wine too. She prayed that the girl would stay awake long enough for their purposes.

Reluctantly, Isobel de Morency got to her feet. The girl watched her, obviously shaken. Her vivid blue eyes were hazed with sexual longing.

'Come along, my dear,' said Isobel a trifle sharply. 'Time to join the lord Aimery.' Isobel was excited herself now at the thought of Aimery waiting for them. She called the maidservant, and watched as Alys dressed the sweetly-scented Saxon slave girl in a silk chemise, fine stockings that were gartered above the knee, and a pretty dark blue gown of softest wool that matched her eyes. The bodice was laced at the front, like Isobel's, and the finishing touch was a lovely silver girdle tied round her waist. Then Alys helped Elena to buckle on some dainty little shoes of dark red leather, and finally brushed out her long golden hair and let it hang loosely, a shimmering gauze around her shoulders.

Isobel, surveying the bewildered Elena in her new finery, suddenly didn't feel quite so pleased with Aimery's latest acquisition. The girl was truly beautiful, more beautiful than perhaps Isobel had realised at first. Her skin was ivory-pale and delicate, not like the nut-brown hue of the other Saxon serfs. And she was young – several years younger than Isobel de Morency.

Isobel frowned. But she could cope with it, couldn't

she? Aimery needed her – she inflamed his blood. No other woman could satisfy him, because he grew bored with their adoration and their desperate, clinging ways. Whereas Isobel was useful to him, because she understood his need to use and humiliate these stupid Saxon girls who became his slaves. For that was all the wench was – a slave – and she'd be reminded of that soon enough. Isobel would see to that.

Only once had she lost him for a while, and that was to that Saxon witch, Madelin, who'd all but destroyed him.

'You look quite lovely, my dear Elena,' Isobel said graciously. Elena overwhelmed by her new finery, smiled shyly up at her, and Isobel took her by the hand.

Aimery was waiting for them in his private chamber. Usually he ate in the great hall below, with his soldiers and retainers, but tonight he'd had food brought upstairs so he could dine alone. He'd almost finished, and the remains of the feast – roast fowl, succulent venison, white manchet bread and pork with honeyed apples – lay about the table.

He dismissed the waiting manservant when Isobel came in with Elena, and stood up. 'Be seated at the table,' he said courteously to Elena, extending one firm, well-shaped hand. 'And take what you want to eat.'

Elena gazed up at him, speechless. Aimery le Sabrenn, the vile beast of rumour, at whose very name the elderly nuns used to cross themselves, was actually smiling at her. And as he smiled she realised, with a little jolt that made her heart pound, that in spite of the cruel scar he was the most devastatingly handsome man she had ever seen. His smile made her feel faint as his thin lips twisted. She sat down suddenly in the chair he indicated and stared at the table, her senses swimming. Isobel sat down too, opposite Elena.

'There is spiced venison here, or perhaps you would

prefer the chicken?' the Breton offered graciously, pushing a dish towards her.

'Thank you, my lord,' muttered Elena, not able to meet his eyes. 'But I am not hungry.'

'Some wine, then?' He thrust a goblet towards her. Elena grabbed at it and drank thirstily, because her mouth was suddenly burning dry. She put it down when it was empty, and closed her eyes as the sweet liquid trickled down her throat.

When she opened them, something had happened. Aimery had sat down again at Isobel's side; and she, Elena, might as well not have been in the room. Most of the candles had been snuffed out; only two remained alight, glimmering from their iron sconces on the wall. Shadows leaped from the log fire, bringing to life the hazy, mysterious figures on the tapestries that adorned the bare flint walls. Her head swam. Aimery and the lady Isobel weren't even touching. But there was something about the way they *looked* at each other . . .

Elena felt her pulse racing, her blood pounding thickly with the wine she'd drunk. She gazed in horrified fascination, unable to tear her eyes away as she saw how the Breton was dipping the sweet red grapes in his wine and dropping them, very slowly, between Isobel's red lips. The lady accepted them with pleasure, gazing all the time into his strange silver eyes; then, as he slowly inserted yet another grape, she nipped at his hand with her perfect white teeth, and caught his flesh between her lips, and sucked and sucked. Aimery smiled slowly, and Elena watched in dazed disbelief as the tiny tip of Isobel's tongue caressed her lord's lean, sun-browned finger.

Elena caught her breath and leaned forward in her chair, her limbs strangely on fire. The soft silk of her chemise tantalised her scented flesh. She clenched her hands.

Isobel looked at her and smiled. Then she gazed into Aimery's eyes again and slowly, very slowly, she

53

unlaced the bodice of her beautiful green dress and slipped it down to expose her white, perfect breasts. They gleamed with the milky whiteness of pearls in the soft candlelight.

Aimery dipped his finger in the wine. Completely ignoring the wide-eyed, trembling Saxon girl, he circled his moist finger round each of Isobel's nipples in turn, totally absorbed his his task. Darker and larger than Elena's, the delicate buds of erectile tissue stood out proudly to meet his sensuous caress. Aimery paused, watching, then reached out both his hands to cup her full breasts together. Isobel shuddered. Then, as Elena watched, hypnotised, the Breton lowered his head as if in homage, and took each of her breasts in turn into his worshipping mouth. Elena could see his sensual, curved tongue licking and circling the quivering flesh. She saw how Isobel threw her head back, her eyes closed, her breath coming in short, ragged pants as she gripped his shoulders with a sudden, fierce hunger.

Elena felt wave after wave of hot, shameful emotion washing over her helpless body. She knew that she should turn and run. But she couldn't move. She felt her own heated blood surge and pulse as Aimery's mouth devoured the lady Isobel's tender breasts. An almost unbearable ache was rising down at the pit of her taut stomach, and her own swollen breasts seemed to be thrusting against the confines of her tight bodice, the turgid nipples hot and painful. Oh, she thought, with a sudden flood of shame, how cool the Breton's cruel mouth would be against her own burning flesh! He was teasing Isobel now, his firm hands lightly spanning her waist; she could see how his tongue was darting and flicking at her thrusting, creamy breasts, while Isobel writhed and panted in his embrace. Elena gripped the edge of the table, and a tiny moan of longing escaped from her parted lips.

They both heard her. Aimery stopped his exquisite torment of his lady; raising his head, he turned slowly towards Elena, and smiled his slow, crooked smile. Isobel lay back in her chair panting, her lovely face flushed and contorted, her body still quivering. As if – as if he had hurt her. But he hadn't, surely? Elena's small face twisted in bewilderment.

Aimery stood up. He lifted the lady Isobel easily in his strong arms and carried her across to a fur-covered bed in the far corner of his chamber. Then he came back towards Elena. She shrank back in her chair, appalled, yet unable to take her eyes from him. He knelt before her on the rush matting, so that his face was at the same height as hers, and let one hand rest lightly on her thigh. He was so masculine, so beautiful in his lithe strength.

'Well, my little Saxon rebel,' he said, his low, cool voice sending renewed tremors through her. 'Did you enjoy that?'

Elena clenched her hands in confusion. 'No! How could I?'

'Then why,' he said, leaning forward, 'did you watch it so avidly?'

She shook her head in desperation, her eyes transfixed by the hard, clear lines of his face. Oh, if only she hadn't drunk that wine! Her brain, like her limbs, was hot and fevered. 'I had no choice!' she whispered.

His strong, capable hands were touching her gown. She caught her breath in horrified excitement. 'But you enjoyed it,' he went on relentlessly. 'Was it because you wanted me to do the same to you, little convent girl? Is that how you and your sweet friends pleasured one another at your nunnery, your nest of rebels? Like this?'

'No! I – oh, please!' Her voice broke off in a gasp of pleasure, because his hands had slipped her silk chemise under her aching breasts so that the taut fabric thrust them provocatively upwards. He began to stroke them, gently. Little arrows of impossible rapture seared Elena's quivering flesh. She gasped and thrust against his big, cool palms, rubbing the tautened globes desperately against his caress. His silver eyes narrowed as he watched her; deliberately his thumbs found her stiffened nipples, and rubbed them tantalisingly. Shafts of hot and cold sensation burned through her. She closed her eyes and shuddered as his hands slipped round her back.

Then a new, impossibly delicious sensation engulfed her trembling flesh. If he hadn't been supporting her, she would have collapsed, because all of a sudden her small breasts felt wet, and hot, and so deliciously sensitive that she was moaning aloud. He was licking her, savouring her with his mouth, in the same exquisite way that he'd tormented the lady Isobel. His long, stiffened tongue rasped slowly, softly to and fro across her engorged nipples, flicking at them, then sucking moistly. Waves of excitement convulsed her flesh; she clenched her legs together, and was suddenly aware of a shameful wetness seeping from her most secret parts.

Oh, could such dreadful things really happen? This must be the work of the very devil, and she would be damned forever for enjoying it . . .

She threw herself back, pushing her quivering flesh hard against his strong sensual mouth, gasping aloud as his teeth nipped deliciously and his firm lips suckled and caressed. Rippling tides of ecstasy washed in mounting waves through her shaking body; she reached out mindlessly to clutch at his wide, strong shoulders, pulling him towards her, pressing his hard-boned face down against her sensitised flesh in an agony of wanting yet more.

In a deliberately calculated move, he stood up, and she sagged helplessly in her chair, gazing up at him with wide, imploring eyes.

'Please,' she whispered, clasping her hands across her still quivering, blue-veined nakedness. 'Oh, please, my lord – '

He stood towering above her, his hands on his hips. The expression on his dark, brooding face was unreadable; the white scar seemed livid in the hard-boned masculinity of his face.

'What did you want me to do next, Elena?' he said in a soft voice that sent shivers through her. 'What did you want me to do to that pretty little nun's body of yours?'

Elena shook her head numbly. 'I don't know, my lord,' she whispered. 'I only know that – I didn't want you to stop – '

He smiled a slow, harsh smile. 'You didn't know, did you?' he said softly, taking her by the shoulders. 'You really have no idea . . .' He turned to Isobel, who was leaning forward, her eyes hungry, on the bed. 'We have a lot to teach her, you see, Isobel. Let us hope that she learns well.'

He let go of her, and she fell in a shaking heap on the ground, burying her head in her arms. Aimery went to the door of his room to open it, and Hamet came in.

'Restrain her,' Aimery said curtly to the Saracen. 'She wishes to partake in our games.' Then he went back to the table and poured himself more wine. He watched impassively as Hamet led the dazed Elena across the room to a darkened alcove and, raising her slender wrists, shackled her carefully to some chains that protruded from the cold stones of the outer wall. Elena's blood was racing wildly at this new degredation. Her bodice was still undone, and she was aware of the big Saracen's hungry black eyes eagerly devouring her nakedness. Her arms were dragged up above her head by the chains, so that her breasts were lifted high. She felt sick with excitement when they began to tingle and burn in anticipation as Aimery le Sabrenn strolled languidly towards her with a full goblet of wine in his hand.

His mouth tightened in mockery as he registered her stiffening nipples. Elena bowed her head in submission. Then, with one hand, he raised her small chin and pushed the goblet against her lips.

'Drink,' he said, almost unkindly. 'Drink it all down, Saxon girl.'

He trickled it down her throat, and she drank thirstily. A lot of it was spilt; she felt it running down her chin, down her throat and across her burning breasts, tormenting her with its coolness. The Breton lord smiled, and reached out to flick the drops away; her body jerked towards him, in automatic reaction. 'Later,' he said softly. 'But first, we must continue with your education.'

He pointed towards the bed. Elena's eyes jerked wide open.

On top of the big, fur-covered bed, the lady Isobel was lying moaning as the big Saracen crouched on top of her. At first, Elena thought that he was attacking her. Then she heard Isobel's low gurgle of delight, and realised that Hamet had pulled Isobels's skirts up around her waist, and she wasn't fighting him. Elena could see how his loose mouth suckled at her exposed breasts, while all the time he was fumbling with his own clothing, throwing his tunic and leggings to the ground and exposing his huge, glistening dark limbs.

Elena closed her eyes in disbelief. The wine swam round in her fevered blood. Aimery raised her head upright again. 'Look,' he commanded. 'You wish to learn? This is your lesson.'

Elena forced her eyes open and watched in dismay. The Saracen's huge male member was fully exposed as it jerked upright between his muscular black thighs. It looked so swollen and massive to Elena that she gasped aloud. She watched, rigid with apprehension, as he seemed to part the lady Isobel's tender thighs and thrust his obscene protuberance against her quivering hips. Elena felt faint; yet at the same time she felt a strange, stirring excitement deep within herself.

She bit her lip as she saw how the big black penis slid into Isobel's private parts, and then withdrew again, glistening with moisture, while a lewd expression of delight contorted the man's face. Surely, Isobel would protest at the intrusion? But no – she was crying out softly, happily, and clutching at the man's shoulders, lifting her swollen breasts into his greedy mouth as he slid that giant shaft into her arching hips yet again.

Elena jerked her head away, feeling that she could watch no more. But there was no escape that way. Aimery, who had been watching her, reached up to her chains, and somehow, by a little ratchet device, shortened them an inch or so, stretching her arms even higher. It was bearable, but made her only too aware of his power over her.

'A warning,' the Breton said softly. 'They can be tightened much, much more. Now, watch.'

Nodding in dumb acquiescence, Elena watched as the little tableau was played out in the flickering, smoky light of the candles. On the bed, the Saracen was now kneeling upright, his swollen member twitching upwards against his belly. The lady Isobel, her slender legs in their silken hose spread apart and an expression of avid delight on her face, began slowly to lower herself onto it, making little squealing noises as she impaled herself. Then she writhed up and down on the slippery shaft; slowly at first, but then, as Hamet's stiffened tongue darted to and fro and guzzled at her pouting breasts, she began to move faster and faster, wriggling in her delight, as the Saracen clutched her to him and thrust himself hard within her. Her gown had ridden up to expose her plump white buttocks. 'Oh, yes,' Isobel was muttering. 'Oh, please . . .'

And Elena felt her own lips echoing those lewd animal noises. Because Aimery, still at her side, had put his arm round her straining shoulders, and was rubbing and stroking carefully at her breasts, still tautly upthrust by the tight chemise, his fingers reawakening the heady, exciting delirium that had gripped her before. He was watching the panting couple on the bed with a little smile on his face; still fingering Elena's breasts voluptuously, he whispered in her ear, 'You like this? I wonder, what do you want next, my little nun?'

Panting, Elena felt the hot, wet liquid seeping down between her thighs. Her whole body burned; she was suddenly aware that this powerful man was reaching down to some deep, dark fire in her own soul that she hadn't realised existed, that the nuns had falsely shielded her from all these years. Her loins twitched and jumped instinctively as she watched the lady Isobel bringing herself close to the very extremity of pleasure. She moistened her burning lips. 'I want – oh, I want – '

His thumb and forefinger gently gripped her nipple, pulling at it; she writhed rapturously against the wall, her shadowy blue eyes heavy with desire. Isobel had almost lifted herself off the man completely; Elena could see the huge, dark pillar of flesh rising from the man's thighs. She saw the expression of glazed rapture that contorted Isobel's face as she carefully slid herself down onto him again.

'What do you want, Elena? Tell me,' came Aimery le Sabrenn's husky voice in her ear.

Isobel was squealing in her pleasure, writhing with little jerking spasms on the hard flesh that impaled her, throwing her head back and thrusting her breasts into the man's mouth. Then she stopped, suddenly, her eyes wide open, and began to moan in a strange, high pitched voice, holding herself rigid as Hamet gently pumped upwards, his big hands on her back, his tongue licking hungrily at her straining nipples. Isobel's delirious cries of pleasure echoed round the candlelit room. Elena couldn't tear her eyes away from the woman's spasming body.

'What do you want?' repeated Aimery relentlessly.

Elena wetted her dry lips, and felt the wine swirling around her heated body. 'I want – to feel a man inside me – like that – ' She broke off with a moan, seeing how Isobel, her face gleaming with sweat, had collapsed at last onto the man's body. 'Oh, God help me! It must be a sin! To want that.'

Aimery, on seeing how the girl couldn't tear her face away from the couple on the bed as Hamet continued to thrust very gently at Isobel's still twitching body, let his mouth twist in a mocking smile. 'No sin,' he said. 'But bodily love between man and woman. You will learn to enjoy it, little Saxon. You will learn to satisfy *me*.'

Elena shuddered, gazing up at his strong, hard body, his lean, scarred face. The thought of doing that, with him . . . The blood rushed to her face, and she felt weak with longing. Dear God. *She wanted Aimery le Sabrenn* . . .

'But first,' he went on carefully, 'you must learn to know yourself – to know your own secret desires.'

Her body quivered involuntarily as he stroked her tender breasts. 'You're learning well, little Saxon,' he said softly. 'But you are not ready for me. Not yet.'

He looked across at the bed. Isobel lay curled in the furs, her eyes closed. Hamet crouched over her, and Elena saw with a shock that he was still fully erect, his massive male member twitching as he waited for his master's instructions. He was looking, hopefully, at *her* – Elena bit back a gasp.

Aimery heard it, and laughed. 'She's not for you, Hamet,' he said to his servant. 'Not yet. Finish with Isobel, then we'll proceed.'

Hamet nodded in obedience, though he still looked at the chained, writhing girl with longing. He turned back to Isobel, and her prone figure fluttered with reawakened pleasure as he rubbed his swollen member across her breasts and swiftly, with one big, practised hand, brought himself to his extremity. He threw his head back and gave a bark of delight as his seed spurted forth; then he rubbed the creamy liquid gently into her soft, trembling flesh with the velvety glans, muttering strange little crooning sounds to himself.

Elena had never before been witness to a man in the throes of his climax. Her face was transfixed in an expression of shock and amazement as she watched the virile, white substance jet forth from the dark nest of his private parts.

This alarming spectacle left Elena in a state of confusion; she had never seen anything like it before. But she didn't close her eyes, and she didn't turn her head away. She felt compelled to watch every second of the explicit moment, and yet she knew that she was observing something which should have been a private act. This knowledge filled her with a feeling of utmost shame. She, an innocent convent girl, was being made to relish the role of a voyeur. Her face flushed at the very thought and she lowered her gaze to the floor, knowing that her ordeal was far from over.

Aimery watched impassively, his hands still fondling Elena's breasts until she sagged in her chains with the unbearable ache of unsatisfied desire.

When Hamet's huge erection had subsided at last, Aimery commanded, 'Isobel. Over here.'

Languidly, like a cat, Isobel rose from the bed and pulled her gown together, a faint flush still staining her cheeks. Hamet too tied up his leggings, and sat cross-legged on the bed, watching Elena intently.

Isobel swayed across the room towards her lord. 'What is your command, my lord?' she said softly.

He glanced with a certain distaste at her swollen lips, her glittering eyes and disordered hair. 'You will attend to the girl,' he said tersely. 'She is obviously untried and ignorant. You will pleasure her gently, as women do. Hamet, come and help.'

Then he reached out, casually, and ripped Elena's gown apart from the waist downwards, exposing her slender legs and her quivering lower abdomen.

Elena gasped aloud. But then the sound of protest died in her throat, because now Hamet had joined his master, and the two men were bending to caress her breasts with their silken mouths. She shuddered with sudden, fierce pleasure as the hot, voluptuous sensation engulfed her chained body. They took one breast each, stroking and licking until she thought she would explode with rapture.

Then she froze, and the men stopped too. Something else was happening. Isobel was kneeling between her legs, stroking her thighs above her gartered stockings. She was pulling aside Elena's ripped gown, and fingering her gently in her most private parts, where she was already melting.

'No – please, no,' begged Elena.

Isobel smiled, gazing at her prisoner's exposed, quivering flesh. Then, before Elena could cry out again, she plunged her head forwards, and started to lick at her most secret place – that place which the nuns said it was a mortal sin even to touch.

The sweet, rasping feel of Isobel's darting tongue, combined with the powerful suckling of the Breton and his servant on each sensitive breast, was too much. Wave after wave of sensation flooded her yearning body, the most wonderful feeling she had ever known.

Then suddenly Isobel's cunning tongue stopped licking, and pushed up, hard and hot and wet, into her inner opening. Elena cried aloud and then shuddered wildly, because the sensation of all three tongues, thrusting and caressing and biting, filled her with a burning pleasure so intense and so unlike anything she had known before. Her brain was flooded with a hot, dark redness and she pushed herself down, jerking against Isobel's pointed wonderful tongue as it circled tenderly inside her pulsing vagina. The men's mouths were caressing her softly, tenderly now as her helpless body shuddered into an exquisite orgasm. Isobel, with a final effort, pushed her tongue hard up inside the climaxing girl so she could grip as it in her final throes of delight. With little whimpers, Elena subsided into the Breton's strong arms.

At Aimery's terse command, Hamet unlocked her from the wall and carried her to the little chamber where she had taken her bath. He slid her torn gown from her sleepy, sated body, and rolled down her silk hose with an expression of rapture. Then he laid her on the narrow bed and covered her with a soft woollen blanket, finally brushing her hair almost tenderly from her flushed face. The Saxon girl didn't open her eyes. He gazed down lovingly at her prone, fragile figure, remembering the luscious taste of her sweet little breasts and the melting cries she'd made as they pleasured her.

The big Saracen thought longingly of the next stage in her education.

Chapter Five

*A*imery's desire, so long restrained, burned hot and hard at his loins. Isobel, watching him, caught her red lips between her teeth and beckoned him across to the bed. But Aimery hesitated, because Isobel was too openly eager for him. The moistness of her excited body was too predictable. Once, when he'd first known her, she was refined and deliciously tantalising. But now . . . He remembered her shameless coupling with Hamet, and frowned.

She sensed his distaste, because she knew him so well. She thought for a moment, then urged in a low voice, 'Aimery, my lord. Tie me up.'

He raised a mocking eyebrow. 'Like the girl?'

She couldn't stop her tongue sliding across her lips in delicious anticipation. 'Oh, yes. Like the girl . . .'

She was already moaning softly as he shackled her arms to the wall.

Aimery felt his excitement surge again. Not troubling to undress, he reached beneath her silk chemise to grip at the hot mound that was the core of her femininity. Down there, she was dark and luxuriant.

The little nun, he'd noted, had a soft triangle of curls, that barely covered her tender flesh.

He thrust up her fine clothing around her hips, glimpsing the soft skin of Isobel's white thighs above her stockings. Her legs parted readily for him and she groaned eagerly as his hands brushed her moist vulva. He unlaced his hose to release his throbbing erection from the constriction of his clothing, and thrust into her without preliminaries. Once his penis was sheathed in her velvety grip, he brushed with his thumb at her exposed clitoris, and she closed her eyes and made soft little noises of pleasure. He realised, with a frown of irritation, that she was trying to imitate the innocent, astonished cries of the Saxon girl.

For once, Aimery had to admit that he had been wrong about the girl. She did indeed seem to be a true innocent, as she claimed – either that, or exceptionally clever. Like Madelin.

Aimery wondered, suddenly, what the Saxon girl would be like when she first felt a man deep within her. He tried to imagine the look of quivering surprise that would transfix her features before the pleasure took over her senses. Had Isobel ever been that innocent? She probably couldn't even remember her first man, he thought grimly.

Isobel, unaware of his thoughts, shuddered with delight as she felt Aimery's wonderful length impale her helpless body over and over again. She wanted to cry out in despair each time he withdrew, leaving her aching with loss. But then she would feel the shuddering, mounting arousal, and her vaginal walls would grip feverishly as he slid slowly back in. It was always wonderful with Aimery le Sabrenn – she would never tire of him. He could sustain his erection for ever, it seemed, he exerted an icy control that was possessed by no other man she had ever known. Any other man, by now, after what had happened tonight, would have been panting with excitement, totally beyond control. Even Hamet, well-trained though he was, was a little too excitable. But Aimery – oh, Aimery was a man . . .

His hands kneaded her trembling breasts as his penis slowly did its magical work. She writhed against him to stimulate her clitoris, the dark pleasure flooding her body, drawing in harsh breaths as her excitement mounted. She wanted to clutch him to her, to undress his wonderful body and stroke his smooth flesh, but she couldn't because she was trapped by the chains. She wriggled in exquisite torment as he thrust himself hard within her and moved his hand down to stroke her engorged clitoris with the pad of his thumb while keeping himself completely still and solid inside her body. Isobel moaned aloud for release, her cheeks flushed with delight. This, this was the blissful part, where Aimery could keep her lingering on that exquisite brink with a finesse that no other man possessed.

'Please,' she begged, with a harsh guttural sound. 'Oh, I beg you – please – '

Slowly he withdrew from her, leaving her empty. She groaned out his name as he stood back and smiled at her. 'Shall I leave you like that, Isobel?' He seemed calmly unaware of his stiff penis twitching hungrily towards hers. 'I have a fancy for a little wine . . .' And deliberately he turned his back towards her and walked towards the flagon on the table.

Isobel spat after his retreating figure. 'Dear God, Aimery! You vile beast! You can't leave me like this!' In her extremity she writhed in her chains, trying desperately to rub her legs together to stimulate her fevered body. 'Bastard,' she moaned to herself. 'You bastard – I hate you – '

Aimery, having refreshed his thirst, came sauntering back and swung her round to face him. 'I thought you, enjoyed being tormented, Isobel,' he said calmly. 'It seemed quite an exquisite game to me, to arouse you so and then leave you chained up, so that even your busy little fingers can't assuage the ache down there.'

He mockingly rubbed the tip of his powerful penis against her throbbing vulva. She gasped and thrust out at him, grasping at the heady sensation. 'Oh, Aimery. My lord, I beg you, have mercy on me.'

He smiled that chilling smile that she knew so well, then shrugged, and coldly sheathed himself within her. She came immediately, jumping and bucking in her chains, her face contorted as the shattering explosions of delight ripped through her yearning body. Aimery leaned his hands against the wall above her shoulders and thrust into her with unbelievable strength.

It took him some time to spend himself within her, and by the time he had finished his breathing was ragged. Isobel, completley sated, let her limp body hang in the shackles and savoured every moment of his wonderful, quivering manhood as he reached his climax deep within her. So, she thought, with an exhausted triumph, even for her masterful Breton lord, the strain of holding on for so long took its toll. She kept very still, wanting him to stay inside her. This was the only time she felt he was really hers.

At last, without saying anything or even looking at her, he withdrew, and turned to straighten his disordered clothing. Then he released her from the shackles.

Isobel swayed against him, her silk gown rumpled and torn, her body weak with wonderfully sated desire. 'If you wish it, Aimery,' she murmered, 'I will spend the night with you.'

He shrugged her off almost impatiently. 'Not tonight, Isobel. Go and wear yourself out with Hamet if you must. I need some peace.'

Isobel was frightened at his outright rejection. That Saxon girl had something to do with it, she was sure.

Pretending not to care that he wanted her to go, she said lightly, 'I'm surprised, my lord, that you've given the little Saxon slut a room up here. She should be bedding down with the serfs in the yard, surely? I thought you wanted to humiliate her – treating her like a lady will hardly do that.'

Aimery's mouth tightened. He said, 'What I do with her is up to me. But I'd remind you that humiliation is all the worse when it is unexpected.'

Isobel frowned and bit her lip. Was he talking about the girl, or about her, Isobel? Feeling a sudden unease, she turned to go.

She paused at the door of the Saxon slut's chamber. To let her sleep, even for one night, in the lord's private quarters was a grave mistake. Tomorrow, she herself would have to remind the girl that she was nothing but a slave. She was smiling a little at the prospect by the time she reached her own luxurious chamber. She wondered whether to send for the inexhaustible Hamet, just to spite Aimery, but decided against it. Hamet was too faithful to his master, like some big dog. He told Aimery everything.

Thinking hard, Isobel nibbled at her white finger and in the end sent her servant Alys to fetch Pierre, the young serf from the kitchens. Pierre was strong, willing, handsome enough, and a simpleton. According to the housekeeper, he wasn't much use for anything, except carrying sacks of grain and turning the iron spits in the kitchen. But Isobel had found another use for him. As well as being simple he was also mute, which meant that he'd never tell anybody anything. Desperate for physical satisfaction, she'd summoned him to her room last night in a moment of inspiration. His eager, if clumsy willingness to pleasure her in every way she could think of was a marvellous physical relief, and a vivid if somewhat startling contrast to Aimery's sophisticated refinements.

By the time he arrived in her chamber, the young man's eyes were already glazed with anticipated pleasure, and his mouth was slack. Isobel could see the bluge of his excited genitals beneath the thin cloth of his homespun tunic; he rubbed at himself surreptitiously as she shut the door. Isobel felt a frown crease her smooth forehead. Pierre was handsome and muscular, but so lacking in any sort of finesse.

Suddenly repelled at the thought of his clumsy attentions, she slapped at his masturbating hand and his face fell.

'Not now, you stupid fool,' she hissed angrily. 'But listen, you can please me very much, if you do exactly as I say. You know we have some new slaves at the castle?'

He nodded eagerly.

'Well,' said Isobel, 'one of them has already seen you, Pierre, and heard about you, and she is very excited at the thought of meeting you – properly. She can see what a big, fine man you are. And she says – she says, Pierre, that she would like to kiss you. In that very special way. You know?'

Beads of sweat stood out on Pierre's downy upper lip. He nodded hard, almost shaking in his excitement.

'Tomorrow,' went on Isobel languidly, 'I will take you to her. She will kiss you and caress you just as you like it, and I will be there to watch. Oh, she might protest a little at first, because that's what she enjoys. But you can do what you like with her, I promise you.' Isobel smiled thoughtfully and touched her own breasts with light fingers. 'Do you know,' she went on, 'at the thought of it, I could almost take a fancy to your services after all . . .'

The serf's hungry eyes, brown and faithful like some adoring dog, widened in anticipation. He gazed with open lust at her full, perfect figure. Then Isobel remembered Aimery. No. After her lord's masterful love-making, she was deliciously replete. A shame to spoil it with this crude wretch. But all the same, she felt like some entertainment.

A little smile pulled at her mouth as she started to unfasten her clothes. 'Alys!' she called out impatiently.

She knew that Alys would be outside the door, listening. 'Keeping watch,' Alys called it, when really the maid was just pleasuring herself by listening to the sounds that emerged when her mistress had visitors. Isobel had actually caught her rubbing frantically at herself one night, when she was entertaining Hamet. Poor Alys was small and ugly. She was almost thirty, and no man wanted her because of her badly pocked skin. Isobel took great pleasure in occasionally providing her with what she wanted more than anything.

As the maidservant hurried into the room, Isobel said in a bored voice, 'I'm going to bed, Alys. But first I want you to let Pierre pleasure you. Do exactly as he says, will you? And don't make too much noise.'

Pierre's face fell a little as he absorbed what Isobel was saying. But his penis was painfully rampant after hearing what was in store for tomorrow, and at least he would be pleasing his mistress.

Alys' ugly face had lit up immediately. Isobel reclined on her fur-covered bed, propped up by feather cushions, and watched the little scene with amusement as Pierre turned to the maid and indicated by gesticulation that he wanted to take her animal fashion, on all fours. A good idea, thought Isobel approvingly, then he doesn't have to watch her face. She sipped with relish at her wine, and made them move around so could see Pierre's swollen, twitching member and tight balls as he rucked up the woman's woollen skirt and felt hungrily for her coarse outer lips.

Isobel reached down and played with herself gently as Pierre thrust his rampant penis between the woman's buttocks and Alys squealed in ecstasy. Pierre withdrew slowly, and Isobel chuckled softly as the glistening shaft came back into her interested view. Really, it was grotesquely ugly, swollen and purple with a strange, upward curve to it. Not that Alys seemed to mind. Pierre impaled her again, and the two of them worked with desperate enthusiasm towards orgasm, bucking eagerly away like dogs in the courtyard. No finesse,

71

sighed Isobel, finding her own engorged clitoris and stroking it tenderly. No style.

The woman came first, crying and moaning with delight. Then Pierre huffed towards his own climax with long, shuddering strokes that took him some time. Isobel was excited by the strength of him, almost wishing that she'd taken him herself, and she brought herself to a pleasantly satisfying little orgasm as she thought of that hot, desperate length of male flesh within her own quivering vagina.

Then she ordered them both quickly out of her sight, because she'd had enough. She blew out the candle, and began to think happily of what the next day would bring.

Alone in his chamber, Aimery le Sabrenn, former penniless mercenary and now lord of Thoresfield, sat restlessly in his carved oak chair toying with his wine goblet.

Something was troubling him, and he knew what it was. He wanted the Saxon girl, badly.

He poured himself some more wine from the flagon, and drank it slowly. A single candle flickered smokily on the wall above his head. He stroked the tight scar on his cheek, which was hurting him more than usual.

The girl, Elena, filled his mind. He told himself that she was a rebel, no doubt responsible for the death of countless of his comrades in arms – a golden Saxon maid, to be enjoyed and cast aside, like the rest. Since his infatuation with Madelin – Madelin, who'd betrayed his brother – he'd humiliated many of them.

Madelin had made the mistake of thinking that she still had some power over him, even after she'd betrayed himself and his brother to the Saxon rebels. When Aimery escaped from the rebels and tracked Madelin down at last, she'd pretended to be sorry about it all and actually welcomed him into her vile bed. She'd even cried over his terribly scarred face, because he used to be so handsome. Aimery had aroused her to her usual state of greedy lust, and then, when she was panting like a bitch on heat, he left her there, with just his bitter, ringing words of accusation for company. At least she still had her worthless life, though his brother Hugh had not been so lucky. The Saxons had tortured him, and castrated him, so that he was glad to die at last.

Aimery's hands tightened round the goblet, remembering. After Madelin, he'd fought the rebels so fiercely that even his own men feared him. And ever since that time, he and his mistress Isobel, had made a game of revenge, by selecting suitable young Saxon girls and making them plead for the pleasure he could bring them, before discarding them. Isobel always had plenty of ideas for their games – no doubt she had plans for Elena.

But, and Aimery frowned, there was something different about the convent girl. She might be one of the rebels, but even so he was strangely aware that he'd never encountered such beauty and innocence before. Soon, the innocence would be destroyed – they'd started on that process this evening. Soon she'd be as eager as any of them for sexual pleasure. She'd sidle up to him hopefully, as Isobel did, and when he grew tired of her she'd turn to other men for satisfaction, like the ever-willing Hamet or that young fool Pierre. Isobel thought Aimery didn't know about Pierre last night, but Aimery had spies everywhere. Since Madelin, he'd trusted no-one.

Aimery felt a sudden craving to know this girl in her innocence before she was changed for ever. He wanted to explore her sweetness for himself, with no-one else watching. He wanted to kiss those firm, sweet young breasts, and feel her yield to his thrusting manhood with all the passion he guessed she was capable of, until she was trembling at the very brink of ecstasy . . .

His mouth twisted mockingly at his fantasy. The little

73

nun had cast a spell on him. All right, so he wanted to try her out. Nothing wrong with that. After all, she was his slave. Afterwards, he promised himself, he and Isobel would begin her training in full.

Elena had drifted into sleep, but it was a sleep tormented by her disturbed dreams. She was back in the bleak little dormitory of the convent; the cold moonlight shone in through the high, narrow window, casting its silvery gleam on the familiar flint walls and flagged floor. Wrapped in her coarse woollen blanket, she felt unbearably, achingly alone.

Then, still in her dream, someone gently touched her shoulder. She moaned and stirred in her sleep, and saw a wide-shouldered, tall figure standing over her little wooden bed, a man with a harsh face that was cruelly scarred. Aimery le Sabrenn. The shadowy horseman of her dreams. He was standing over her, slowly removing his clothes, and Elena cried out his name in soft disbelief. What was he doing here, in the convent? In her dream she felt no fear, only wonder, because she'd never seen anything so beautiful in her life.

In the smoky candlelight, his naked body was hard and strong, and marked by old sword scars that only accentuated the muscled smoothness of his skin. His hips were lean, his thighs heavily muscled, and his pulsing manhood was jerking upwards from that dark, mysterious cradle of soft curling hair, waiting for her, wanting her. With a soft cry of need, Elena reached out to him, and he was beside her on her small bed, cradling her to him, pushing back her long golden hair and closing her tear-stained eyes with his kisses. His cool, flat palms slid beneath her silk chemise to caress her small breasts; she moaned with soft delight and nuzzled against the smooth, muscled wall of his chest, a sweet, undefinable longing tugging painfully at the very pit of her stomach. Her dream had never been so clear, so sweet before. She never wanted to wake.

'Slowly, *caran*,' his voice came cool in her ear. 'We have all night remember? And you have so much to learn, little Elena, before the dawn . . .'

'*Caran*,' she repeated wonderingly. 'Please – what does it mean?'

He smiled softly, playing with her hair. 'In my own language, the language of Brittainy, it means *beloved one*.'

Elena gazed wordlessly up at him, her eyes soft with desire. She reached out to touch the cruel scar that split his cheek, and felt the tense ridge of white skin against the tip of her finger.

The feel of it brought her to her senses. That face. That scar. *That voice*. Dear God, this was no dream!

With a cry of alarm, Elena wrenched herself back into reality. She was not in the convent, but in Aimery le Sabrenn's castle! And she was in the Breton's naked arms . . .

'No!' she cried out. 'No!'

But it was too late. Already, she was his prisoner. His hands continued their gentle stimulation, and he was still smiling at her. Her heart turned over. Heaven help her, but she *wanted* to be here like this! He had imprisoned her with some dark, potent magic, and she couldn't have torn herself away, even if she'd wanted to.

His erect manhood stirred heavily against her soft belly, sending strange, liquid sensations flooding through her helpless body. She let out a little, quivering moan and arched against him so that she could feel the rasping hardness of his long, muscular thighs against her own trembling legs. To lie in his arms, like this, to breathe in the warm masculine scent of him, was indescribable bliss. With a little shock, she realised that *this* was what she had always longed for, in her wistful daydreamings at the convent.

'You want me?' he whispered softly, his tongue flicking her earlobe, his hands slipping her chemise

75

from her shoulders. 'You were dreaming of me? Tell me, *caran*.'

She shook her head helplessly, her blood already fevered. 'Yes, I was dreaming. I often dream.'

'You have the sight?'

'No!' How often had the nuns warned her not to tell anybody about her strange premonitions? 'No . . . But this *must* be a dream.'

In answer she felt his skilful hand slide down to her private woman's place, where her flesh churned, soft and melting. 'No dream,' he said, 'but a reality. Elena, let me teach you.'

She caught her breath as he parted her moist lips and stroked, very gently with the pad of his thumb. He found her little bud of pleasure, and stroked it lightly so as not to over-stimulate her tender sex; Elena gasped aloud and went rigid, her eyes dark with sensation. 'Wh – what are you doing?'

His voice came softly out of the darkness. 'This, my little Saxon maid, is the heart of all your bodily delight, the tiny bud that flowers into sweet passion. You have never given pleasure to youself?'

She gasped again, because as his thumb stroked she felt the sweet, melting yearning spiralling like flames through her helpless body. She shuddered in his arms, realising that even if she had the choice she could not leave him now.

He bent his head to suck gently at the pink, tender tips of her breasts, and she writhed in rapture as the sensations poured through her. He raised his head to gaze at her. 'Your first lesson,' he went on softly, 'is to learn that it is not wicked, but wonderful, to pleasure one another so. As the lady Isobel pleasured you tonight. You enjoyed it, didn't you? The way her hot little tongue flicked at you – like this – and like this – '

Before Elena could speak, he had moved down the bed, and parted her unresisting thighs. Dear God. His head was lowering to her belly; she felt the hot warmth

76

of his tongue at her navel, and then it was sliding down her flat abdomen to slip between her lips and stab gently at that unbelievable pleasure place, just as Isobel had done earlier, only Aimery's moist, silken tongue was so firm, so fulfilling. She moaned, and writhed against his wonderful, rasping mouth.

He lifted his head to gaze at her, and his teeth gleamed whitely in the darkness as he smiled. 'You liked that, Saxon girl?'

Her body arched violently against him in reply, desperate for release. He could feel the waves of urgent desire spasming through her. 'Not yet, little one,' he murmered warningly. 'Not yet. You want to learn, do you not, about this wonderful instrument of pleasure?'

He reached to take her small, trembling hand and enfolded it round the throbbing shaft of his manhood.

Eleanor gasped aloud at the hot feel of it in her fingers. It was huge and velvety soft, beautiful to touch, yet so full of pulsing power. Would the lord Aimery do to her, now, what the terrifying Saracen had done to the lady Isobel? How could she ever take it within herself? Such a huge, swollen thing – almost like another limb – surely it was not natural! And yet she ached desperately to feel its silken caress inside her secret parts.

She snatched her hand away, trembling with confusion.

Aimery gave a low chuckle, and said, 'You will learn soon enough, *caran*, to worship my instrument of love. And, whether you realise it or not, you are more than ready to pay homage . . .'

His wonderful, teasing hands slid down once more between her moist thighs. He ran a finger up and down her quivering flesh, caressing that wonderful point of pleasure with his circling thumb, until Elena was crying aloud with pleasure and thrusting her swollen breasts against the hard, muscular wall of his chest.

'Ready, little one?' he whispered. And he arched himself above her.

Elena stopped breathing when she felt the velvety smooth head of his penis stroking between her lips. There was no room for him! There couldn't be room! And yet, that swollen glans caressing her own engorged, melting entrance was a feeling so exquisite that she wanted it to go on for ever.

'Surrender to me,' he was whispering in her ear. 'Give in to me, Elena. Do you not desire me?'

'Oh, yes. Nothing more . . .'

With a husky groan of satisfaction, he thrust gently into her melting flesh.

And then, something happened. Elena felt the long shaft slip inside her, between her throbbing lips, and slide slowly up, into the very heart of her. There was a sudden, sharp pain that made her cry out, but the Breton kissed her mouth, and she forgot it in the wonder of feeling his manhood moving so slowly, so masterfully within her.

She lay back, breathless, her eyes wide open. He caressed her parted mouth with his skilful tongue, and then he began to thrust, gently.

It was the most wonderful thing Elena had ever known – beyond her dreams, even. Aimery was sending wave after wave of hypnotic pleasure flooding through her with each slow stroke. Once, he paused, and gazed down into her transparent, wide-eyed face; she gasped and clutched him to her, running her fingers up and down his muscular back. 'Don't stop,' she pleaded. 'Oh, please don't stop – '

For answer, he lowered his head to suckle at her aching breasts. Then she moaned with pleasure and instinctively coiled her slender legs round his thighs as he slid his hard length deep within her again. He continued to lick her breasts, sucking hard at the taut nipples, and Elena cried out with a new fever of delight as his hand moved down to touch her engorged clitoris, very gently. Her blood was on fire, her breath was coming in short, ragged gasps as wave after wave of rapture engulfed her dazed body.

'*Oh!*' She gave a long, shuddering cry and bucked wildly against him as her senses exploded in a shimmering orgasm of pleasure. 'Oh, dear sweet Christ . . .' He continued to move gently within her, his lips flickering at her jutting nipples, and she gripped his penis fiercely with her inner muscles, clenching at the wonderful, hard length of him with wild sensuality. She cried out, again and again, as he used all his skill to prolong her ecstasy. Then, as her strange little animal cries subsided, he lifted himself high above her, so that she could see the engorged shaft wet with her own juices in the darkness, and he plunged into her, over and over, driving himself to his own fierce, shuddering release. Elena quivered with renewed orgasm at the feel of his hot release within her. She held his sated body tight in her arms, glorying in the feel of his hard nakedness, her body still warm with delight.

Aimery was shaken as he lay there in the darkness. It was a long time, almost longer than he could remember, since he'd taken such pleasure in conventional love-making. She was truly innocent, just as she had claimed. Perhaps, too, her claim that she knew nothing at all about the Saxon rebels who visited the convent was true as well.

He reflected with some surprise that normally, a clinging, innocent girl such as this one would bore him out of his mind, and he'd turn away in disgust to find more sophisticated pleasures. Yet the Saxon girl's rapture had moved him strangely as he watched her exquisite face light up the darkness.

Not part of his plan, he reminded himself. His plan was to coldly arouse her, as he'd aroused others; to make her hunger desperately for him, then reject her. Remember Hugh's death – remember Madelin. Wasn't this girl tainted with the same Saxon blood?

He withdrew sharply from the girl's innocent, tender embrace and stood up. Elena looked up, bewildered, and saw how harsh his scarred face was in the shaft of moonlight that glanced through the shutter. She felt suddenly cold. 'My lord . . .'

Aimery reached for his clothes. He said, flatly, 'Not bad for a first time. But you still have a lot to learn. Isobel will teach you some new tricks.'

She shrank back as if he'd struck her. 'No! Not Isobel!' She put out one trembling hand. 'My lord – I only want you!'

Again, Aimery le Sabrenn felt that stupid wrench at the heart he knew he no longer possessed. He buckled his belt over his tunic and said abruptly, 'Isobel; Hamet; you will submit, Elena, to whoever I decide will teach you. Remember that you're nothing but a slave. You will do exactly as I say.'

The girl gazed up at him from the bed, her soft face dazed with misery. 'I am your slave, lord,' she whispered. 'I will do whatever you command. Only – will you come to my room again – like you did tonight?'

Aimery's mouth twisted as he glanced down at her. Her little breasts were adorable, her sweet face still flushed by that intense, fevered orgasm. Damn it, but if he stayed any longer he'd be making love to her again in a few moments.

'Perhaps,' he forced out coldly. 'But not for some time. As I said, you have much to learn.'

As her dark blue eyes clouded over in sudden pain, Aimery turned and swiftly left the room.

Elena lay on the cold little bed and hugged her aching body. She was racked with an empty sensation of loss at the memory of the sweet, dark pleasure the Breton lord had bestowed on her. Already, she yearned for him again.

She'd given herself, body and soul, to Aimery le Sabrenn, and she knew that she'd do anything, anything, to persuade him to return and pleasure her again in his powerful, exquisite way. And she knew, she was sure, that he desired her.

She had much to learn, she knew. But he was all that she wanted; and if this was to be a contest, then she resolved that she would win him.

Isobel, who had heard Aimery go to Elena's chamber and had suffered a violent hour of intense jealousy as the stupid girl gasped away her virginity, heard her lord return to his own room at last. Only one hour, and he had had enough of her.

Isobel cheered up immediately, and revised her plans for tomorrow. Pierre would be a part of them, of course. But what else? With a sudden smile of pleasure, she remembered the little wooden chest where she kept her most precious possessions. She found the key and unlocked it, and fingered thoughtfully through its contents. At last, she withdrew a wonderfully carved piece of ivory that had once been brought to her by a traveller from the Mediterranean lands. It was shaped like a man's phallus, of more than generous proportions, and was designed, with careful carvings and protuberances, to stimulate a woman's pleasure zones; though not all women were capable of taking the huge shaft within themselves, especially not virginal Saxons. By the time Isobel and Pierre had finished with her, the girl wouldn't even *want* Aimery to touch her again for, oh, a good while.

Isobel fondled the instrument, rubbing it gently against her still tingling breasts until her nipples peaked and strained against the fabric of her shift. She smiled, imagining the Saxon slut's innocent face when confronted with this formidable weapon. Would Isobel show it to her first? Or would she wait for Pierre to finish with the girl, and then . . .

Her green eyes gleaming with anticipation, Isobel kissed the ivory phallus and locked it away in its box. Then she went to bed, and laid her plans for tomorrow.

Chapter Six

*E*arlier that same night, soon after the slave convoy had arrived at the castle, Morwith, the young, redheaded Saxon woman, had been herded into a low, thatched hovel along with the other female serfs. Disconsolately, she lay in the darkness on her crude, straw-filled pallet with just a rough blanket for cover, and turned her back on the other women. After all, she Morwith, was different. Hadn't she, in the most delightful way possible, entertained the lord of Thoresfield and his Saracen servant on the way here?

A Saxon reeve, who'd been here in the days before Hastings when Thoresfield had been no more than a fortified manor house, had brought the women food: dry bread, and stale cheese. Morwith had caught his arm before he left, and said haughtily, 'I think there must be some mistake. You see, I shouldn't be in here, with the others. I wish to speak to the lord Aimery.'

The man had laughed sneeringly. 'They all say that,' he mocked. 'Will I do instead, wench?'

Morwith was disappointed that a mistake had been made, and that she'd been put in this hovel. But she was confident that the lord of Thoresfield would send for her, in his own good time. Since the sacking of York last winter, she'd lived with a band of homeless Saxon outlaws in the forest, and was used to looking after herself. She would wait, and watch for her chance.

While the other women tossed and muttered in exhausted sleep, Morwith lay awake, her pale blue eyes glittering, her ripe body in its tattered chemise feeling unbearably warm and restless in the stuffy air of the windowless hovel.

She remembered every minute of that wonderful encounter in the half-ruined hut in the forest. The Saracen's muscular, gleaming body and dusky skin; the lord Aimery's coldly handsome face as he looked on impassively. She'd serviced the Saracen well, hadn't she? Used all her practised skill to tease him with her warm tongue; taken him smoothly into her willing mouth, huge though he was, while cupping and stroking the heavy pouch of his testicles until he had groaned aloud in ecstasy.

The Breton lord could hardly have failed to be aroused. But he'd taken her silently, impersonally, so Morwith had not been able to witness his powerful release.

She stirred restlessly on her scratchy pallet and her hand closed round her aching breast as she relived that sublime moment when the Breton's wonderful, iron-hard shaft had slipped slowly inside her juicy love-passage from behind. Oh, she'd never known such masterful, exquisite pleasure. While the Saracen's eager mouth had suckled her dangling breasts, each slow, muscular thrust of the Breton's phallus had built up the waves of sensation shamelessly quivering through her body, until the final orgasm had washed through her in warm floods.

She gave a little moan and cupped her aching vulva with her cool palm, feeling how it pulsed moistly, hungrily, at the memory of the Breton's darkly satisfying manhood. She would have him again, the Breton lord. Her chance would come, and she would take it.

She stroked her clitoris, rubbing quickly with her fingers, imagining the Breton's long penis soothing her hungry flesh. She spasmed quietly, biting on her lip to stop herself crying out.

Morwith slept at last.

Early the next morning, Elena woke with a start. She sat up jerkily, feeling frightened and confused. Then the sounds of the castle courtyard came floating up through her narrow window, and she remembered. The early morning sunlight danced across her bed. Somewhere, a distant bell tolled.

The hour of prime. At the convent, the nuns would be filing into the little chapel for the first service.

No. The convent no longer existed. That life was over.

Elena slid from her rumpled bed, her skin golden in the sunlight, and ran her hands dreamily through her tousled blonde hair. Her naked flesh was warm and sensitive; her breasts softly flushed. Had last night really happened? Or was it all a dream? The colour rose in her cheeks as she remembered. Walking slowly to the window, she pushed the oiled hide shutter to one side and peeped out.

It was all true. She was really here, in the very heart of Aimery le Sabrenn's northern stronghold. The courtyard below was already a hive of early morning activity, full of bustle and noise. Servants from the kitchen were hurrying across to the bakehouse carrying trays of warm, scented bread; young squires frowned in concentration as they carefully polished their masters' armour on the trestles set up outside the guardhouse; a groom was leading a big warhorse from the stables, while some female serfs giggled and gossiped as they scattered grain to the hens.

Aimery's castle. Aimery's people. And last night, Aimery le Sabrenn had taken her in his arms . . .

Elena breathed in deeply, the sunshine warm on her

face and her bare shoulders. This was to be her new life. There was no going back now. She knew that, and accepted it willingly. Her heart stirring in that knowledge, like a challenge, she turned to pick up her silk chemise from the floor, where the lord Aimery had cast it so carelessly last night. She held the soft fabric to her cheek.

Suddenly, the door opened. Elena looked up, startled, as the lady Isobel glided in; she looked exquisite in her beautiful green silk gown, with her dark hair coiled smoothly at the nape of her neck. Over her arm was a folded garment of rough homespun wool.

'My dear,' she purred, 'I trust that you slept well after our little *entertainment* last night?'

Elena, conscious of Isobel's slanting green eyes flickering with interest over her vulnerable, naked body, clasped the silk chemise she'd just picked up close to her breasts and said quietly, 'Thank you, my lady. I slept well.'

Isobel's words were kind enough, but there was something cold, assessing, in her eyes. Elena shivered suddenly, in spite of the warmth of the room.

Isobel's eyes rested on the beautiful silk chemise Elena was holding, and her mouth curled in amusement. 'As for today,' she went on briskly, 'I'm sure you understand, Elena, that as a serf you are expected to earn your keep. Edith, the housekeeper, is expecting you in the kitchens this morning. Here – I have brought you suitable clothing.' And she pressed a coarse serf's tunic into Elena's hands.

Elena's blue eyes widened; she could not stop her gaze wandering to the beautiful gown she had worn the night before, lying on the oak chest at the foot of her bed. 'The – the kitchens?' she stammered out in confusion. 'But last night my lord Aimery said – '

Isobel's eyes snapped with annoyance, and she arched her exquisitely shaped dark eyebrows. 'Oh, dear. I do hope you're not going to be difficult, Elena.

85

Naturally, I am informing you of Lord Aimery's specific commands, however could you think otherwise?'

Elena swallowed down the sudden ache in her throat. Last night she'd been too eager, too open. She'd repelled him. 'If it is my lord Aimery's wish,' she said in a low voice, 'then of course I will obey.'

Isobel smiled, satisfied. So, this was the way to subjugate the girl! My lord Aimery's wish. What an innocent little fool she was! Lord Aimery, in fact, knew nothing at all about all this, as he had ridden out on the dawn patrol with his men and would not be back till this evening. But how was the Saxon slut to know?

In fact, Isobel had felt a desperately fierce pang of jealousy as she'd entered the room and seen the unclothed girl standing there as if she was in a dream. The sunlight had played magically on her high, perfect breasts, on her slender hips and long legs; on that soft golden fleece at the top of her thighs and the clouds of glorious silken hair cascading round her shoulders.

Isobel vowed anew in that moment that she would subjugate this girl herself, if Aimery would not.

Elena was slowly lifting the rough woollen tunic over her head when Isobel reached out languidly to stroke the exposed, taut skin of her abdomen. Elena gasped and froze; Isobel, with a smile, trailed her fingers towards the juncture of the girl's thighs, where the soft gold hair curled so delicately.

'My dear,' she murmered, 'just like gold silk! So delicate. Quite, quite charming. But you really do need educating, don't you? So sadly lacking in any refinement. And Aimery really does not care, you know, for unsophisticated women.' Isobel's thumb brushed tantalisingly at the top of Elena's secret place, stroking the pleasure bud, pinching the outer lips swiftly, then withdrawing her hand. Elena gasped and flushed at the sudden burst of pleasure that assailed her, and Isobel laughed at the girl's consternation.

'So,' she went on, 'the lord Aimery has given me

something for you. A little gift, if you like. He made it quite clear that he wished you to wear this special garment.'

Elena, her spine tingling with unease, said suddenly, 'Where is lord Aimery?'

'Gone out with his men. He then has to escort a convoy from Lincoln through his territory, so he will not be back for some time. But he left this for you, my dear. Here – let me show you.' And, reaching into the recessed folds of her skirt, she drew out what looked to Elena like a small leather belt.

Elena, still naked, clutched the serf's tunic to her defenceless body, and shivered with apprehension. There was something sinister about the belt that Isobel dangled teasingly before her, with its buckles and straps. 'I would rather not wear it,' she whispered.

Isobel, watching her, felt a renewed surge of hatred. This girl was fresh, young, innocent. *And Aimery had gone to her room last night* . . .

'Oh, dear,' chided Isobel in her sweetest tones. 'Disobedience already! I shall have to tell Aimery – he will be most disappointed in you – '

She saw how the girl's face became drained of blood. She was obviously terrified of Aimery's disapproval. Poor girl, she was besotted, like all the others before her. And therefore well on the way to her downfall . . .

'So, of course,' Isobel went on brightly, 'you will wear the belt, won't you, my dear? Here, let me help you.'

'It is the lord Aimery's wish?' said the girl quietly.

'Of course.'

The girl bit her lip and nodded mutely. With a secret smile of satisfaction, Isobel helped her into the little belt that was one of her own favourite devices. Elena had to step into it because, although the main strap was buckled round her waist, there was a further piece of leather that pulled up tightly between her legs, cradling the soft mound of her femininity, narrowing at the back to slip between the rounded cheeks of her bottom.

Elena gasped at the unfamiliar feel of the cold leather against her outer flesh lips. 'It is too tight!'

'Nonsense!' retorted Isobel briskly as she nimbly tightened the big buckle at Elena's small waist, thus drawing up the strap between her legs even further. 'This is how it is meant to be worn. You will soon be perfectly used to it. It is quite customary for favoured female slaves, I assure you!'

She let her fingers trail along the firm leather that pressed against the girl's delicious femininity, secretly revelling in the exquisite combination of soft, tempting flesh and dark, thick leather. The girl, with her stupid, innate modesty, recoiled with a shudder from her touch; but Isobel knew that already the cunningly-made love belt would be doing its work. Because where it pressed against Elena's pink folds it was slightly ridged, so that it would exert gentle yet persistent pleasure on her tender flesh lips. It would eventually part them, chafing against her sweet pleasure zones with every step she took, preparing her for the entertainment that Isobel had in mind for the afternoon.

Already, Isobel could see that the girl was breathing raggedly with the secret combination of shame and promised pleasure. Isobel smiled. 'The lord Aimery will be most pleased to know that you are obeying him,' she lied softly. 'Now I will send my maid Alys, to take you down to the kitchens.'

And with that, the lady Isobel left the room.

Elena stood very still after she had gone, trying desperately to order her reeling thoughts. She would run away from Thoresfield! She would not suffer this humiliation!

Pulling on her coarse woollen gown, she moved purposefully towards the door. The castle gates were open. No-one would notice yet another serf heading off towards the fields.

Suddenly, as she moved, the ridged leather slipped up between her flesh lips and rubbed with heart-stopping sweetness at her secret parts. The delicious warmth, the novel feeling of constriction, flooded her belly, and she felt her nipples tingle suddenly where the woollen gown chafed them.

She remembered Aimery's dark embrace; her body's awakening in his arms. Already, the leather belt was moist between her legs. She moved again, tentatively, towards the door; the leather rubbed softly against that very heart of her pleasure, nudging at the little bud that the Breton had caressed so sweetly last night. Maybe tonight he would come to her again.

Elena knew then that she would not, could not run away. She knew that a day of exquisite torment lay ahead, like a challenge – a challenge issued by the lady Isobel. She drew a deep breath and turned back into her room, to await her next orders.

She would rise to that challenge, and win.

Beyond the castle, in the great south field that bordered the encroaching forest, Morwith was growing hot, tired and rebellious. Since daybreak, when they had meagrely broken their fast on bread and weak ale, she and the other serfs had been working their way up and down the field gathering armfuls of the hay, newly mown by the lines of men with scythes. The midday sun burned into her face; the sweat gleamed on her arms; the blades of grass tickled her legs unbearably. Everyone else passively accepted the barked orders of the Saxon reeve and his men, and trudged obediently across to the big cart with armfuls of grass. But Morwith, who knew she was different, felt the irritation boiling up inside. Somehow, she would find a way to get to the lord Aimery! He, surely, would not expect her to labour like this, to sleep in a hovel with the other women! There must be some mistake.

'You, there!' The reeve called out sharply to her. She swung round defiantly, pushing her hair from her face. 'You, who think yourself too good to be a serf – yes, you, the red-headed wench! Go to the kitchens, and fetch more ale for the mowers. And be quick about it!'

Glad at least to escape from the backbreaking work for a while, Morwith bit back her retort and hurried across the fields towards the castle's gates. At the kitchen, they gave her a big earthernware jug and told her to help herself from the ale cask in the store room. She found her way there slowly, taking her time; it was shadowy and dark in the cask-filled store room, and cool out of the heat of the sun. She filled the jug with the creamy, fragrant ale and took a long drink of it herself. It slid down her parched throat like nectar. She drank more, then set down the heavy jug and went to stand in the doorway, running her hands through her thick red curls.

'You are in trouble, lady?'

The soft, dark voice broke into her thoughts. She turned with a gasp of alarm; someone was coming along the side of the storeroom towards her. The dark-skinned man, Hamet – the Breton's servant.

Morwith stammered, trying to collect her thoughts, 'I – I was but resting for a moment, sir. They sent me for ale. Ale for the reapers.'

He nodded, his arms folded across his burly chest, watching her. He wore a sleeveless leather tunic; his hugely muscled shoulders glistened with perspitation in the midday heat. Did he remember her from that night in the forest? Surely – surely he did. He had taken such pleasure in her. Morwith's heart beat furiously. Now. Now was her chance. Hamet the Saracen was the lord Aimery's personal servant. If she could find favour with him, then surely he would take her to his master again.

Morwith moved slowly and thought fast. Picking up the heavy jug, she gave the Saracen a shy smile and moved to go past him. Suddenly, she swayed and lost her balance; the jug crashed to the floor, and the big

Saracen caught her quickly, his hands steadying her waist. 'Lady, you, are not well?'

Morwith swayed hungrily against him, feeling her loose bodice slipping from her shoulders. 'No,' she whispered, gazing up at him hungrily and moistening her full lips. 'I am not well. But you can make me feel better. So much better . . .'

Slowly, tantalisingly, she reached up to run light, provocative fingers over his strong arms. Then she licked her forefinger and touched his lips, half-closing her eyes. With a harsh foreign oath, Hamet crushed her to him and devoured her mouth. Morwith leaned back, panting, against the cold stone wall of the store room. 'Oh, yes,' she gasped through his kiss. 'Please . . .'

Her eyes opened wide in lascivious delight as Hamet cupped and lifted her ripe breasts, freeing them completely from her ragged gown. Then he ran his hungry tongue greedily across her pouting flesh, lapping and sucking at her turgid nipples. Eagerly, Morwith reached for his belt, but Hamet anticipated her. Swiftly he untied the lacing at the top of his leggings, and freed his huge erection. It sprang out, quivering with tension, already fully rigid.

Morwith gasped and coloured at the sight of the dusky, throbbing shaft as it reared towards her. 'So magnificent,' she breathed huskily, reaching with trembling fingers to stroke its satin length. 'My lord, you are truly a stallion.'

With a throaty groan of delight, Hamet reached to pull up Morwith's full skirts. She was wearing nothing underneath; the plump, freckled flesh of her inviting thighs drove him insane. Devouring her luscious mouth, Hamet lifted her in his arms to prop her against the wall, supporting almost all of her weight while he thrust eagerly against her.

Morwith, breathless with excitement, arched her own moist, pouting secret flesh towards the Saracen's lunging hips, wrapping her thighs tightly round him as he held her off the ground. Hamet prodded blindly, at last finding the quivering entrance to her love-channel. With a sigh of satisfaction, the Saracen slid up inside her.

Morwith gasped, her arms clutching convulsively at his leather-clad shoulders. Her hungry flesh was a riot of delight as he licked and suckled her pouting breasts. Oh, the feel of his massive penis, gliding so slickly in and out of her greedy flesh! She felt herself rising inexorably to a shuddering, delicious climax as he serviced her; felt him thrust his hips powerfully towards his own release, his penis jerking and spasming within her luscious, grateful body.

The pleasure washed over her, again and again. Simple, crude and wonderful. Sated, she clung to him still, licking the smooth dark skin of his cheek, caressing his soft earlobe. Slowly she felt his subsiding manhood slip out of her and nuzzle her damp thighs.

'Good,' she murmered. 'So good.' Gently she unwrapped herself from him, smoothing down her crumpled skirt. 'Hamet, you like me, do you not?'

He groaned in acknowledgement, swiftly lacing up his leggings. 'Lady, with you, the pleasure is wonderful.'

'Then,' whispered Morwith, 'why do I not come to you again? You sleep within the castle itself, do you not? Near to the lord Aimery?'

Hamet visibly hesitated. 'I do. But – '

'Send for me,' she whispered. 'Your master need not know. Send for me, Hamet, and I will be yours, all yours, for the night!' She reached up to kiss him languorously. He began to harden again, against her belly; she released him with a soft laugh of delight and whispered, 'Now, go quickly, before we are seen. And remember – this is our secret.'

At a tiny window overlooking the courtyard, the lady Isobel de Morency, who had seen everything, moved away with a smile of satisfaction playing around her full lips.

When Isobel had first caught sight of the redheaded Saxon serf talking to Hamet, distracting him from his duties as Aimery's deputy, she'd frowned, and been on the point of sending someone down to chastise her.

But then, as Isobel saw how swiftly the lascivious hunger took over their bodies, she felt her own excitement rise. Hamet was so straightforward in his pleasures, and so undeniably well-endowed. And the redheaded slut, who must be new to the castle, how ripe and voluptuous she was as she took her greedy pleasuring from the big Saracen! No innocent she; why, she positively crowed with delight as Hamet slid his willing shaft up into her juicy flesh. What a contrast to the pale, virginal convent girl, who would be slaving away in the kitchens, no doubt tormented by the belt that would be chafing so deliciously between her slender thighs! Surely, the redhead would be more suited to Aimery's needs?

Isobel felt pleasantly aroused from watching the little scene in the courtyard. Smiling to herself, she revised her plans – just a little.

Later that afternoon, Isobel lounged back on her fur-covered bed, sipping from a silver goblet filled with sweet, heady wine. 'You see,' she was explaining, 'I need a very *special* kind of servant . . .'

Morwith stood in front of her, hands clasped together, head meekly bowed. She'd just enjoyed a luxurious bath, a blissful experience for her, and she'd been given an old but serviceable woollen gown of Isobel's to wear instead of her serf's tunic. Her glorious red hair, newly washed, hung in silky tendrils around her shoulders. She looked the picture of meekness; but Isobel, having seen her antics with Hamet earlier, was not deceived.

Thoughtfully, Isobel poured herself more wine and

inspected her new prize. The young woman had a lovely figure, voluptuous yet firm, with full breasts and swelling hips. A trifle plump, perhaps, but all femininity.

Isobel ran her finger round the rim of her goblet and stretched her legs languorously beneath her silk gown. Leaning back against the soft down-filled pillows that were piled up behind her, she went on casually, 'You know, I take it, that you are in the stronghold of Aimery le Sabrenn?'

The woman seemed to flush slightly; then nodded.

Isobel continued, 'My lord Aimery, like all great and powerful men, needs his relaxation, Morwith. He likes me to arrange certain little – entertainments for him. I wonder if you understand?'

There was certainly now no mistaking the brightness in the redhead's pale blue eyes. Isobel slid languidly from the bed, still holding her wine, and walked over to her. Morwith's gown, a little too tight, strained provocatively across her chest; Isobel ran a slow hand across the woman's constrained breasts, felt the instant hardening of her nipples, heard her sharply indrawn breath.

'Are you a good servant, Morwith?' Isobel said softly. 'Are you going to be truly obedient to your lord?'

The Saxon woman moistened her lips eagerly. 'Oh, yes, my lady,' she breathed.

Isobel's hand whipped up and struck her hard across the cheek. Morwith bit back a cry and staggered back, her flesh glowing red where Isobel's hand had caught her.

'You lie to me!' You are far from obedient! I saw you earlier today, out in the courtyard with the Saracen! Who gave you permission to pleasure yourself so vilely, to distract my lord's servant from his duties? You will be punished, Morwith!'

The young woman sank to her knees, trembling. 'My

lady, I crave your pardon. I humbly beg your forgiveness. Please, please don't send me away!'

Isobel watched her thoughtfully, a little smile playing at the corners of her lips. Morwith, on seeing that smile, shivered and felt a sudden dark excitement leap in her breast. Isobel said very quietly, 'You will most certainly be punished. Remove your gown, and abase yourself.'

Morwith, still kneeling, her eyes lowered, slowly lifted the woollen gown over her head, then her cotton chemise. She crouched naked before the lady Isobel, her red hair sweeping her pouting breasts, her plumply rounded thighs splayed just a little so that Isobel could glimpse the secret flesh veiled by the tightly curling red hair. Her flesh was creamy white, dusted with light freckles like a sprinkling of gold dust.

Isobel licked her lips and said, huskily, 'You are ready, then, for your punishment?'

Morwith lifted her pale, glittering eyes. 'My lady,' she whispered. 'Only tell me how can I do sufficient penance for my dreadful sins?'

Isobel laughed aloud. Without bothering to reply, she eased herself onto her bed and leaned against her pillows. Then she drew her silk gown up above her stockinged thighs, and whispered, 'Pleasure me.'

Morwith could not belive her luck. Her heart pounded. First the encounter with the Saracen, and now, for some reason, the lady of Thoresfield; this beautiful, sophisticated woman who was lucky enough to be Aimery the Breton's mistress, had singled her out!

Entertainment, she had said. Entertainment for the lord Aimery . . .

Keeping her head low, so that the lady Isobel would not see the lascivious gleam in her eyes, Morwith said meekly, 'Anything you say, my lady.' Then, with a slow, wicked smile, she walked to the foot of the bed and climbed up between Isobel's parted thighs.

With a little groan, Isobel reached out for the Saxon woman's dangling breasts. They were heavy and full, with large, dark brown nipples that already jutted fiercely. Isobel leaned forward to suckle hungrily, stroking the turgid flesh with her fingertips, then she leaned back against her pillows, her eyes closed dreamily. 'Kiss me, Morwith. Kiss me, down there.'

Breathless with excitement, Morwith stroked softly at Isobel's thighs above her gartered stockings, parting them still further. The sunlight from the narrow window fell across the bed; she could feel it warm on her back, though Isobel was in the shadows beneath her. Now she could see the lady's most secret place; the softly curling dark hair, the crinkled flesh lips; such a luxuriant contrast to the white smooth skin of Isobel's belly and thighs! Morwith, already excited by Isobel's urgent suckling of her breasts, felt the heat begin to churn in her own loins. Hungrily she dipped her head between Isobel's thighs and licked softly, parting the dark outer folds with her gently exploring tongue.

This, to Morwith, was new; the pleasuring of a female, the feel of the moist, wrinkled folds of flesh against her tongue. But she knew only too well what she herself enjoyed; knew how the tongue's soft, teasing delicacy could be a most delicious replacement for a man's rigid phallus. Delicately she drew her tongue between the soft labia that were already engorged with desire. If this was how fine ladies lived, then she, Morwith, would be a fine lady!

Gliding her tongue steadily up the smooth pink slit, Morwith's pointed tongue at last found Isobel's sweet bud of desire, already enlarged and sensitive. Careful not to abuse it, knowing how easily a harsh touch could kill pleasure. Morwith let her tongue circle the quivering stem, caressing it tantalisingly. Isobel threw her head back and clutched at Morwith's heavy breasts with desperate fingers. 'Kiss me. Oh, your tongue is so sweet, Morwith. Let me feel your tongue, deep inside – oh, yes, yes!'

With a little smile, Morwith drew her sensuous

mouth in a swirling caress round Isobel's tender flesh. Then, pointing and stiffening her ready tongue, she glided lightly up and down between Isobel's inner flesh lips and thrust it gently, teasingly in and out of the entrance to Isobel's juicy love channel.

Isobel groaned aloud and jerked her hips desperately towards Morwith's teasing mouth. Morwith gave a low chuckle and continued to slide her tongue up and down, but more firmly now; lightly swirling Isobel's engorged pleasure bud, then gliding down to thrust slickly inside her, to satisfy her. So close now – so close . . .

Her tongue glanced, then flickered on the shaft of Isobel's swollen clitoris. Isobel's body arched violently into the air, her buttocks tight and straining in her extremity. Morwith, taking a deep breath, stuck her tongue as far as she could inside the other woman's love passage, making little jabbing motions to simulate a man's phallus, using all her skill to satisfy her new mistress.

Iosbel exploded, uttering fierce little cries. She spasmed again and again against Morwith's busy mouth, almost throwing her off the bed, then she collapsed, sated with exquisite pleasure.

Slowly, Morwith slipped from the bed, the coverlet of wolf pelts exciting her own heated, sensitised skin as the fur brushed her belly and thighs. She kneeled on the floor at the foot of the bed, her heart beating wildly. Unbearably excited herself, her own secret flesh was moist and slick and hungry. She bowed her head, submissive but hopeful.

After some moments of utter stillness, Isobel stirred and drew herself up, stretching in lazy contentment. Her cat-like green eyes regarded the kneeling, naked serf thoughtfully.

'You show some promise, Morwith.'

Morwith looked up, her eyes bright, her body flushed with her own eager desire. 'My lady?'

Isobel chuckled as she surveyed the wet pink flesh between Morwith's parted thighs. How the woman begged, wordlessly, to be pleasured! But she would have to wait. 'You must learn patience, Morwith, if you are to progress. I can see that you are all too eager for your own satisfaction.'

Morwith licked her lips, her eyes pleading. Isobel slid from the bed and smoothed her silk gown so that her skirts fell in rich swathes to the ground.

'But first,' Isobel went on calmly, 'you must help me in another task. You seem to have forgotten, Morwith, that we have someone else to punish.'

Morwith's eyes widened. 'My lady, if I can help in any way –'

Isobel poured herself more wine, and drank contentedly. Aimery would not be back for a long, long time. Which was as well, because there was so much she had to do. She went on, 'You can help me indeed. You see, we must punish Hamet the Saracen for neglecting his duties, and for serving you so lasciviously. Don't you agree, Morwith?'

Morwith gulped and nodded, her heart pounding with excitement.

The hot afternoon sun beat down relentlessly on the procession of wagons and horses travelling slowly northwards along the sandy track. The clumsy wooden wheels of the baggage carts kept embedding themselves in the ruts; the drivers cursed impatiently, whipping on the plodding horses, sweating and grumbling in the baking heat.

Aimery le Sabrenn rode at the head of the armed escort, watchful and wary. Here, at least, bracken and thorn scrub replaced the dense oak forest to the west, making visibility better and Saxon ambush less likely.

Though if the Saxons knew that the twelve baggage wagons contained arms and provisions for the isolated garrison at York, Aimery had no doubt that they would attack, and kill.

'My lord, a horseman! Coming down the track – about a mile away – '

Aimery nodded acknowledgement at the hurried warning from the sergeant-at-arms, his hand tightening briefly on his sword. He reined in his big black destrier, aware once more of the sun's heat burning through his chainmail hauberk, and ordered his men to halt. Another wagon was stuck anyway; at least a dozen of his men were heaving and grunting at the wheel where it was embedded in a deep, sandy rut.

He could see the horseman himself, could see the glint of armour through the cloud of rising dust. Leaning back against the high cantle of his saddle, Aimery pushed his hand through his dust-streaked hair and silently gestured to his men to fan out around the convoy, all of them warily scanning the bracken wastes that surrounded them. Perhaps the horseman brought news of battle. He was aware of a swift, unusual regret, that his return to Thoresfield might be delayed. The fair-haired Saxon girl had haunted his thoughts all day.

'One of de Ferrers' knights, my lord, by my reckoning,' muttered the sergeant at his side.

The horseman rode up in a cloud of dust, pushing back his helmet from his sweat-streaked face.

'My lord Aimery?' he gasped.

Aimery pushed his horse forward, but there was no need; his air of natural authority had already identified him. 'You have a message for me?' he said quietly.

'Aye, my lord. You are shortly to be relieved of your escort duties, by a convoy of Henri de Ferrers' men travelling northwards to York for garrison duties. They will converge with you shortly, my lord, at the next crossroads. They carry all the necessary papers, by your leave . . . '

Aimery turned round to his silent, waiting men. 'It

looks,' he said, 'as if we shall be returning to Thoresfield earlier than planned.'

His men grinned and relaxed. 'That's good news, sir,' said the sergeant. Escort duty was never popular, with the constant fear of ambush and the possibility of scrappy, isolated fighting in the outlaw-ridden forest, though Aimery knew that his men would follow him to hell and back if he asked them.

Aimery smiled back at the burly sergeant, his scar twisting his firm mouth. 'Good news indeed,' he replied softly, half to himself.

He found that he was thinking of the girl again. Remembering her soft, tender body in his arms last night, he grew hard. He gritted his teeth silently against the harsh, burning desire that leaped through his body.

Chapter Seven

*T*hroughout that day, Elena had struggled to do her work alongside the other serfs. She knew, without being told, that she was hopeless at it. She could barely carry the heavy trays of dough to the bakehouse; the great cauldron of stew that she was ordered to stir burned and stuck to the sides of the pot; and as for plucking chickens, the other serfs took the half-feathered birds from her in disgust when they saw how little progress she made. Everything about the busy, bustling place confused her; people shouted and scolded, and try as she might, she succeeded at nothing.

And all the time, the love belt chafed insistently at her flesh, filling her bewildered body with unfamiliar sensations, like a secret caress. A reminder that she was a prisoner. Every minute of the day, the lord of Thoresfield's scarred, beautiful face haunted her mind; the look of tenderness in his steel-grey eyes as he murmured, 'We have all night, *caran* . . .'

She struggled on alone, because Isobel had told her it was Aimery's command, and only once did someone try to help her.

She was carrying two pails of milk across the yard, for the cheese-making. The wooden pails were so heavy, she was afraid of dropping them; but she did not dare to put them down. The sun burned down on her and her arms ached as she struggled on.

Then someone came up behind her, and took the pails from her, swinging them easily into this own strong hands. 'Let me take those,' a strangely familiar, male voice said quietly. 'Just follow me across the yard – don't trouble to express you thanks, or people will notice us.'

Elena gasped as she gazed up into the man's face.

The tall, golden-haired Saxon – the rebel. The man she had met coming from Father Wulfstan's house. The man she had taken water to, that night in the forest, the night she had first seen Aimery. 'You!' she whispered, gazing up at him as he stopped outside the kitchen.

He put down the heavy, frothing buckets. 'My name is Leofwin,' he said quietly. 'I am a serf. A prisoner here, like you. But, lady, if you need help of any kind, then summon me. I will do anything I can to help you.'

Elena felt her breath catch in her throat. Even in the ragged tunic of a serf this man was breathtakingly handsome, with his tanned, muscular body gleaming with perspiration in the heat of the day, and his sun-streaked mane of hair. And the way he looked at her, so tenderly, with those fathomless blue eyes . . .

Elena suddenly felt the tight love belt rub between her thighs, and a hot, liquid, churning sensation in her stomach. She knew instinctively that this man Leofwin would hate Aimery le Sabrenn with a burning hatred; would want to kill him, for what he had done to her last night.

From inside the kitchen, someone called out, 'Hey, you there! With the milk! Are you, going to be all day?'

Hurriedly Elena picked up the heavy pails and struggled to haul them inside, while the Saxon, watching her with his hands on his hips, said quietly, 'Remember me if ever you need a friend.'

* * *

In the afternoon, after a meagre lunch of rye bread and weak ale, Alys, the lady Isobel's maid, showed Elena how to wash the fine household linens in buttermilk, then peg them out in the sun to bleach them dry.

'You are lucky, Elena,' sighed poor, pockmarked Alys, suddenly stopping her work and regarding the slender blonde Saxon girl with envy. 'It won't be long before one of the men chooses you for his own. No such chance for me!' And Alys squeezed fiercely at the linen sheet she was dousing in the big tub of buttermilk.

Elena, her heart wrung with pity in spite of her own suffering, said quickly, 'You may well meet some good man who will wish to marry you, Alys. Looks should not be so important!'

'It's all vey well for you to say that, when you are so beautiful!' sighed Alys. 'It won't be long before one of lord Aimery's fine knights takes you for himself, I'll be bound.'

Elena remembered Aimery in her bed last night, and a slow blush stained her cheeks. As she knelt to peg out the linen, the leather belt tightened at the soft flesh between her legs, sending little arrows of desire burning through her belly and breasts. How long would she be kept in this exquisite torment?

Someone shouted across the yard at her. 'You! The new girl! The lady Isobel wants you up in her room. Make haste!'

Elena paled, and felt suddenly dizzy as she stood up. Alys said laconically,

'Better hurry, then, girl. My lady doesn't like to be kept waiting.' Elena bit her lip and set off towards the castle; Alys watched her go enviously.

Alys knew what the summons from Isobel meant. She knew what kind of things were in store for the beautiful blonde Saxon girl, and envied her wildly.

Elena blinked, disorientated, as she was shown into the lady Isobel's chamber.

The hide shutters had been drawn across the window embrasures, blocking out the sunlight. The heat from a brazier in the corner was intense. Two candles burned in silver holders placed on an oak coffer, their flames casting glimmering, unreal shadows around the tapestry-clad room. At first, accustomed as she was to the dazzling sunshine outside, she felt blinded.

Then she began to see. And what she saw made her want to turn, and run.

Isobel reclined in a carved wooden chair in the corner. Even in this claustrophobic darkness she looked as cool and elegant as ever, with her beautiful green silk gown and coiled black hair. Taking no notice of Elena, she continued to gaze at a little tableau in the opposite corner of the room, and a hazy smile played round her full red lips. Elena followed her gaze, and the breath caught in her throat.

In the near-darkness, Hamet, Aimery's servant, was kneeling on the floor. He wore leggings, but his gleaming dark torso was completely naked. His hands were tied behind his back to an iron ring in the wall, and he was blindfolded.

In front of him, with her back to Elena, was a redheaded woman wearing nothing but a strange, tight bodice made of black leather. She was leaning over the Saracen, dangling her large ripe breasts lewdly in his face, as he strained hungrily up towards her. Apart from the laced bodice, which thrust up her breasts and emphasised the curvaceous flesh of her rounded bottom, she wore nothing.

Elena leaned back against the closed door, feeling suddenly faint. Isobel glanced across at her, and laughed. She had plenty of time, to punish this stupid Saxon girl and get rid of her before Aimery got back.

'You are just in time, little Elena,' she said caressingly. 'Just in time to witness Hamet's punishment. Hamet, you see, has disobeyed me. He is now paying the price of his disobedience, and you, Elena, are to take part in his punishment.'

Elena felt her throat go dry. 'No! I – '

Isobel went on briskly, 'My dear Elena, I thought you understood. This is what the lord Aimery wishes; what the lord Aimery commands. And you want to please him, don't you?'

Elena was breathing shakily. The door behind her was unlocked. She was not in chains. She knew she should turn and run from this decadent, shadowy chamber, with all its dark promise. But the love belt squeezed gently, insistently at her fevered flesh, and just the mention of the Breton's name was enough to set her blood on fire. The redhead in the corner, oblivious to everything but the powerful man imprisoned beneath her, continued to torment him by rubbing her creamy breasts against his face. Elena felt the dark hunger in her secret places burn more fiercely than ever. She moistened her lips and whispered steadily, 'Yes. I wish to please the lord Aimery.'

Isobel nodded her satisfaction, and leaned forward. 'Then let me explain. Hamet here has behaved badly, with Morwith, the Saxon slave who torments him so with her lascivious body. He ravished her, serviced her crudely in the yard as if she were some animal on heat; drove his massive member into her quivering flesh.'

Hamet, in the corner, let out a soft moan of despair at her crude words. Isobel stood up, and Elena saw that in one hand she carried a small leather whip, its lash trailing on the ground as she walked slowly across the dimly lit room towards the imprisoned Saracen. Morwith saw her coming and stepped silently back into the shadows; Elena saw, with a jarring shock, that the red-gold hair at the juncture of her plump thighs was slick with moisture.

Isobel stood in front of Hamet, who gazed blindly up at his lady. He let out another moan as Isobel trailed her whip across his broad chest and let the lash dangle across the swelling bulge at his crotch.

'And Morwith too,' Isobel went on, turning suddenly on the redhead. 'Your punishment is not yet complete. Slut, I remember your face – how you enjoyed every wicked second as Hamet's rampant shaft slid up inside you. I saw you as you flung your head back in ecstasy! I heard you squeal with pleasure as you felt him impale you!'

The redhaired Saxon woman hung her head, but her nipples were dark and turgid above her leather bodice, and her pale blue eyes glittered with repressed excitement. 'My lady,' she whispered, 'I deserve further punishment. I wish to do penance.'

'Then,' said Isobel sternly, 'you must prepare yourself. Go and lie down on the bed. And Elena, who has been brought here to join in your punishment, will carry out that punishment. Come here, Elena.'

Elena stood immobile by the door as Morwith sprawled back luxuriantly on the fur-covered bed. She couldn't move. The heated blood coursed through her trembling body; the taut love belt pressed more tightly than ever, riding high between the soft pink folds of flesh at the top of her thighs. She knew that she couldn't bear this exquisite torment for much longer, and that even to move would send ripples of pleasure coursing through her body.

'Come here, Elena, dear,' repeated Isobel sweetly, fondling the handle of her whip, 'or the lord Aimery will be greatly displeased with you!'

Drugged with her own dark desires, her abdomen strangely heavy, her breasts tingling, Elena moved towards Isobel slowly, as if in a dream. Isobel smiled.

'Look, Elena,' she whispered, 'see how hungry Morwith is for love. Look at her sweet, ripe body, that drives Hamet to such torment!' Swiftly, Isobel opened up the chest by her bed, and drew out a length of fine silk cord. 'Here, Elena,' she said, 'she is yours. Tie her wrists to the bed. See, how she writhes, longing for her punishment!'

Elena stood hesitantly, her dark blue eyes wide with uncertainty. Isobel said softly, 'Now, we don't want to have to tell the lord Aimery how disobedient you are, Elena, do we? Why, he might even send you away! And you don't want that, do you, my sweet Elena? You don't wish to leave, never to see Aimery again?'

Swallowing hard, Elena shook her head. She was completely in this woman's power. Because Isobel knew she would do anything, anything, to obey Aimery's wishes.

Taking the rope numbly from Isobel's outstretched hands, she silently bound the redhead's wrists to the wooden frame of the bed, as Isobel indicated. While she worked, the musky heat of Morwith's voluptuous body reached up to her, inflaming her even more. With a little shock, she saw the wet pink flesh of her woman's parts protruding excitedly from the nest of red hair between her thighs, waiting desperately for a man's touch. Elena thought of Aimery's mysterious, proud phallus, and it was like a dark shaft through her soul, possessing her.

Isobel watched contentedly. Good. The fair-haired convent girl was learning obedience at last. The leather belt would be driving her to distraction by now. No doubt she was eagerly awaiting her own reward. Perhaps she even had illusions that Aimery would come to her again.

By the time Isobel had finished with her, Aimery wouldn't even want to set eyes on her, ever again. Isobel sighed with satisfaction at the way her plans were working out.

She suddenly became aware of Hamet, kneeling blindfolded and chained at her side. Poor Hamet, already he was breathing raggedly with suppresssed excitement. And Isobel, fondly imagaining how his rampant penis would spring out when freed from the constrictions of his clothing, decided that some speed was now necesary, before he was driven to extremity.

'Poor Hamet,' she said softly. 'Can't you picture Morwith as she writhes on the bed, longing for you to fill her with your hungry flesh? But her wish is not to be fulfilled, Hamet. You see, you are going to have to wait, and listen, as Morwith is pleasured by Elena.'

Isobel saw, with satisfaction, how the blood drained from the Saxon girl's face. She reached, again, into the chest. 'With this.'

And she pushed her prized possession into the trembling girl's hands – the ivory phallus – so beautifully designed for a woman's extremity of pleasure, so thick and long and cunningly carved. Morwith, on seeing its size, gave a little squeal of delight; Isobel pushed impatiently at Elena.

'Use it, Elena. Use it. Do I have to explain how? Pleasure her. You see how eager she is, how she spreads her legs and writhes towards the ivory? Pleasure her, Elena, and your lord will reward you well!'

Elena shook her head helplessly, the ivory phallus cold and heavy in her hands. 'I – I cannot. I do not know how.'

Isobel frowned impatiently, her slanting eyes becoming dark emerald slits. 'Aimery will be displeased, Elena, you realise that? Very well, we shall have to show you; and soon, very soon, you will feel the kiss of the ivory yourself. But first, poor Morwith. See what torment she is in. And Hamet too.'

Taking the phallus from Elena's nerveless hands, Isobel moved across to the bed, where Morwith sprawled, her knees raised, her legs wide apart. Carelessly Isobel ran her hands over the tight leather bodice, over Morwith's full, pendulous breasts. Then, without preliminaries, she thrust the giant phallus deep into Morwith's hungry, moist entrance. Morwith cried out, and squirmed her hips in delight, ravished by the cold, rough feel of the ivory's protuberances sliding deep within her. Isobel, holding it firm and still as Morwith writhed around it, looked scornfully across at Elena. 'Go and sit down,' she hissed out. 'Watch, and learn. Then perhaps next time the lord Aimery is foolish enough to visit your bed, he will not find you quite so totally incompetent!'

Shaking and humiliated, Elena did as she was told. Everything she saw, everything she heard, made her yearn unbearably for the hypnotic presence of Aimery le Sabrenn. As she sat down, she felt the shaming moisture seeping from between her legs, dampening the leather strap that tormented her so with its promise of pleasure. She wriggled on the chair, but that only made it worse.

'Watch, I said!' hissed Isobel.

Slowly, the lady of Morency was working the ivory phallus in and out of the bound woman on the bed, while Morwith twisted against her ropes, groaning her pleasure, her stretched flesh lips clutching obscenely at the creamy shaft. Hamet listened avidly, breathing harshly as he knelt in his dark corner, the bulge at his groin sufficient indication of his huge arousal. Glancing across at him, Isobel moved suddenly away from the bed, taking the phallus with her, slick and wet with Morwith's love juices. The redhead moaned her disappointment, rubbing her thighs together to ease the fierce ache. 'Remember your punishment, Morwith,' said Isobel coldly. 'It is not over yet.'

And as Morwith writhed helplessly on the bed, Isobel walked across to Hamet. 'Here. Smell, taste these juices; feel how she longs for you, Saracen.' She thrust the big phallus at Hamet's open mouth; avidly the blindfolded prisoner licked and sucked and tasted. 'Are you sorry now for your greedy lust?'

'Yes, oh, yes, my lady!' Hamet groaned in despair as Isobel kneeled to probe at his concealed erection with the cold ivory.

'You will not pleasure the redhead again, so lewdly, so publicly, without my permission?'

'No, I swear, never!'

'And do you want to watch now, while I pleasure her with this?'

Hamet gasped, nodding his head. With a few deft movements. Isobel ripped the woollen blindfold from his eyes. Then she unlaced his leggings.

His dark phallus sprang out, immense and straining, quivering against his taut belly with excitement. Already a clear drop of moisture gleamed at the swollen tip. Elena, hypnotised, felt a spasm of almost unbearable excitement shudder through her loins. Shutting her eyes, she fought for control. Isobel moved purposefully across to the bed and once more slid the huge ivory phallus into Morwith's hungry flesh, sliding the cool, ridged shaft teasingly in and out, twisting it so that its protuberances pulled at her swollen lips, rubbing at her hot, throbbing clitoris. Morwith, shuddering as the ecstasy built up inside her desperate body, turned her head and glimpsed the pinioned Saracen's huge, dusky erection rearing up helplessly from his loins. In that instant, she imagined wildly that it was Hamet's throbbing penis that she gripped so tightly within herself; that it was the Saracen himself who thrust his rampant, hardened shaft within her.

It was enough to take her over the brink. With strange, delirious little cries, she clutched at the ivory phallus with her inner muscles, and was convulsed in wave after wave of blinding pleasure, squirming about the bed as Isobel, frowning in concentration, pushed the ivory deep within her spasming flesh.

Hamet, watching avidly, was unable to control his body any longer at the lascivious sight. His hands still tied behind his back, he clenched his buttocks tight and let out a wild cry of abandon as jet after jet of milky white semen began to spurt from his throbbing penis.

Isobel waited silently for their climaxes to subside.

Then she turned slowly to view the white-faced, anguished girl in the chair. 'Now, Elena,' she said silkily, 'I think it's your turn. Don't you?'

Elena, her whole body now throbbing with the torment of desire after the pleasure she had witnessed, shuddered in refusal. She longed unbearably for her burning flesh to be assuaged – but not so shamelessly, not in front of them all!

Isobel, seeing her shake her head, frowned. So, it was not going to be as easy as she thought! Swiftly releasing Hamet from his chains, she ordered him abruptly to dress and depart. She'd decided that Hamet was too loyal to his master to witness what she had in mind. Morwith watched silently, curled on the big bed in the shadows, as Isobel turned back to Elena.

'You would refuse my orders?' she queried in surprise. 'You would displease the lord Aimery? You mean to say that you do not wish for his favours, do not wish him to visit you shortly?'

Elena's head jerked upwards, her delicate face suddenly flooded with colour again. Aimery. All she wanted on this earth was for Aimery to come to her, to release her from this sweet torment. 'He is coming here? Soon?' she whispered.

'Oh, indeed,' lied Isobel. 'And how do you think he will wish to find you, my dear? Ready and waiting, of course.' She lowered her voice. 'Now remove your gown and lie upon the bed.'

And then Isobel had the satisfaction of watching, as the trembling Saxon girl, whose innocent beauty she so hated, started despairingly to lift the coarse serf's gown she wore above her head. Isobel noted avidly where the rough fabric had scratched the girl's small, tender breasts, which were such a contrast to Morwith's freckled voluptuousness; saw where the tightly buckled belt cut into her tiny waist; saw how the leather between her thighs was moist with her sweet juices.

Elena started to unbuckle the tormenting belt with shaking fingers.

'Oh, no,' said Isobel swiftly. 'Not yet. First, you must make a promise. Do you swear to submit to whatever the lord Aimery wishes? To – anything?'

Elena moistened her lips. 'Yes, I swear it.'

Nodding, Isobel jerked the belt upwards; the tautening of the strap still higher between her legs sent waves of dark pleasure through Elena, like a secret promise. *Oh, Aimery . . .*

'Lie on the bed,' soothed Isobel in her ear. 'Let Morwith tie you up, and Aimery shall come to you!'

Blindly, Elena did as she was told, and Morwith moved in.

Morwith had watched the unfolding scene with interest, and a certain amount of pity. The girl Elena was a Saxon, like herself; and Morwith could see that she was on fire, tormented by her own longings, yet afraid to give in. Gently, Morwith started to fasten the silken cords round Elena's blue-veined, slender wrists and ankles.

'Don't be afraid,' she whispered in Elena's ear. 'Such pleasure in store, Elena, I will teach you!'

There was a soft knock on the door. Isobel went to answer it impatiently, and came over to the bed. 'Bind her mouth with this,' she instructed curtly, handing Morwith the black cloth that had been used to blindfold Hamet. 'We don't want her crying out and making a stupid fuss. Morwith, you know what to do, I'll be back very shortly.' She turned and left the room, slamming the door behind her. Morwith smiled to herself.

Carefully, she knelt up on the bed beside the frightened Saxon girl, stroking her inner wrist gently. 'Don't worry, I won't do anything to hurt you,' she whispered. 'Believe me, there is only pleasure in store. Were you taken prisoner by the Normans, like me?'

Elena shifted in anguish on the bed, terribly aware of the sensuous wolf pelts caressing her buttocks and the back of her thighs, of the pleasure that seared through her threateningly as her bonds tightened. She nodded her head desperately.

Morwith had a sudden inspiration. 'I know, you are from the convent!'

That explained so much – why this girl was so ripely feminine, so ready for love, and yet knew so little! On a sudden impulse, she reached out to stroke Elena's firm, lovely young breasts, noticing how the sudden spasm of pleasure shot through the girl's helpless body. 'Submit to me,' she whispered. 'Submit while I prepare you for Aimery's love, and you will find everything so much the sweeter! Listen, isn't this better than being out in the hot fields gathering hay, or slaving in the kitchens? Elena, you and I can be friends. Such friends! Let me show you what your body longs for . . .'

One of the candles guttered and went out. The room was almost in darkness, hot and oppressive. Carefully moving down to Elena's hips, Morwith stroked the leather belt. Then her fingers slipped downwards, parting the girl's tender, swollen lips, so that the pink flesh protruded in moist silken folds on either side of the taut strap. Then she dipped her head and started to lick softly, caressing the oversensitised flesh, curling her tongue beneath the thick leather, lapping up the sweet moisture that trickled down her secret cleft.

Elena went rigid with shock. Then, as the other woman continued so gently with her wonderful tonguing, she gave a muffled groan, and closed her eyes helplessly as the warm, soothing pleasure washed over her. Her belly tightened and her breasts throbbed unbearably as Morwith's long tongue licked so sweetly up and down her love channel. She arched her hips; the leather band pressed against her throbbing bud of pleasure, chafing at it, driving her almost to the brink of which she'd so long despaired.

She didn't hear the door open; neither did Morwith. But they both heard Isobel's voice, as she said, approvingly, 'Well, well. Morwith, you exceed your duties, I think. It seems as if we have arrived just in time.'

Elena, warm and flushed with shameful pleasure, jerked her head round to the door. *Aimery. Isobel had brought Aimery to her, as she had promised* . . .

Her eyes widened in shock.

Not Aimery, but a strong, muscular young serf whom she'd seen working in the kitchens. Isobel drew him forwards into the dark, heated room. 'Let me introduce you both,' she said huskily, 'to Pierre.'

The young serf's brown eyes had lit up with disbelieving pleasure as he saw the two beautiful women on the bed. He stumbled eagerly forward; Isobel stopped him with the lash of her tongue.

'Not yet, Pierre! First, you must show us that you are ready! Remember?'

Nodding avidly, Pierre started to fumble eagerly with his clothing. Elena, suddenly all too aware of her extreme vulnerability, struggled in her bonds, and felt her heated flesh growing cold. Surely – surely Isobel did not intend this youth for her? Morwith was crouching very still on the bed, watching and waiting. She said, almost accusingly, 'You told the girl that Aimery would be coming here.'

'In a while,' Isobel replied. 'In the meantime, we have a special treat for our convent girl. Dear me, Pierre, you are a little slow tonight. Would you like some encouragement?'

The handsome, strapping youth nodded fiercely, his hands still fumbling beneath his shabby tunic. Isobel glanced across at the bed and caught the look of blind rebellion on Elena's face.

'Oh, dear, Elena,' she sighed. 'And I thought you were so eager to learn, to carry out my lord Aimery's wishes!'

Elena squeezed her eyes shut. Aimery wished this? On her? After the tenderness he had shown her last night? No, she would not believe it! She struggled, trying to free herself again; Isobel watched her, her face hardening.

This was going to be more difficult than she thought. And yet, Pierre was an essential part of her plan. Elena must be desperate for pleasure by now after her day of torment, truly desperate for the feel of a strong man inside her hungry flesh. Surely, once she glimpsed Pierre's exceptional appendage, she would be begging for it, pleading wildly for him to pleasure her, to drive himself within her! And then – then, she could tell Aimery how his precious little Saxon slave had degraded herself with a common serf, a simpleton, and he would turn from the girl in utter disgust. Isobel turned her attention to the expectant redhead.

'Now, Morwith. As you can see, Pierre is a little shy, but he is truly, exquisitiely well-endowed. Encourage him a little, will you? You will find yourself well rewarded, I promise.'

Morwith glanced anxiously at Elena's white, despairing face. Then, obediently, she got up from the bed and swayed sensuously across the room to the muscular young serf, her breasts jutting proudly above her tight leather bodice. As she reached him, she sank to her knees and slowly began to unfasten the belt that supported his thonged trousers. 'Show me,' she smiled softly up at him. 'Show me, Pierre, what a man you are.' And she reached inside his clothes, licking her lips.

Pierre gasped, and clutched at her mane of red curls. Carefully, happily, Morwith drew out his already thickened penis, and cradled it between her palms, watching enraptured as the engorged shaft stiffened and grew. The lady Isobel was right. It was of exceptional proportions, long and solid, with an endearing curve towards the end that made it appear proud and eager to do service. Pierre was quivering with excitement, his penis jerking desperately towards her soft lips. Taking pity on him, Morwith stuck out her pink tongue and circled him lasciviously, licking slowly round the edge of the swollen purple glans, pushing back the foreskin and mouthing him delicately until he gasped with delight.

Isobel, seeing the perspiration standing out on Pierre's forehead, broke in swiftly. No, not yet. He must save himself for the convent girl, who trembled in her bonds as she gazed at Pierre's huge, glistening purple erection. 'Stop, Morwith. That is enough.'

Obediently but reluctantly, Morwith withdrew her mouth from Pierre's penis, so that it swung free, pointing blindly into the empty air. Pierre's face fell; his big hand moved swiftly to soothe his engorged shaft, sliding up and down in smooth, powerful strokes while his eyes closed in rapture.

'Stop that, Pierre!' cried out Isobel sharply. Pierre's hand fell swiftly to his side; he hung his head. Isobel went on, more gently, 'Now for that special treat I promised you yesterday, remember? A young Saxon girl, who is most eager to try out your splendid equipment – are you not, my dear Elena?'

Already the serf had turned eagerly towards her naked body on the bed, a grin of anticipation spreading across his blandly handsome features, his purple protuberance jutting out in excitement. Elena wrenched wildly at the silken cords that bound her wrists and ankles. *No*, Aimery could not want this for her. He could not!

Morwith, seeing what was happening, crouched quickly by her side. 'You'll enjoy it, Elena!' she whispered urgently. 'Don't be afraid! See what a man he is – see his fine instrument of pleasure – oh, don't your love juices flow for him? Don't you long to feel him inside you?'

Isobel, overhearing, chuckled in agreement. 'How right you are, Morwith! Pierre, get on with it. The girl is ready and waiting. All this protest is just part of some silly game that she likes to play. Take her, Pierre – she is yours.'

116

With a grunt, Pierre knelt on the bed between Elena's spread thighs. Eagerly he bent over her and began to struggle with the buckle that fastened her love belt, his huge purple member quivering and straining as he worked. Licking his lips, he drank in greedily the sight of those moist pink flesh lips protruding so sweetly from her soft golden fleece, longing to thrust himself in that honeyed passage.

The door to the chamber flew open suddenly, letting in a draught of fresh air and daylight. Pierre kneeled up, blinking.

Aimery le Sabrenn, lord of Thoresfield, stood outlined in the doorway, and in the shadows his scarred face was black with rage.

Chapter Eight

Aimery slammed the door shut. The draught blew out the final candle, throwing the room into complete darkness except for the glowing brazier in the corner.

Isobel moved quickly to relight the candles. 'Why, my lord! We did not expect you back so soon, but you are most welcome. We were preparing a little entertainment for you . . .'

Aimery's strong mouth curved in the dangerous smile that always sent a shiver of fear through even his closest friends. His tense, powerful figure dominated the room; it was as if everyone had stopped breathing, waiting for his reply. He still wore his leather gambeson, though he had removed his armour. The heat and dust of the long hours in the saddle were with him still, streaking his tawny hair. His eyes were like cold steel as he surveyed the still figures on the bed in the corner. Elena, lying helpless in her bonds, shivered when she saw the icy scorn in his glance.

He hadn't known. He hadn't wanted all this for her. Isobel had lied. And now, thinking that she'd willingly submitted to this degradation, he despised her with all his heart. She had lost before the game had even begun. Isobel had won.

Pierre, bemused and more than a little frightened by the lord of Thoresfield's presence, slid from the bed and backed into the shadows, his erection drooping quickly.

'So,' grated the Breton to Isobel. 'This is how you spend your afternoons when I am absent?'

Isobel moved swiftly towards him. 'It was all for you, my lord!' She ran her dainty hand down his muscular shoulder, gazing up with rapt emerald eyes into his tired, harsh face.

'And the girl?'

'You mean Elena? Why,' said Isobel, thinking quickly, 'your new acquisition has been most willing to join in with everything, my lord! She has displayed a touching eagerness, you wil be delighted with her progress! So enthusiastic, so passionate! Hamet, Morwith, Pierre – she has enjoyed them all!'

Aimery le Sabrenn felt suddenly sick. The dark bitterness rose in his soul. Once more he'd been mistaken, deceived. As he'd been deceived by the Saxon, Madelin . . .

Abruptly, he crossed to the chair and sat down, pouring himself a full goblet of wine from the silver jug resting on the nearby table. He drank it down and poured again. He felt a sudden, wild rage that transmuted itself into a hardening lust, a familiar tightening at his loins. So, they'd all pleasured the Saxon girl. Very well, then he, too, would take his pleasure from her, before throwing her out – off his property, his land, his demesne.

Elena had given up struggling. She was gagged still, and even if she were not, she knew, from the look on the Breton lord's face, that there was no point in trying to deny what Isobel had just told him. He would not believe her. He looked so tired, so bitter; and she burned desperately with longing for him.

Isobel, not sure which direction things were taking, said quickly, 'My lord, you are weary. I will dismiss these others, send for food, and you and I can spend some time alone.'

Aimery's face twisted cynically. 'What, Isobel – send them all away, when it seems that I have missed most of the entertainment already? Surely you can exercise your imagination and share a little of your diversion with me?'

Isobel, uncertain of the strangely harsh tone in his voice, felt suddenly uneasy. 'My lord – what is your will?'

Aimery let his black, bitter glance scald them all. His gaze alighted on the bewildered Pierre, who hovered, still hopeful of pleasure, in the shadows. 'What about him?' Aimery grated out. 'Your new favourite looks disappointed, Isobel. Have I interrupted him? Let him choose his pleasure – presumably he had finshed with the slut on the bed. Let me see him try the other one, the redhead!'

At this, Pierre brightened considerably; so did Morwith, who had been kneeling in stillness, breasts pouting, naked thighs just slightly apart, hoping desperately that she would catch the Breton's attention. Now was her chance! If she performed well, the Breton might take her himself.

Shivering at the very thought, Morwith moved voluptuously to crouch on all fours, her heavy, brown-nippled breasts dangling, her full buttocks wide and plump beneath the leather corset. Pierre, his erection suddenly jerking into life again, kneeled joyfully behind her, feeling for her juicy cleft, and with a soft hiss of delight thrust himself deep within her ripe, glistening folds. Morwith groaned aloud in ecstasy as his long, thick shaft possessed and filled her silky inner flesh. 'What a fine lad you are, Pierre,' she muttered in encouragement. 'Let me feel all of it, all of it – ah, yes, that's it.'

Meanwhile, Isobel kneeled hopefully beside her lord and let her fingers rest on his strongly-muscled thigh.

He ignored her and drank more wine, seeking oblivion, of the body and the mind. He was strongly aroused by the crude coupling going on in the shadows, and felt once more the urgent need for his own release. Not with Isobel. Not with the redheaded Saxon, whom he remembered from that midnight journey through the forest. She was doing all this for him, he knew, casting sideways glances at him through lascivious eyes. Dismissing her, his eyes strayed to the bed.

Elena lay very still, her eyes to the wall, the black cloth still fastened crudely round her mouth. Her beautiful blonde hair cascaded in disarray over her slender shoulders; her small, firm breasts rose and fell slightly with every breath she took, the rosy nipples tender and sweet. Her legs were drawn apart by the cords at her ankles; he could see the tender pink flesh of her femininity peeping out from either side of the tight leather belt. How many of them had used her today. Which of them had she enjoyed most?

Last night, he had thought she was different. But now he knew that she was just like all the rest.

He could feel his penis rearing up against his belly, hot and hungry. 'Untie the girl,' he rapped out to Isobel at his side. Isobel got up slowly, slanting a look of venomous hatred at the fair-haired Saxon bound to the bed. Pierre and Morwith were by now totally engrossed in their copulation; the young male serf kneeled above her, his muscular hips pumping away enthusiastically, while Morwith's face flushed with delight as Pierre's satisfying length of iron-hard flesh worked vigorously up and down her moist love channel.

Elena, freed by the coldly furious Isobel, the gag removed from her mouth, got to her feet and stood with her head held high.

'Come here,' said Aimery flatly, and she obeyed slowly, still not looking at him.

Blood of Christ, but she was beautiful, swore Aimery silently. Her wide, vulnerable eyes were dark sapphire pools in her pale, delicately shaped face; her glorious hair framed her head and shoulders like moondust. Her body was slender and graceful. Even in that tight leather belt, which must have been driving her into a frenzy of lust all day, she looked so pure, so untouched. Surely . . .

Isobel, crackling with jealousy, said with a light laugh, 'You will find dear Elena somewhat exhausted, my lord. She has such enthusiasm for our little games! Spare her your attentions as well, my lord, the poor girl can barely stand, so sated is she with pleasure.'

Elena's head jerked at that. She looked as if she were about to speak and gazed almost imploringly at Aimery le Sabrenn, her fathomless blue eyes dark with some kind of pain, then she changed her mind and lowered her eyes, her full lower lip trembling with passion.

So, she was ashamed. Aimery's empty stomach curdled suddenly on the strong wine he'd been drinking so freely. He said in a low, venomous voice, 'You mistake me, my lady Isobel. The girl is to give me pleasure, not to take it for herself. Obviously, you are taking her training very seriously. I wish to see the results so far.'

Elena stood before him with her hands clasped and her head bowed, so that her golden hair almost obscured her face. Her whole body burned for this man. His mere presence melted her; his voice, harsh though it was, sent impossible arrows of desire quivering through her helpless, naked flesh. He despised her so utterly, that she knew he would scorn anything at all that she tried to say in her defence. Would he take her word instead of Isobel's? Never.

Behind her, Pierre and Morwith reached their noisy climax, bucking wildly in each other's arms before collapsing, sweaty and sated, onto the floor. Aimery waited till they were still, then bit out roughly, 'Very well, then, Elena. Show me what you have learned.'

Elena gazed up at him, bewildered; Isobel gave her a

little shove, and hissed in her ear, 'Pleasure him, you fool! Have you learned nothing all day? Kneel, and pleasure your lord!'

With sudden realisation, Elena fell to her knees. Pleasure him. As Morwith had pleasured Pierre, when he first entered that hateful room.

Her cheeks flooded with colour now, Elena bowed her head so that her swathes of golden hair hung like a silk curtain across the Breton's strongly muscled thighs and brushed the tops of his leather boots. With trembling fingers, she reached for the lacings that fastened his woollen hose. Oh, if only men's clothing were not such a mystery to her! Unintentionally, as she fumbled beneath his leather tunic, she brushed the Breton's heated groin, saw his strong hands suddenly tighten on the arms of the chair. Her throat went dry. His bare forearms were tanned and sinewed, the skin covered with fine, sun-bleached hairs that she longed to kiss . . . She was this man's slave, she acknowledged hopelessly, in more ways than one.

As she knelt on the ground before him, the leather belt pressed in again on her soft, moist flesh. Already this afternoon, Morwith's sweet mouth had aroused her almost to breaking point. Now, with the Breton so near, she felt the drugged desire build up almost unbearably. She tried to hold herself very still, so that the leather strap would not slide any further between her swollen lips, but already her breathing was short and ragged.

Isobel's sneering laugh mocked her as she struggled with the stubborn laces. Then she found the opening, and her fingers shook as she caught a glimpse of smooth, taut thigh, darkly covered with soft, secret hairs. And then – between his thighs was that thickly curling pelt, from which grew his mysterious phallus, already thickened and stirring with life . . .

Forgetting her anguish, she gazed silently at its beauty, her breath catching in her throat. This was the heart, the dark, masculine core of this man who dominated her every thought.

From behind her, Isobel hissed, 'Go on, you little fool. Don't just stare!' She was aware of Morwith and Pierre, too, watching avidly from the shadows behind her. She panicked. What was she supposed to do?

Suddenly, she remembered how Morwith had taken Pierre's manhood in her mouth, when he first entered the room. She had been horrified then by the act, by the redhead's blatant sexuality. But this was different.

Elena felt herself filling up with an exquisite, yearning tenderness. No-one else in the room mattered, no-one else existed, except for Aimery. She leaned forward gently, to press tiny, delicate kisses on the warm flesh that stirred so strongly between the Breton's powerful thighs. As she did so, the root thickened still more, nudging her, caressing her parted lips. Elena kissed it again, carefully, along the now rigid shaft. Her heart thudded slowly as she felt the veined silken skin pulsing, tautening, lengthening. It was so beautiful, so warm and full of life.

Dimly, she heard Isobel exclaim impatiently, 'My lord, would you rather I gave you satisfaction instead? Clearly the girl has much to learn yet!'

Aimery, not taking his eyes from the girl's bowed head, said coldly, 'Isobel, your interruptions annoy me. Can't you find something, or someone else, to occupy your time? Another crude kitchen serf, perhaps?'

Isobel gasped aloud, as if he'd struck her. With a swirl of her silken gown, she turned and left the room, slamming the door behind her. Pierre, watching the kneeling Saxon girl as she paid homage to her Breton lord, was stirring with excitement again; Morwith too watched with moist, open lips.

Elena was oblivious to them all. All except her lord, Aimery. This suddenly seemed to be the only way she could express her love for this proud, bitter man, and her whole body hungered to serve him. All her yearning self, all her pulsing flesh, so exquisitely tormented during that long day, centred on her slow, deliberate caresses. His penis stood proudly erect now, straining at the flat, hard muscle of his belly; with a little gasp at the sight, almost frightened by it, she leaned forward on impulse and rubbed her small breasts, one by one, against the throbbing, silky glans.

The feel of his strong phallus against her tender, rosy nipples excited her unbearably. Sweet flames of sensation burned through her flesh, to meet in a molten blaze at the pit of her abdomen. Oh, to feel that massive pillar of flesh deep within her, caressing her, filling her!

Aimery groaned aloud at the unexpected delight of her breasts against his fevered phallus. Reaching out blindly, he clutched at her mane of hair and pulled her face down close to his throbbing erection. Shyly yet defiantly, Elena parted her lips and kissed him there, softly running her small tongue around the ridge that encircled the swollen glans. Then, drawing a deep breath, she took him in her mouth, sliding her moist lips down the straining shaft as far as she could, sensing rather than hearing the Breton's harsh gasp of pleasure.

He tasted exquisite. Warm, silken, aromatic – the very essence of masculinity. Knowing that she could take no more of that imposing shaft into her mouth, she instinctively gripped the base of his phallus with her hand, and continued to run her soft mouth up and down up and down the rigid flesh, shuddering with pleasure herself as he gasped and clutched at her shoulders.

Suddenly, Elena, her blood pulsing by now with almost unbearable excitement, felt the Breton's taut hips go very tense and still. With exquisite sensitivity, she continued to lick and suck, pouring her whole heart into her caresses; his strong hands moved to cup her breasts, his palms working deliberately to and fro across her stiffened nipples. Conscious of her own surging rapture, Elena gasped and felt the leather belt rub more tightly than ever against her secret parts. She thrust her breasts against Aimery's cool hands, rubbing the swollen globes desperately, dipping her head to pleasure him more fiercely than ever.

Then, the Breton suddenly withdrew. She feared she'd displeased him, but he soothed her, stroking her hair, restoring her confidence. At the same time his fingers squeezed her heated breasts, kneading and pinching her engorged nipples; the leather belt seemed to press harder between her moist inner lips, rubbing unbearably against her clitoris; until at last, with a wild shudder of ecstasy, Elena's racked body arched and exploded, all her senses obliterated by the shimmering waves of pleasure that rolled through her exquisitely-tormented nerve endings.

Still dazed with sensation, she felt an overpowering urge to bring him to the same plateau of rapture. Pushing her hair back from her flushed face, she leaned forward to draw her tongue tip around the sensitive glans of his urgently throbbing phallus, taking as much as she could into the soft cavern of her mouth, while with her hand she stroked and gripped the base of his rigid shaft. She felt a wonderful sense of power as he started to thrust strongly, uncontrollably within her mouth, and when his first spurt of semen shot out, she felt her body ripple in renewed orgasm. Dazed with the pleasure of it, she continued to suck and swallow the salty, exquisite emissions as his penis jerked powerfully at the back of her throat.

At long last he was still, and she felt the rigid shaft begin to soften within her mouth. She kissed it tenderly and knelt before him, her head bowed in silent homage. Surely, he would realise now what he meant to her. Tears of emotion welled in her eyes, making them translucent.

She felt his hand cupping her chin. He raised her head gently, compelling her to look up at him. His scarred, handsome face was stern and expressionless, the grey eyes cold. Yet behind it all, she knew, she was triumphantly sure, that there was some tenderness for her! He had sensed her own approaching release and urged her towards it, with infinite skill, even though he was so close to his own climax of passion.

Then suddenly, Aimery le Sabrenn saw the unshed tears of emotion in Elena's eyes, and stood up so abruptly that Elena almost fell.

'My lady Isobel has failed in her tuition,' he grated out sharply. 'You are not supposed to shed tears, Elena. Even if I am the person you hate most in all the world.'

'My lord!' she stammered out, shocked. 'I –'

'Enough.' He cut her short. 'From now on, you can take your pleasure with the rest of Isobel's rabble – presumably they please you more!' Swiftly, in less time than it took to blink an eye, he fastened his clothes and left the room. Elena drew a deep, shuddering breath of despair and gripped at the legs of the chair he had just left, fighting back the sharp pain that seared her. He had misunderstood. She would go after him.

From behind her, Morwith said softly, 'Dear me. You've got a lot to learn, haven't you? A lot they didn't teach you at the convent.'

Elena whirled round. Pierre, sated, was asleep on the floor; Morwith was watching her with a strange light in her pale eyes. 'Was I so bad then?' Elena whispered brokenly.

Morwith frowned. In fact, she'd been wildly jealous of the Saxon girl's exquisitely natural, sensual caresses, and she'd seen, only too well, the effect they'd had on the Breton.

But she wasn't going to tell her that, because Morwith wanted Aimery too, and she hoped that she might be able to turn this incident to her own advantage. 'Not bad,' the redhead conceded grudgingly. 'Not bad – for a first time. But I'd be very, very surprised if he came back for more. I'll tell you what, I'll give you lessons sometime.'

Pierre stirred in his sleep, and emitted a gentle snore.

Elena went slowly over to the bed and started pulling on her serf's tunic, her heart unbearably heavy. Suddenly, she wanted more than anything to be out of this room, away from the heavy, overloaded atmosphere. 'Thank you, Morwith,' she said. 'I will remember your offer.'

Then she went back to her own little room further along the gallery and lay on her bed, the despair washing over her.

In the great raftered hall, brightly lit by scores of smoking wax candles set in iron sconces on the walls, the evening meal was drawing to a close. Knights, men-at-arms, stewards and reeves relaxed noisily at the trestle tables set up through the length of the hall; shouting for more ale from the serving wenches, telling bawdy stories, picking at bones and mopping up the last morsels of juicy gravy with slabs of manchet bread. In front of the great log fire that always burned, day and night, several shaggy hunting hounds sprawled on the freshly-strewn rushes, gnawing contentedly at the half-finished scraps that had been thrown to them.

Only at the high table, raised on its dais at the end of the room, was the company subdued. Aimery le Sabrenn, lord of Thoresfield, was in a dangerous mood, and even his friends, the loyal knights who had campaigned with him in the old days in France and Sicily, were wary. One by one they left, to see to their horses, or their armour, or to join the cheerier company in the body of the hall as stories were told and dice were rolled. Aimery watched them go, stirring himself briefly to rap out some brief, curt orders to the sergeant-at-arms who was responsible for the night watch. Then he poured himself more wine and gazed into the smouldering logs of the fire. Even when his favourite deerhound came loping up to him and nuzzled hopefully at his hands, Aimery barely noticed him, and his face remained set and hard.

The girl obsessed him. With what pleasure Isobel had told him how the Saxon girl had enjoyed her tuition! Hamet, Aimery could almost forgive; but to think of her with that coarse serf, Pierre, was too much.

Why had he hoped she'd be different? Was it because of last night, when she'd surrendered so sweetly to him in her room? A fresh stab of bitterness coursed through his blood. Perhaps she wasn't even a virgin. Last night, he would have sworn, as he sheathed himself so deeply within her tender flesh, that she'd not known a man before. But perhaps she was especially cunning, like Madelin. Perhaps it was one of the tricks she'd learned, while servicing the rebels who stayed at that rat-hole of a convent, to look and sound innocent – as if it was her first time, every time.

Even this afternoon in Isobel's oppressive chamber, when the girl had taken him in her mouth, she'd seemed exquisitely innocent, yet so tender and loving that he thought he'd never known such pleasure.

At least, he should be grateful that her tears of revulsion had given her away in time. She'd not been able to conceal them. Aimery had no doubt that she'd reached a shattering plateau of pleasure herself – her shuddering climax was no pretence – but then, when she came to her senses and remembered who she was with, she hadn't been able to hide her true feelings.

He was her enemy, her people's enemy, and he was also hideously scarred. He thought he'd got used to that, but perhaps he hadn't.

Madelin. Madelin, the Saxon witch who'd killed his brother, was the one who'd scarred his face and embittered his soul

He drank more wine, remembering. The flames in the fire died down; a log settled, sending sparks flying. The noise and merriment of his soldiers at the lines of trestle tables seemed suddenly very far away.

Madelin, the young widow of a Saxon cloth merchant, lived in a house in York, while the brothers were garrisoned there under the command of William fitz Osbern. Hugh, who was in love with her, had been slightly injured in a skirmish with Saxon rebels and was confined to York castle. That night he asked his older brother to visit Gudrumgate, where Madelin lived, to tell her.

Madelin's maid, thinking perhaps in the darkness that Aimery was his brother, sent him straight upstairs to Madelin's chamber. When Aimery opened the door and went in, he realised the mistake; but by then, it was too late.

Madelin, the golden witch, lay on the bed, with a tall candle burning on the table beside her. It was a small, shabby room, but he didn't notice that. He only noticed her.

She was waiting for his brother. She was sitting up against her pillows, the cool linen sheet just touching her hips. Otherwise, she was naked. The candlelight turned her pale, smooth skin to gold, its incandescent flame shimmering on her wonderfully full, pouting breasts, on the glistening fair hair that hung in swathes round her shoulders. Her shadowed eyes were violet, her mouth was wide and full; and she smiled as she said huskily, 'Welcome, Aimery le Sabrenn.'

Aimery felt the heat scorching through him and said harshly, 'My lady, there has been some mistake. I come with an apology from my younger brother, Hugh.'

She sat forward then, so that the sheet fell back and he saw the smooth curve of her raised, silken thigh.

'No mistake,' she said softly. 'I have been waiting for you, Aimery le Sabrenn, since the day I saw you ride into York.'

Aimery still felt sick when he remembered how quickly he had betrayed his brother.

She sat up, the Saxon witch, in her soft bed, and slowly spread her raised knees, so he could see the smooth, completely hairless folds of flesh that framed her femininity. Then, still gazing at him with those

130

drowsy, violet eyes, she'd put one hand on her full breasts, caressing it softly until the scarlet nipple grew heavy and turgid. With her other hand, she reached down to her thighs, and started to stroke herself, playing with delicate fingers at her naked love mound and making little soft noises of longing at the back of her throat while she gazed at the man standing motionless by her bedroom door. With a slow shudder, she dipped her index finger between her lower lips, inserting it carefully into the moist pink flesh, then she drew it out and sucked at it, rapturously, with her mouth.

'Aimery,' she murmured. 'Oh, Aimery.'

Aimery the Breton was no saint. At his first sight of her, his penis had reared up, darkly massive, chafing against the thick belt that girded his tunic.

Freeing his phallus from his leggings with abrupt, jerky movements, he pulled her spread legs to the edge of the bed and took her standing up, planting his hands on either side of her reclining shoulders and sheathing himself up to the hilt in her soft, juicy love passage. Madelin seeemed to almost faint with pleasure as he slid his stiff rod between her legs; she dragged her fingers lasciviously across his broad, muscled shoulders, crying out huskily and arching fiercely against him as he lowered his head to suckle at her full breasts. She felt so good. Shuddering, Aimery bent over her, his feet still firmly planted on the ground, taking his weight with his arms. Slowly he slid his massively erect member in and out of those hairless, pouting lips, savouring her moist, delicious wantonness.

'Oh, Aimery,' she whispered. 'I have dreamed of this, since first I saw you. Fill me, fill me to the brim.'

Suddenly she wrapped her supple legs around his hips, clutching him to her; and Aimery, driving his engorged penis deep within her hot, pulsing flesh, reached a fast, shuddering climax deep within her as she writhed and bucked against his spasming body.

They lay entwined on the bed, slick with sweat, dark

with shame. Aimery drew away at last, and started to tell her that this must never happen again. She had gazed up at him with those wonderful violet eyes, her face soft and drowsy, and nodded.

'Oh course,' she murmured. 'Whatever you say, Aimery le Sabrenn.' Then she'd knelt above him, and positioned herself carefully, her tongue between her pearly teeth, so that those wonderful, scarlet-tipped breasts stroked heavily against his somnolent penis. With a life of its own, it began to stir thickly again. She knelt lower to take his testicles in her mouth, sucking at the rough, tautening globes one by one, nipping and licking at the coarse flesh until his phallus reared jerkily again, its powerful length all too ready for her soft, enticing flesh.

'Take me like this, Aimery,' she'd whispered, swiftly turning so she was on all fours, her secret flesh wet and glistening between the ripe roundness of her bottom cheeks. 'Take me, drive yurself into me, with your wonderful shaft. Yes, oh yes . . .'

Aimery had left the house in Gudrumgate two hours later, degraded and bewitched. He told his brother Hugh that he'd delivered his message; and from that night on, the intimacy, the trust between the two brothers had gone for ever.

He remembered it all now, only too clearly, as he sat in the great raftered hall; surrounded by all his men, and yet alone.

Since Madelin, he'd hated all Saxon women, and hated himself as well, for betraying Hugh.

Seeing that his goblet was empty, and the jug beside it, Aimery beckoned for more wine, and looked up to see that it was Hamet the Saracen who brought it to him. Hamet had been missing at the evening meal and Aimery had assumed that it was because the Saracen was ashamed to see his master, after what he had done with the Saxon girl.

Hamet started to fill his goblet from the jug, but

Aimery gestured curtly for him to stop. 'Leave me the jug. I'll pour.'

Hamet hesitated a moment, then sat down carefully on the bench at his master's side. 'I think,' said the big Saracen in his soft, musical voice, 'that you have perhaps had enough, my lord.'

Aimery's face twisted sardonically. 'I shall be the judge of that, I think. Where have you been this evening, Hamet? Sleeping off the afternoon's excesses in your room?'

Hamet's face shadowed in puzzlement at his master's bitter tone. 'My lord? I have been out on patrol, with a dozen men-at-arms – we left before your return. There were reports, this afternoon, of a band of armed rebels, down near the river. That is what I wished to speak to you about. We found no Saxons, but there were hoofprints, a good number of them, down by the ford. If your lordship thinks fit, perhaps we should mount extra guards tonight.'

Aimery frowned, forcing the potent wine fumes from his brain. 'I appreciate your excess of zeal, my friend. But if it's because you feel guilty about the Saxon girl this afternoon – '

Hamet looked down at his big hands. 'Then the lady Isobel has told you,' he said humbly. 'I apologise, my lord, for temporarily neglecting my duties. But the girl waylaid me, around noon. She was wanton and eager – I swear, it was all over in a few minutes!'

Aimery felt the bleak anger rise within him. God's blood – wanton and eager! His fist clenched. If Hamet had not been his friend of many years, he would have struck him down to the rush-strewn floor in that instant.

'It seems,' Aimery said, with a voice like splintered ice, 'that she deceived us all last night. Either she has learned very quickly, or her feigned innocence was all a pretence.'

Hamet's head jerked up at that, his dark eyes

puzzled. 'My lord – last night? I swear to you, I did not even see the redheaded Saxon woman last night!'

It was the Breton's turn to look surprised. 'A redhead? This – coupling you spoke of this afternoon – I gathered it was with the convent girl, Elena . . .'

Hamet's heavy brow cleared in relief. 'Why, no, my lord! The Saxon I spoke of was the redhead, Morwith. You might remember her from the woodcutter's cottage, on our way here!' He coughed awkwardly. 'I came across her in one of the outhouses at noon. She recognised me, and . . . and . . .'

Aimery le Sabrenn was watching him strangely. 'Then the fair-haired girl, Elena. The one who was in my room last night. You are telling me that you have had no contact with her today?'

Again, Hamet cleared his throat in embarrassment. 'My lord, the lady Isobel arranged for myself and Morwith to be punished for our misdemeanour. The girl you speak of was brought in, to watch. But she took no part in any of it, my lord!'

'She was there willingly?'

'I think not, my lord. Though,' and Hamet added this hastily, on seeing the Breton's expression, 'as far as I saw, she was not touched or harmed in any way; but merely made to witness our chastisement.'

With an oath, Aimery was on his feet. The wine jug on the table went crashing to the floor with the violence of his movement.

Hamet, confused, said, 'My lord. The extra patrol I mentioned?'

'Speak to the sergeant-at-arms,' called Aimery over his shoulders as he left the table. 'Tell him what you think fit.' Then he was gone, taking the stairs up to the sleeping chambers two at a time. Hamet, totally perplexed, turned back to ruefully survey the spilled wine.

Elena sat on the edge of her small bed in the darkness, thinking still of Aimery. At every encounter with the

Breton lord, she needed him more and more. Yet he despised her, openly.

She clenched her hands in her lap, trying to think coolly and calmly. Later tonight, she would try to escape from the castle. She didn't think she could bear to see the Breton again, to be so flayed by his cold scorn. She knew that she must leave, before he destroyed her completely.

The door to her room started to open, slowly. Her throat dry with fear, Elena leaped to her feet. *Aimery . . .*

Chapter Nine

*T*he Breton shut the door very deliberately behind
him, and stood there, watching her. Elena, standing
by the bed, felt herself trembling. His strange silver
eyes blazed with light above his hard, jutting cheekbones; his strong, curved mouth, so cruelly twisted by
the long white scar that slashed his cheek, was com-
pressed in a thin hard line. Her heart hammered against
her ribs, because he looked so *angry*.

Aimery said, in a low voice that seemed to her to be
filled with menace, 'So, Elena. Tell me exactly what
happened this afternoon.'

Elena moistened her dry lips. Somehow she stammered out her reply, forcing herself to look up into his
stern, compelling face.

'The lady Isobel summoned me. I – I was working in
the courtyard, bleaching the linen – '

Aimery bit out an oath. 'You were bleaching linen?'

He looked wildly angry. Elena, frightened and confused, said defiantly, 'Yes, my lord! I worked in the
kitchens all morning, and in the afternoon, I washed
linen, as you commanded! Was it not your will?'

Aimery said softly, dangerously, 'Go on. Tell me
more. You were summoned inside, by the lady Isobel.
And then?'

Elena bit her lip; the colour blazed in her cheeks. 'They were punishing him,' she whispered. 'Your servant – Hamet. Isobel and Morwith were punishing him. Then Morwith, too, was punished . . .' Her voice trailed away helplessly as she remembered the ivory phallus that gave Morwith such pleasure, remembered the Saracen in his extremity, his pulsing phallus spurting seed across the room.

Aimery was saying quietly, 'And you helped with their punishment?'

'I – I secured Morwith to the bed.' Her voice was scarcely discernible. She added, again with that note of desperate defiance, 'The lady Isobel told me that it was your will, my lord!'

'And the love belt that you wore? Your own bondage? You submitted willingly to all that?'

'Yes – because it was what you wanted! Wasn't it?'

Aimery ran his hand wearily through his thick hair. 'And you were so frightened of me that you would submit to anything Isobel said?'

'Not – not *frightened* of you, my lord,' Elena whispered.

A throbbing silence hung in the darkened room. Aimery suddenly realised how very tired he was. The girl stood before him in the darkness like a flame, pale and golden, shimmering with beauty and a quiet strength that defied him, defied all of them. He said, heavily, 'The lady Isobel told me that you joined in willingly with the others this afternoon – with their games. That you encouraged them to pleasure you. Was this true?'

The girl's face went white; he noticed how she clasped her hands rigidly at her side. 'No, my lord!'

'Then why, in the name of Christ, did you not deny it earlier?'

Elena gazed up at him, her dark blue eyes burning with some emotion he could not name. 'How could I?

When I had been told that the lady Isobel was merely carrying out your commands?'

His commands. The girl was right. More right than she would ever know. His commands, to choose a vulnerable Saxon slave from the latest batch of newcomers, to pleasure her, humiliate her, destroy her. His own revenge, for Madelin. His own soul, dark with a hatred that needed to feed on innocence.

With a bleak gesture of despair, Aimery le Sabrenn turned to the door. 'I will give orders, Elena, that you are not to work in the kitchens any more. And you may leave the castle tomorrow, if you wish. You are no longer a serf. You are free.'

Her incredible blue eyes widened with emotion at his words; numbly, still gazing at him, she whispered, 'My lord, as you wish!' Aimery, somehow expecting more reaction, paused with his hand on the door.

'One last thing. This afternoon, in Isobel's room. I would have you know that it was not my intention to grieve you so.'

The girl's face jerked upwards. '*Grieve* me?'

'Your tears. I did not mean to cause you such distress.'

She took a step towards him. 'My lord. Those tears – they were not caused by distress, but because I felt so completely unable to express how I felt . . .'

Aimery had gone very still. 'And how do you feel?'

Elena took a deep, steadying breath. 'All my life,' she said softly, 'I have been a captive, of sorts – in the convent. I was not unhappy, or ill-treated. But nevertheless, I was captive; I had no choice, nowhere else to go. Here, in your castle, I find myself a prisoner again. And now you offer me my freedom. But,' and her clear voice sank to the merest whisper, 'I do not want to leave, my lord. All I want in life is to be yours. In whatever way you wish.'

In three strides, Aimery le Sabrenn had covered the ground between them and caught her slender figure in his arms. She gazed up at him silently, her delicate face pale, her eyes dazed with helpless love.

'Elena,' he muttered as his strong hands gripped her shoulders. 'Oh, Elena. I thought, this afternoon, that you hated me. I thought I repelled you.'

Steadily she reached up her hand to smooth back his hair, and drew one delicate finger down the white ridge of scar tissue. 'My lord,' she said simply, 'at the convent, I used to dream. You are all I ever dreamed of – and more.'

Slowly, she began to lift her tunic over her head. Then, as Aimery gazed mesmerised at her slender, graceful figure, she sank to her knees and reached beneath his tunic for the lacings that fastened his hose. As her fingers did their work, she continued to gaze up at him, her face radiant. 'You will find me your most willing slave, my lord,' she whispered. 'Command me – I am yours.'

His penis was already thick, hanging lengthily down his inner thigh. With gentle little caresses, she bent to run her pointed tongue lovingly round its tip, kissing the swelling shaft until it sprang rapidly into a magnificent erection, jerking hungrily towards her soft, moist mouth. Aimery groaned aloud with pleasure, his hands clutching at her shoulders; she heard it, and caught her breath. She longed to feel him within her. But she was his slave; she was obedient to his commands.

Gently, he moved her head away. She looked up at him, dismayed. 'I do not please you, my lord? I know I have much to learn . . .'

He laughed, a soft, smoky laugh. '*Caran*, you are exquisite, all that a man could desire. But I would pleasure you too. Come, let me show you . . .' Slowly, he too sank to his knees, with his shoulders back against the wall, facing her. He too, pulled his tunic over his head, and Elena gasped with pleasure at the sight of the thick, rippling muscle that ridged his chest and shoulders. He bent to kiss her mouth, tenderly; she responded wildly, clasping at his back, running her fingers over his smoothly-tanned skin, fingering the old sword scars that adorned his soldier's body with burning pity, conscious all the time of his proudly erect phallus jutting up from his loins, like a dark, thrilling promise of delight.

'Spread yourself, Elena,' he whispered softly, 'Kneel astride me – I will support you. Spread your thighs, and let me slip into you, like this, ah . . .' With a gasp, Elena did as he said, straddling his strong, bent thighs. He eased himself into her, gently at first, inch by inch, rocking slightly to ease his entry into her tight, slick passage, trying his best not to hurt her with his massive erection.

Elena threw her head back, gasping with pleasure, rubbing her small breasts against his hard chest. All day, she had longed for this, and now it was unbelievably exquisite, to feel his thick, strong penis sliding up into her, totally within her control. She quickly discovered that if she raised herself so that the long shaft was almost free of her, and then slid slowly down again, clutching with her inner muscles, Aimery's face darkened with rapture; and her own pleasure mounted in relentless waves as the solid rod of his phallus filled her plump, tender flesh.

Then Aimery's fingers slid down to her little pleasure bud and softly stroked. With delicious little cries of pleasure, she closed her eyes and rode him, up and down, faster and faster, her jutting nipples grinding against his chest, until at last she exploded in a cataclysm of rapture, quivering and clutching with her inner muscles at that hot pillar of flesh that filled her so deliciously. Holding her tightly, Aimery pumped with his strong thighs to find his own driving release, spurting up within her; then she slumped against him, murmuring his name, knowing a moment of perfect peace as his lips gently kissed her tangled hair.

Then suddenly, somewhere out in the darkness of a

castle courtyard, a horn blared shrilly. Elena, her senses lulled by pleasure, barely heard it, thinking that it signalled the change of watch as usual. But then she realised that Aimery, still enfolding her in his arms, had become suddenly tense.

The horn brayed again, nearer now, a raucous, searing sound from beneath the window. Elena, still dazed with love, murmured in sleepy protest as Aimery moved into action. Carefully but swiftly, he lifted her up, laying her on her cold little bed, and began to dress himself.

'*Caran*, I must go. No time to explain.'

Elena lay shivering, suddenly cold. 'The horn, Aimery, what does it mean?'

He was buckling on his sword belt. 'It's the alarm. It could mean that the Saxons are about to attack.' He bent to kiss the top of her head. 'Wait for me, little one. I will be back.'

Then he was gone, the door slamming shut behind him. Shivering with premonition, Elena pulled the linen sheet from the bed around her shoulders, and tiptoed on bare feet to her little window.

The courtyard below was ablaze with the light of torches and lanterns. Men ran to and fro in a purposeful melee, seizing arms and horses, shouting barked orders to grooms and squires. The great gates of the palisade were already being swung open; the first mounted band was preparing to ride out into the darkness of the night, to face the enemy.

And the enemy, she knew, would be the Saxons, her own kind. She shivered suddenly.

Aimery plunged down the stairs to the hall below, where all was in a state of uproar. His faithful squire stood silently ready, holding out his armour and his sword. Hamet was already buckling on his own swordbelt.

'Scouts we sent out earlier have spotted a large band

141

of rebel Saxons moving through the forest from the east,' Hamet told Aimery grimly. 'Planning, no doubt, to surround Thoresfield and take us by surprise.'

Aimery nodded, making for the door. 'Leave twenty men-at-arms to guard the castle.'

A soldier came running in up the steps to the main door, and stood panting in front of the Breton. 'Sire, there are rumours that the Saxon serfs are planning to escape tonight, to join the rebels!'

Aimery gritted his teeth. 'Then impound them. Lock all the Saxons securely away until our return.'

'Sir!' The soldier acknowledged the command, and ran off towards the armoury. Aimery made for the stables, where his big black warhorse was ready for him, and sprang into the high saddle. With a harsh shout of command, his sword held high, he led his knights out through the wide-open gates, their horses' hooves trampling the beaten earth, their weapons glinting in the smoky torchlight.

Isobel watched them go, her heart burning with venom. She knew, because her spy Alys had just told her, that Aimery had been in the Saxon girl's room when the alarm sounded. Now was her chance to get her revenge, and put paid to the troublesome convent girl for good.

Elena too watched Aimery le Sabrenn ride out through the gates at the head of his men. Silently she watched the band of horsemen gradually disappear into the darkness of the night; saw the flickering light of their torches as they crossed the river by the ford and plunged into the dense silence of the great forest. Shivering, she turned away forlornly from the window and pulled on her serf's tunic.

There was a sudden loud hammering at her door. Bewildered, she hurried to open it. At once, two burly manservants shoved their way in, wrenched her hands behind her back, and started pushing her out of the room.

'No!' She tried to struggle out of their grasp. 'There must be some mistake!'

'No mistake,' growled one man. 'All rebel Saxon scum to be locked away until the lord Aimery returns. Are you saying you're not a Saxon, wench?'

'Yes! I'm Saxon but – '

'All Saxons,' repeated the other man grimly. That was what the lady Isobel had told him a moment ago, wasn't it? Especially, she pointed out, the little Saxon in the top chamber. She'd made a point of mentioning her, said she was to be locked in the dungeons along with the other women.

The men half-pushed, half-dragged their captive down the stairs and winding passages to the stone cellars beneath the castle. They opened up a dark doorway and roughly pushed her through; she stumbled down the stone steps and fell heavily on the straw-covered floor. Behind her, the door thudded shut, and she heard the chilling sound of the heavy bolt being slid into place.

Slowly, her head aching from her fall, she opened her eyes. There were other people, women, in here with her; she could hear their soft whispers as they crouched against the walls in the darkness.

'Here, take some of this,' said a sympathetic voice in her ear. 'It's only stale water, but it's all you'll get down here.'

Elena looked up jerkily, her cheeks smeared with dirt and tears, and recognised the plump, pretty face of Joan, one of the kitchen serfs, bending over her in the darkness.

'M – my thanks,' Elena stammered out, drawing a deep breath to steady herself and taking the proffered wooden beaker in her trembling hands. Then she tried to withdraw into the shadows, but Joan rocked back on her heels, and studied her with interest.

'Why,' she said, 'it's the new girl! You were working in the kitchens this morning, weren't you? You were the one who couldn't pluck chickens to save you life! And then you disappeared – what happened to you?'

The others, all young fair-haired Saxon women, had crowded around now in a circle on the straw, avidly curious about this newcomer. One of them chuckled huskily at Joan's question. 'Perhaps Aimery le Sabrenn carried her off to his chamber!'

Elena caught her breath *Did they know?*.

'What, her?' laughed one of the others scornfully, tossing back her thick golden braids. 'That little waif? She's from a convent, isn't she? A lot of good she'd be to the lord Aimery! Why, she wouldn't know what to do with a man like him! Now, if it was me . . .' And she whispered something in another girl's ear that had them both rippling with laughter.

Elena blushed and clasped her hands tightly in her lap.

'That redhead, Morwith,' another of the girls was muttering, 'she boasts that she lay with the lord Aimery on their journey here!'

'Ah, she's a stuck-up piece, that Morwith,' scoffed another, sprawling back in the dry, heaped-up straw. 'Lying again, no doubt. Anyway, why isn't she here with us? She's a Saxon serf, isn't she?'

'Lying or not, she described it all in perfect detail! Apparently,' and the speaker lowered her teasing voice, so the others crowded in close to listen, 'apparently, our fine lord is most exquisitely equipped. It's not only his sword that he has skill in wielding, they say!' She gurgled with laughter. 'Oh, what wouldn't I give for just one hour of his fine company?'

'Stop, stop, I can't bear it!' sighed another girl, tossing back her long hair. 'Gytha, how can you talk of such impossible delights, when we're locked up down here, with only each other for company?'

Suddenly, she whirled round on Elena. 'And what

about you, little convent girl? I saw you, blushing away in the darkness. Bet you don't even know what we're talking about, do you?'

'Yes, what was it like in the convent?' challenged Gytha, laying her hand on Elena's shoulder. 'Did you lie awake, little nun, dreaming of some fine man coming to your lonely bed?'

'Or,' whispered another one, rubbing close up to Elena's side, 'did you enjoy yourself with your friends? Did you pretend that you had a man to pleasure you?'

Suddenly they were all giggling, teasing, touching. One of them clutched laughingly at her tunic; it ripped, and they sighed with pleasure as her small white breasts were revealed to their avid gaze.

'No,' begged Elena, flushed with shame. 'No, I beg you—'

But they took no notice. The woman Gytha bent her head swiftly to suckle at the rosy crest; it pouted and stiffened beneath her teasing lips. 'Imagine,' she whispered hungrily, 'that it's the lord Aimery pleasuring you. Oh, just imagine little nun, that he's preparing to enter you with his great thick penis, getting ready to slide it into that hot, juicy little nest between your thighs . . .'

Elena felt the wild, dark pleasure rise in her just at the sound of his name. The women, sensing her shameful excitement, moved in on her quickly; two of them held her thighs apart, while Gytha gently ran her hands up beneath her tunic. Elena gasped as the exploring little finger caught tantasingly at the secret folds of flesh between her thighs; she twisted and turned, but there was no escape, and Gytha's cunning finger sliding up into her yearning, moistened flesh was so delicious that she let a soft moan escape from her parted lips.

Gytha gave a secret smile of satisfaction, and held up the finger that glistened with Elena's love juices. 'Such a sweet, hot little love mound, girls,' she whispered gleefully. She used two more fingers to stroke Elena's flesh lips, parting them softly and rubbing with gentle insistence so that the flesh around her swollen clitoris was stretched and pulled. 'Our little nun is more than ready, it seems, ready to feel a strong man slide his thick shaft inside her, to feel him pleasure her until she squeals for mercy. Is this what you did at the convent? All of you using your eager little fingers, to give yourselves pleasure? Girls, let's show her that we can do the same!'

Instantly two of them bent to her pointed little breasts, suckling and licking at her exquisitely sensitised nipples as Elena writhed helplessly beneath them. The dark pleasure flooded her; she was terrified that she was going to climax hotly beneath their teasing fingers and hot busy mouths. Slowly, she was being drawn into a whirling vortex of sensation that it was impossible to resist –

'Stop!' hissed Gytha suddenly. 'Someone's coming!'

Elena was abandoned. She rolled over into the shadows, clutching her torn tunic across her breasts, her whole body aching with wild, unsatisfied desire. The other girls, suddenly silent, flew apart and shrank back into the shadows against the bare stone walls.

The bolt grated back slowly, ominously, and everyone held their breath. The door opened, and the light of a torch fixed at the top of the stairwell flooded in, temporarily blinding them. A soldier was coming warily down the few steps into the cellar, carrying a stone pitcher of water and a big wooden platter piled high with coarse rye loaves.

Suddenly, someone darted up to the door and slammed it shut, blocking out the light so that they were plunged into pitch darkness again. Within seconds, the soldier, tripped up by a slender ankle, was on his back in the straw, with the water and bread scattered to the four corners of the cell; two of the girls had seized his wrists, while two more straddled his muscular thighs, pinning him down. He opened his mouth to yell, but Gytha had already whipped the sharp dagger from his belt, and now she held it to his throat.

'Keep very still, soldier,' she said throatily, her blue eyes dancing in the shadows. 'I rather think you're the answer to our prayers.'

The French soldier, who was young and darkly handsome and understood barely one word of Saxon, lay very still.

Then, one of the girls who sat astride his thighs started to slowly lift her ragged dress above her head. He watched, hypnotised, and swallowed thickly, aware that even in the midst of his terror his eager phallus was stirring between his imprisoned thighs. Cursed Saxon witches, he muttered silently to himself. What devilment were they planning?

Then another girl, laughing softly, reached beneath his leather tunic and unlaced his leggings. With soft, busy little fingers, she released his genitals, cupping his hairy balls and giving a little gasp of pleasure as she felt how his penis had already thickened. He continued to struggle instinctively, his eyes on the sharp knife; he almost choked with fear as his own dagger pricked at his vulnerable throat.

'What is your name?' someone whispered throatily in his ear. 'Your name, soldier.'

Struggling to comprehend, he muttered, 'Henri.'

'Well, then, Henri,' said the voice smoothly, 'lie still, and watch.'

The girl who had removed her tunic leaned forward, and the young soldier groaned aloud as her full, ripe breasts brushed across his loins. His penis jerked upwards from its bush of black hair, yearning to savour those rosy nipples; the girls surrounding him gave soft murmurs of delight at the generous length of his throbbing erection, and watched avidly.

'Who's first?' whispered one, licking her lips.

'Take turns,' commanded Gytha softly. 'Isn't that fair, soldier?'

Needing no encouragement, the naked Saxon girl who was so busy rubbing her hardened nipples against the soldier's swollen glans moved swiftly to straddle his hips, and lowered herself, licking her lips, onto the swollen red shaft. She closed her eyes with delight as he slid up her and threw her head back, wriggling in a delirium of sensation as the thick, engorged penis hungrily filled her aching flesh.

The others watched avidly, enviously. Gytha murmured, 'We must make the most of this, girls. This fine young fellow will earn his keep tonight.'

And, pulling her own tunic deliberately over her head, caressing her own flushed breasts, she crouched above the soldier's head to face the girl who was riding his hips, her secret flesh poised above his mouth.

'Lick me, Henri,' she whispered. 'Lick me. Push your fine, hard tongue up into me – ah, yes, that's it – ' On the verge of spasming already, she leaned forward to grasp the other girl's breasts in her cupped hands, pinching at her nipples, so the other girl cried aloud and rode herself harder and harder on the imprisoned man's rigid shaft.

Elena, hot with shame, was unable to tear her eyes away, aware that she was almost on the brink of explosion herself, her love-channel slick with juices, crying out for satisfaction. She could see the thick base of the soldier's rigid penis as the excited woman slid up and down his shaft; the thought of feeling that long, hot stem sliding within her own juicy passage made her feel faint with desire. At the same time, she could see how the solider lapped avidly at Gytha's moist vulva, licking and tasting greedily, sliding along her inner lips and thrusting high into her swollen pink flesh.

Suddenly, with groans of ecstasy, the three of them began to explode; the two girls writhing their hips as they clutched hungrily at the young man beneath them, while the soldier pumped deliriously hard with his penis, at the same time swirling and licking at Gytha's wetness with his mouth. With a great cry, the soldier, feeling his seed gathering relentlessly, arched his hips as his climax overtook him in spasms and he thrust hungrily into the juicy loins of the Saxon girl above him.

Exhausted, sated, the three of them stretched out alongside one another's bodies, still licking and caressing softly, as the afterwaves of orgasm melted deliciously through their contented bodies. The other girls watched in envious silence.

Gytha got up first, her eyes glittering brightly in the shadows. 'Whose turn next?' she whispered softly.

The young soldier, lying back with his eyes closed, caught the gist of what she was saying and gave a weak groan of protest. Gytha smiled wickedly at him, admiring his fine, muscular body. 'That's only the start, soldier,' she grinned. 'You're here to service us all – you realise that?'

Henri shook his head, not understanding, but he smiled. Gytha's eyes darted intently round the room, until they rested on Elena, still curled in her corner. 'Well, well. I think I have just the thing for you, Henri. How does an innocent convent girl take your fancy? Joan, you others, hold her down.'

With a scandalised cry of rebellion, Elena tried to wriggle into the shadows. But there was nowhere to run. Laughing huskily, the four girls held her down, just as they'd pinioned the soldier, and pulled her ripped tunic apart once more so that her quivering breasts were exposed. Gytha, standing over her with her hands on her hips, gave a slow smile of satisfaction.

'Now, my handsome young friend Henri,' she said softly. 'On your knees before her. See how her flesh burns for you! See how the little convent girl yearns for a real man's caress! Bow down before her – taste her – kiss her – '

Henri understood not one word, but he did understand what he was meant to do. Eagerly he kneeled between Elena's spread legs, and she wrenched her head aside, closing her eyes in shame.

But then, as she began to feel his slow, rasping tongue wriggling along the folds of her secret flesh, the hot tide of pleasure began to build up inside her like an unstoppable flood. His touch was exquisite. Skilfully, he drew his long, pointed tongue up and down the entrance to her inflamed love channel, sliding lingeringly along the moist plump flesh, flicking at the pleasure bud at the end of each stroke, until she cried aloud with the sweetness of it. The girls who pinned down her arms were licking moistly at her distended nipples until she squirmed with pleasure; still she fought desperately to hold back, because she couldn't bear the thought of these women witnessing her shameful delight in this degradation.

Then the young soldier slowly slid his stiffened tongue up inside her, gently thrusting against her pulsing inner walls. At the same time, the two girls nipped and sucked at her swollen breasts, drawing out her aching nipples with their teeth; and Elena, lost in a haze of voluptuous sensation, crashed into a violent frenzy of rapture, writhing her hips against the man's delicious tongue, and rubbing her breasts against her tormentors' sweet mouths.

In endless waves, the exquisite pleasure washed over her and slowly receded. The girls smiled down at her, pleased with themselves, and looked round for their next entertainment.

The soldier had enjoyed Elena's cries of rapture, and was fully erect again. The girls on seeing his proud, handsome appendage thrusting out so eagerly, squabbled fiercely over him. They ended up in a confused tussle in the corner; until three of them crouched over on all fours in a row, desperately thrust their juicy, naked hips towards him, openly parting their moist flesh lips with eager fingers. Henri, taking his time and thoroughly enjoying himself, crouched on his knees to

150

fondle their plump bottoms and to service each one of them briefly; then he withdrew, and moved on. Each girl panted breathlessly with excitement as her turn approached; each girl savoured every second as his glistening red phallus drove passionately into her hungry flesh; then moaned in despair as he withdrew and moved on with a grin. Every eye was on his long, jutting penis, every eye watched enviously as he lingered at last with the third girl, who convulsed into orgasm the minute his rampant shaft slid up her tight, aching love channel. Her little gasps of pleasure were too much for the soldier. They all watched avidly as he clutched at her plump hips, pumping hard into her until, with a groan of shattering delight, he spasmed into her quivering flesh, the sweat glistening on his ecstatic face.

'Hush! Someone's coming!' hissed Gytha.

They all froze. They could hear heavy footsteps coming down the stairwell beyond the wooden door. The soldier Henri, exhausted though he was, sprang to his feet in alarm and pulled down his leather jerkin; the women rearranged their rumpled tunics and shrank back into the shadows, completely silent. Elena felt as if everyone must be able to hear the heavy pounding of her own heart. She had watched, transfixed, as the young soldier drove the three women to distraction, her own body still awash with delicious sensation. Oh, if only it had been Aimery, she yearned silently.

Rusty hinges grated, and the door slowly opened. The light from a lantern poured into the dark, airless dungeon.

A captain of the guard stood outlined in the doorway, his sword drawn, his grim face menacing.

'Henri!' he grated out. 'They have been looking for you this past half hour. Your turn for the night watch, lad, or had you forgotten? A good job someone remembered you were due to take bread and water to these sluts.'

The young soldier Henri, his face admirably straight, said, 'I stumbled and fell down the steps, sir.' He gestured apologetically at the scattered loaves, the spilled pitcher of water. 'Gave myself a knock on the head. These girls were – most helpful, sir.'

Someone stifled a giggle; the captain raised his lantern and scoured the shadows suspiciously. They all gazed back at him, wide eyes innocent. Meanwhile, Henri had bent to pick up his fallen dagger.

'Move yourself, then, lad!' said the captain gruffly. 'Your turn at the gate!'

'Sir!' said Henri smartly, and hurried through the door and up the stairs. The captain turned one last time to glare at the women. Damned Saxons, he muttered to himself. All the same, a good-looking young bunch. And the air in here was strangely heavy and scented, musky, almost as if – as if . . .

Shaking his head, he followed Henri out of the cell and slammed the door.

Back in the darkness, the girls collapsed with laughter, and huddled in a circle to relive the delightful ordeal of their all-too-willing prisoner. Someone gathered up the scattered rye loaves that Henri had brought, and they devoured them greedily. Then Joan sat back suddenly, and sighed. 'I wonder how much longer we'll be shut up in here?'

Gytha said curtly, 'You heard the orders when they rounded us up. All Saxon serfs are to be locked away until Aimery le Sabrenn returns.'

'Perhaps,' murmured someone longingly out of the darkness, 'the lord Aimery himself will visit us . . .'

'Then we could kidnap *him*!' murmured another girl excitedly. 'Oh, every time I see him riding out through the castle gates, I go hot and cold all over. That face, that voice, that body! I tell you, the things I'd do to him, if the lord Aimery were my prisoner!'

Gytha said sharply, 'Best steer clear of him if you've any sense.'

Elena, kneeling at Joan's side, almost stopped breathing. 'Why?'

'Because, little convent girl, I've heard stories. About the Breton.' She looked around the hushed circle, seeing how their pretty young faces watched her avidly. 'I've been here longer than any of you. And, believe me, I've heard tales of how the Breton likes to amuse himself.' She paused; the silence was absolute.

'Our fine lord Aimery,' she went on softly, 'has a liking for Saxon girls.' Someone gave a murmur of excitement. 'Yes, girls like you. Any of you. He picks on a pretty serf, and takes her upstairs, to his private chamber. Lavishes her with fine clothes, wines from his own cellar, the finest, most delicate food. And nights of exquisite pleasure. Unimaginable pleasure.'

'How do you know all this, Gytha?' someone whispered eagerly.

'I heard it with my own ears from the lady Isobel's maid, Alys. You know how she's always eavesdropping, spying at keyholes. Poor Alys, she's so desperate for a man, she'd tell us any secret, if we find a sturdy Saxon to service her. She told us – ' and again her voice dropped – 'that's it's the Breton's twisted idea of entertainment to choose himself an innocent Saxon girl, one who's new to the estate, then he drives her mad with devilish pleasure, and when she's quite besotted, demented with longing for him, he casts her out again. Back onto the dungheaps, where he reckons all we Saxons belong.'

It seemed suddenly cold in their dark cell. 'But why?' someone faltered. 'Why would he do that, when he can have his pick of anyone?'

Gytha shrugged grimly. 'I've heard it said that he hates all Saxons – especially women – with a deep, poisonous hatred. There's something hidden in his past, that's burned into his very soul.'

The others sat in silence, absorbing what they'd just heard.

Elena, glad of the near-darkness, was clenching her knuckles until her nails dug into her palms. *No.* She wouldn't believe it. He had called her *caran* – his beloved. She wouldn't believe it. She was different!

But wasn't what Gytha spoke of happening to her already? Already the powerful Breton lord dominated her every thought, her body, her soul. Even at the height of sensual pleasure bestowed on her by the soldier, Henri, it was Aimery's name that rose to her lips. And, if what Gytha said was true, then it explained why she was imprisoned down here, at Aimery's command.

'Are you all right, Elena?' Joan, who'd been watching her, put a friendly hand on her shoulder. Elena pushed her tousled hair back from her white face.

'I'm tired, that's all.' She tried to smile.

'Then sleep,' said Joan soothingly. 'We're friends, you know.'

Elena nodded silently, and curled up in a corner on the straw. Someone covered her with a tattered cloak, and she slept through the night, exhausted.

She awoke with a start. It was morning. The daylight flooded down the stairwell through the open door of their cell. She was aware of lots of noise and confusion, with armed guards standing by the doorway hustling the women out.

Elena scrambled to her feet; Joan reached out to grab her hand, pulling her urgently towards freedom. But at the last moment, two of the guards seized Elena roughly and pushed her back into the cell so that she stumbled and fell.

'Let her go, you oafs!' said Joan sharply. 'Isn't she to be freed, like the rest of us?'

'That one stays,' said the guard warningly. 'You'd argue with the lord Aimery's orders, would you, wench?'

Joan was pushed, protesting, out of the cell. The guards followed and the door was locked.

Elena lay on the straw in the corner, her arms wrapped around her shivering body. 'The lord Aimery's orders?'

Gytha had been right about the Breton, but her warning had come too late for Elena. Already, her punishment was beginning.

Morwith should have been locked up with the other women. In fact, she'd been rounded up with the rest of the Saxon serfs when the order for their restraint first came through; but she'd quickly pointed out to the guard the error of his ways. In fact, she'd whispered in his ear and the young guard, confused and excited, had promised to take her to the guardroom instead, to keep her safe while the alarm was on.

Two other guards were rolling dice at the roughly-hewn oak table as she was shown into the barely furnished guardroom that lodged by the main gates to the castle. The candles flickered as the door opened; the soldiers looked up from their game, and grinned slowly as the young guard ushered in his prize.

Morwith returned their challenging stares with a slow smile, tossing back her thick red curls, and smoothing her plain woollen gown tightly over her voluptuous hips.

One of the seated soldiers said slowly, 'Tell you what. We'll play dice for her.'

'What a good idea,' said Morwith, moistening her lips as she surveyed them. They were all young, all sturdily built and sternly attractive, with their leather gambesons and sunburned faces framed by close-cropped dark hair. Her own excitement surged. 'Just as long as you *all* win . . .

The soldier who'd brought her in, the youngest of the three, gulped noisily. With a wicked smile, Morwith untied the girdle at her waist and pulled her long gown over her head, dropping it on the hard earth floor. Then she slipped out of her cotton chemise and stood provocatively before them, clad only in a pair of Isobel's silk hose, that were gartered with silk ribbon around her plump, freckled thighs. She clasped her hands demurely across her ripe mound, where the red-golden hair so tantalisingly outlined her sex. In doing so, her upper arms squeezed her full breasts up and together, so that the large brown nipples, already stiffening, pouted hungrily.

She felt the heated excitement licking like tongues of fire at her belly, here in this bare guardroom, with three fine soldiers and all the trappings of war, the armour and the weapons, scattered about the room. This was the kind of power she'd only dreamed of, when she was a shabby, homeless outcast in the forest!

All three of them – why not?

'Well, lads,' said one of the guards thickly, scarcely able to tear his eyes from Morwith's glorious body. 'Looks like we've got ourselves a tasty, willing morsel for tonight. Which one of us first?' and they began to roll the dice with feverish haste.

A straw pallet intended for the use of off-duty soldiers lay in the shadowy corner of the guardroom. Morwith swayed tantalisingly across the room towards it and sprawled languorously on her back, her hands behind her head, watching the three intent soldiers as they played by the light of the candle. 'Come on, then,' she murmured provocatively. 'Show me what you can do.'

With a cry of triumph as the dice settled, one of the soldiers jumped to his feet. Swiftly he unfastened his belt and loosened his leggings. He had no time for any further preparation, and Morwith soon saw why; he already sported a huge erection. Her eyes widened with joy as he kneeled eagerly between her parted legs and, frowning with concentration, gripped at his throbbing member.

'Ah, soldier,' she breathed, drawing up her knees to

display her ripe, moist flesh. 'That's a beauty! Stick it up me – oh yes, yes!' She wrapped her legs eagerly round his muscular hips, and her words were lost in a delighted cry of pleasure as he slid his engorged shaft up her juicy love passage and began pumping eagerly away.

And now the second soldier had won his game of dice; he pulled down his leggings swiftly, and his angry red penis reared up from his loins, searching blindly for an orifice. Morwith's mouth, gasping with pleasure as the first soldier made his deep, searching thrusts, was open and tempting; with a groan he kneeled astride her face and thrust himself within that velvety opening, feeling her soft lips adjust instantly to receive the swollen glans, her insolent tongue darting, licking, sucking as hard as she could.

The third soldier, the youngest and the one who'd brought her here in the first place, stood watching enviously, his hand pumping despairingly at his own slim, pulsing shaft as he watched.

Then he noticed the first man's buttocks, tight and muscular as he drove himself in and out of the Saxon wench. He saw the man's heavy balls dangling between his thighs; saw the shadowy curls of hair that outlined the dark mysterious crevice between his bottom cheeks; caught a glimpse of the tightly puckered brown hole that he knew would be pulsing with excitement.

Eagerly, the young soldier spat into his hand, and rubbed the moisture over his ravening penis. Then he knelt behind the other man, smoothing his hands lovingly over those muscular bottom-cheeks, parting them, rubbing his finger along the dark, hairy crease and poking his forefinger exploratively into the tightly collared hole.

Then, swiftly, he pushed himself into the tiny aperture, groaning aloud with delight as the narrow anal rim caressed his hot, angry phallus. The other man shouted aloud as he felt the intrusion; gasped with excitement, and began, almost immediately, to climax into the redhead with harsh, spasming jerks. The young soldier who impaled him was also carried over the brink, his own orgasm washing over him in hot, flooding waves; while at Morwith's head, the man who occupied her mouth let her wonderful, silky lips suck him into a rapture so extreme that he cried aloud in delight as his seed gushed into her throat.

As for Morwith, she had never known anything like it. Three virile, splendidly-equipped, muscular men, all writhing in ecstasy above her, within her. She arched her hips convulsively as the ripples of exquisite sensation coursed through her body and exploded in a blinding torrent of pleasure.

Slowly, grinning somewhat sheepishly, the men withdrew and got to their feet. Morwith lay on the pallet, flushed and sated, her red hair billowing about her shoulders and her eyes drowsy with delight.

'Gentlemen,' she said softly, 'consider me your prisoner for the night. Another game of dice? Only this time, I'll join in . . .'

Chapter Ten

*I*t was late afternoon when the lady Isobel de Morency, flanked by guards, stood expectantly in the sunbaked castle courtyard. She had come to witness a punishment.

The sergeant-at-arms pointed brusquely to where a man was fettered on his knees against the stable wall.

'That's the man, my lady. Just some Saxon clod, a serf. My men caught him trying to escape from the armoury where he'd been locked in with the rest of the rabble. An informer warned us – said he intended to escape and join the rebel army. He's been in chains all day, without food or drink and now, by your leave, my lady, he'll be flogged, as an example to the rest of the rabble.'

Isobel nodded, her green eyes narrowing as she surveyed the prisoner kneeling on the hard cobbles, trapped in the full glare of the hot summer sun. Without water to ease his thirst, he would be suffering. She felt a pleasurable pulse beat in her white throat.

She'd known he was Saxon by the striking colour of his ragged, shoulder-length blond hair. He looked young and muscular, a fine figure despite his ragged breeches. Out here in the dusty courtyard there was no relief from the sun and his bronzed back glistened with sweat. Moistening her full lips, Isobel drank in the subtle interplay of taut muscle and assessed the stretched tendons and corded sinews of his powerful, imprisoned arms as he knelt there in his humiliation, his hips upthrust into the air.

Isobel smiled to herself. Suddenly, life didn't seem quite so tedious. Walking slowly across the yard, the guards following, she stopped in front of the bowed prisoner. Then she reached out for the sergeant-at-arms' leather quirt, and trailed the lash of the whip softly across the serf's broad shoulders.

The man shuddered briefly, then looked up at her in silent defiance.

Isobel's eyes widened, taking in the regular, tanned features; the strong, square jaw shadowed with blond stubble; the proud yet sensitive mouth and the vivid blue Saxon eyes that were filled with a natural arrogance, even in this hopeless subjugation. A find indeed.

'They tell me,' she said softly, 'that you were trying to run. What a coward you are. What is your name?'

The proud Saxon moistened his parched lips and grated out, 'I am no coward, lady. And my name is Leofwin.'

'Well, Leofwin. You may know that I am in charge of this castle while my lord Aimery is absent. And it is my duty to see to your punishment.'

'May your precious lord Aimery rot in hell,' said Leofwin the Saxon, slowly and clearly. A gasp went up from the guards at Isobel's shoulders; she held up her hand to restrain them.

'Have a care, my fine Saxon,' she said silkily. 'Remember that it is up to me to determine the severity of your punishment.'

His eyes flickered with lazy scorn. 'Do what you will. You can think of nothing new.'

Isobel's eyes danced. 'Oh,' she murmured, 'you would be surprised. I can think of lots of things,

Leofwin.' She turned suddenly to the sergeant at her side. 'Take off his clothing.'

Leofwin's head jerked up at that and he gritted his teeth as the sergeant ripped at the ragged breeches that were his last vestige of modesty. Leofwin closed his eyes briefly, as if bracing himself, as his nakedness was revealed.

Isobel gazed with pleasure at the heavy pouch of his balls hanging amidst the blond nest of hair between his legs, at the long, thick phallus that lay prone between his powerfully muscled thighs. Raising the whip, she drew the tip of its lash gently along his buttocks, thrust into prominence by the posture that the fetters forced on him. Then she let the lash dangle between his cheeks, drawing the leather up slowly. The man Leofwin bit his lip to stifle a groan, and Isobel saw, with delight, how his phallus was beginning to stir into life. The soldiers, gathered around, were grinning openly at her subtle torment of the prisoner. Isobel turned again to the sergeant. 'Encourage him,' she said pleasantly. 'Our poor guest seems a little – reluctant – to entertain us.'

With a grin, the sergeant thrust out his big fist and bent down to grip Leofwin's swelling shaft. Swiftly he pumped up and down a few times, drawing back the foreskin so the smooth glans was revealed. The other men murmured in appreciation as the Saxon's tumescent member throbbed and grew to impressive proportions, jerking up against his belly as the sergeant gave it a last, appreciative rub and reluctantly let go. Leofwin had closed his eyes; his mouth was set in a gaunt rictus of mingled shame and pleasure. Isobel, watching with rapt pleasure, brought the whip sharply down across his tautly-muscled buttocks and Leofwin groaned aloud as his now rampant penis jerked hungrily into thin air.

Isobel said, 'So, my proud Leofwin. Do you still consider that we can think of nothing new to torment you?' She picked up the man's discarded clothing and tossed it at the sergeant. 'Make him decent again, and have him taken down to the lower dungeon. In chains.'

'But my lady, the girl is still down there, as you commanded.'

'You heard me!' Isobel snapped dangerously. 'Do it – now!' As her men started to unfasten the stocks, she fingered the whip softly, with pleasure.

Elena, lying on the straw in the corner of the dark cell, looked up with a start. She heard footsteps; someone was coming down the stone steps outside. Perhaps they brought bread and water again. Or perhaps Aimery was back? No. She swallowed hard at the ache in her throat. Hadn't she heard, with her own ears, that it was Aimery who'd ordered her to be kept in solitary confinement down here? Gytha's words had haunted her all day, *He hates all Saxons – especially women – with a deep, poisonous hatred.*'

The bolt was rasped back. The door was flung open; the sudden light from the stairwell all but blinded her. A man in ragged breeches, with his arms chained behind his back, was kicked and shoved down the stairs; he fell, and the two guards behind him started to pull him up roughly. Behind them stood the lady Isobel de Morency who carried a gleaming torch, which she stuck into a cresset fixed to the wall.

The prisoner was pulled to his feet and held upright by the guards, his arms still in chains. He spat out a harsh Saxon oath at his captors; Elena, pulling herself to her feet, stared into his familiar face.

Leofwin. Leofwin, the captured rebel, with his gaunt, proud features and his blazing blue eyes.

Her own eyes widened in distress at his humiliation. He caught her gaze and shook his head very slightly, as if to say, 'No. Don't talk now. Don't let them know that you know me.'

Isobel, her hands on her hips, was saying with silky relish, 'We've brought a friend for you, my little Elena.

One of your own kind, to keep you company down here. You Saxons are used to wallowing in filth, aren't you? I should think this cell is quite luxurious for you both!'

Leofwin jerked himself free, sending his guards flying; they scrambled to get a grip at his chains and wrestled him, still struggling, to his knees.

Elena, unable to bear any more, launched herself towards Isobel. 'Leave him alone! What harm has he done? Why should he be punished like this?'

Instead of answering her, Isobel turned towards the guards. 'Get out,' she told them.

'But my lady – '

'I can deal with them. Both of them. Get out.'

The guards reluctantly obeyed, closing the heavy door behind them. Isobel turned towards the still kneeling Leofwin. 'Well, my fine Saxon, it seems as if you have found yourself a little champion here. A soft heart, hasn't she, our little convent girl? A pity, though, that she's a slut.'

Elena whitened. 'No. I beg you . . .'

Isobel advanced slowly on her, her silk gown rustling against the straw scattered on the floor, the flames of the torch bringing the fine fabric to life. 'Oh, yes, a slut. Tell Leofwin here, convent girl, how you let the Breton ravish you – how you welcomed him into your lonely bed on your very first night here, and moaned aloud with pleasure – go on, tell him!'

Leofwin looked up at her steadily. 'It's all right, Elena. I know she's lying.'

Elena hung her head, feeling sick. Isobel chuckled.

'No lies, my fine Leofwin! Why, she couldn't wait for it, could you, Elena? Show him – show him that tender, luscious body that you allowed lord Aimery to use as a plaything!'

'No,' whispered Elena. 'No . . .'

Isobel moved meaningfully towards the kneeling Leofwin, and Elena saw that she was carrying a small but lethal whip, which she trailed lightly across his bronzed, muscular shoulders.

'Show him, Elena. Or he will suffer. I mean it.'

Her heart thudding with shame, Elena slipped her ragged tunic from her shoulders and stood very still, her cheeks burning with silent degradation in that dark prison cell. The torchlight flickered on her soft skin, on her high, pouting breasts, on the shadowy triangle of soft golden hair at the apex of her slender thighs. Isobel jerked Leofwin's face upwards with the handle of her whip. 'Look,' she commanded exultantly. 'Isn't she pretty? A pity my lord Aimery tired of her so quickly, but then he gets his fill of these eager, insipid Saxon wenches – '

Leofwin looked, but it was as if his eyes did not see. The strained sinews of his powerful torso gleamed in the half-light; his handsome face was bleak as he said quietly, 'I'll take no part in your games, lady.'

'No?' Isobel laughed, and moved suddenly to crouch on the straw at his side, heedless of her fine gown. 'Well, my proud Saxon. What have we here?'

And she reached out delicately, to cup the Saxon's groin. With a low chuckle of satisfaction, she brushed her fingers along his ragged breeches, then reached for the opening, ripping it apart.

Between the man's powerfully-muscled thighs, his phallus, so recently erect, was again stirring helplessly. Isobel stroked it gently, lasciviously, with light, teasing fingertips, then moved her hand carefully to cradle the heavy bag of his testicles in her smooth palm. The Saxon groaned aloud in despair and closed his eyes; Elena stood frozen, watching, equally trapped by Isobel's power.

Isobel continued to stroke lightly, relentlessly at Leofwin's hardening flesh until the long, thick shaft reared high against the man's flat, muscled belly, throbbing angrily.

'Such a fine big weapon,' murmured Isobel huskily

as she stroked the silken skin with her fingertips. 'How I wish I had time to savour it fully.'

Elena's head jerked up. The lady Isobel was about to leave? Then this humiliation, for both of them, was about to end?

Isobel, rising slowly to her feet, caught the sudden flare of hope in the naked Saxon girl's haunted blue eyes. 'As for you, my dear Elena,' she went on softly, 'you, I am happy to say, will have all the time in the world. He is yours. My present to you. Use him well, won't you?'

Elena said, with quiet scorn, 'I will do nothing of the sort.'

Isobel arched her dark eyebrows mockingly. 'Still defiant, my dear?' Then she gazed thoughtfully down at the helpless Leofwin's still massively rigid penis, and trailed the tip of her lash along the velvety, purple glans. Leofwin shuddered in spite of himself at the subtle promise of pain.

'If you do not obey my orders, Elena,' said Isobel silkily, 'then this man will be punished. By me, personally.' Elena rubbed her hand across her eyes in fresh despair, Leofwin clenched his jaw. 'Do as I command,' continued Isobel sweetly, 'and you will both be rewarded by your own gratification. Is it so very much to ask? A satisfactory – more than satisfactory, I should think – mutual pleasuring?'

She started to walk towards the door, and at the top of the stairs she turned round. 'By the way, don't think to deceive me. I assure you, I have very reliable ways of knowing whether or not my orders have been obeyed.'

Then she was gone, the heavy door bolted behind her.

Elena sank to her knees, and wrapped the torn tunic forlornly round herself to hide her shame. How Leofwin must despise her. How she despised herself.

* * *

Isobel climbed the stone stairs quickly, and went down a long, dark passage at the back of the great hall. No-one was around to see her; the castle seemed strangely deserted in Aimery's absence. Using one of the keys fastened to her girdle, she opened a recessed door and went quickly inside, shutting it behind her. Good; Alys had prepared everything, as she asked.

The room was small but luxuriously furnished, with silk hangings covering the bare stone walls and rush matting on the floor. There was a low bed and a carved wooden chest and, because there were no windows, the room was lit by two wax candles in wall holders.

Isobel went purposefully over to the far side of the room and knelt down on the floor, lifting up the edge of the matting.

Yes. This was the place. Below her was a crack in the wooden floorboards, that had been cunningly, secretly enlarged to form a spyhole into the room below. Pillowing her cheek on her arm, she gazed through the crack. The glowing torch she'd left for them lit the scene perfectly. She was directly above the cell where the chained prisoner Leofwin was locked up with the insipid Saxon girl. How virginal she looked, with her pale golden hair and girlish figure! How, oh how could Aimery be so besotted with her?

And what, she suddenly thought, would the Breton say if he knew what she, Isobel, had done?

Frowning angrily, Isobel turned her gaze on Leofwin. She felt herself soften and melt as she gazed on his proud, handsome face, his mane of fair hair, his heavily-muscled torso that gleamed so enticingly in the flickering light. She'd have him later, perhaps. She made herself a secret promise. Then, filled with eager anticipation, she settled down to watch.

Still kneeling in the straw of the cell below the castle, Elena lifted her pale face and pushed back her tangled blonde hair. 'Leofwin,' she said quietly, 'I would do anything to save you from punishment. But I must tell you that everything the lady Isobel said was true. I have no excuses to make. I – I understand that you will have nothing but scorn for me, will not want to touch me . . .'

She tried to keep her voice steady, but it broke slightly at the end. Leofwin, who had listened in silence, said huskily, 'Elena. Come here.' Puzzled, she moved slowly across towards him and knelt on the straw to gaze anxiously up into his face.

Leofwin, taking a deep breath, drank in the sight of her; the pale gold, tousled hair framing that lovely, innocent face; those dark blue, anguished eyes and the small rosebud mouth. Even in her rags, he realised, she was still the loveliest girl he had ever seen.

Softly, he said, 'Elena. You are beautiful, and your body longs for pleasure – the pleasure that only a man can give you. There is nothing wrong with that. But did you know that Aimery le Sabrenn bears a personal hatred for all Saxon women?'

She nodded, the sudden pain clouding her eyes. 'I know now. But why, Leofwin? I had heard that most of King William's commanders were stern, but fair, that the king himself is anxious for peace between Normans and Saxons. Why does the lord Aimery hate us so?'

'I have heard that he was once betrayed by a beautiful Saxon lady, with whom he was in love – betrayed by her to the rebels. He escaped, but was scarred for life. That, it seems, is the reason for his cruel vengeance.'

She tried to look calm and sensible as she nodded again, but he saw the tears glitter suddenly in her translucent blue eyes. 'Oh, Elena,' he groaned out suddenly, 'that you should suffer so. Elena, kiss me . . .'

With a little gasp, she suddenly flung her arms around his neck, running her hands through his thick, tangled mane of hair. He was pressing hot, burning kisses against her cheek; finding her lips, his mouth devoured her, his tongue thrusting and probing, and

167

she responded dizzily. Her torn tunic slipped unnoticed from her shoulders; her soft breasts nuzzled the hard, ridged muscle of his broad chest, teasing his brown nipples into hardness, until his breathing became harsh and ragged. He strained at the chains that shackled his hands behind his back, but he was cruelly pinioned still. Elena, seeing his silent struggle, bent to kiss his straining shoulder muscles, to lave the hard buds of his nipples with her small tender tongue.

'See, Elena,' he grated out hoarsely. 'See what you do to me . . .'

With a little gasp she looked down, and saw how his penis, darkly-engorged, had reared anew from his ragged breeches. The blood pounded dizzily in her temples at the throbbing masculinity of it. With a soft moan, she reached to caress its magnificence softly with her fingertips; it quivered, jerking towards her eagerly. Her flesh was on fire for this proud, beautiful Saxon man; already she could feel a melting in her loins, a soft ache in her secret parts, a sweet yearning not properly assuaged by the girls' caresses and the French soldier's lascivious kiss. She wanted him; oh, she wanted this man, to take him within her yearning, quivering flesh . . .

With a little whimper, she kneeled upright, her hand gripping and stroking at the long, bone-hard phallus, as she thrust her breasts eagerly into his mouth.

He lapped hungrily, wickedly, laving her heated nipples with cooling saliva, sucking on them with deeply satisfying caresses that made her throw her head back in blissful arousal, her hand still clasping the strong silken shaft of his penis. 'Oh, Leofwin, please . . .'

'Turn round,' he muttered huskily. 'Turn round, my Saxon princess. On your knees. Ah, yes, that's it . . .'

In a drugged haze of desire, she turned to do his bidding, and Leofwin sighed aloud as her slender yet rounded buttocks were presented to his hungry gaze. By the light of the glimmering torch, he could see her pouting sex between her bottom cheeks, could see the moist pink flesh, so hungry for him. He narrowed his eyes and leaned forward, his rampant penis searching hungrily for her entrance.

His chains made it difficult; but she thrust her hips wantonly towards him, driven wild by the merest touch of that huge throbbing glans against her secret places. Leofwin, his wildly-excited member almost out of control, aimed as carefully as he could, sliding his long, thick shaft between her thighs, rubbing higher and higher against her soft pink folds, hearing her little sighs of eagerness, until at last he found her.

Slowly, catching his breath, he slid his rampant rod between her silken flesh lips and into her tender, hot love passage. He was wild to thrust deep within her, to the very hilt; but he was careful not to hurt her, knowing the power of his fully erect member.

Elena trembled in an agony of delight. Crouching on all fours, her swollen breasts dangling free; she laid her cheek on her arm and cried out softly in her pleasure as the big Saxon entered her from behind. Her whole body was on fire as that deliciously long shaft slid into her hungry love channel, stroking her, driving her slowly to the very edge of rapture. Surely – surely, she couldn't take any more! But still, he filled her with his gentle but powerful thrusts, and waves of delicious heat began to spread upwards into her belly, into her breasts. She moaned, and thrust against him finding his rhythm, feeling herself exquisitely impaled on that hot, hard length of male flesh. 'Please,' she groaned, 'please, Leofwin . . .'

The torch glimmered smokily on the wall above them. She closed her eyes, shivering with exquisite pleasure, hearing Leofwin's harsh breathing above her, picturing his magnificent, naked body crouching above her with his arms chained behind his back, servicing her, driving his wonderful penis slowly in and out of her juicy, clutching flesh. She was so near. And yet, and yet . . .

169

'Touch yourself, my princess,' murmured Leofwin huskily in her ear. 'Your sweet little pleasure bud – it longs for release. Touch yourself, gently.'

In a daze, she did what he said, finding with a shock that the little pinnacle of flesh was hotly aroused and exposed. Carefully, she touched it, while Leofwin paused in his movements, leaving his swollen penis nudging hungrily at her inflamed entrance. The sensation sent a violent spasm coursing through her; carefully she touched again, and began to rub, slowly, along her own exquisitely sensitised little shaft.

'You are ready?' murmured Leofwin gently.

'Oh, yes! Leofwin – I beg you please – '

He gave a throaty chuckle that drove her wild. 'Very well, my princess. Then you shall have it – all . . .' He plunged into her, with solid, powerful thrusts that sent wonderful sensations coursing through her blood. Elena cried out in rapture, panting greedily as she worked herself against him; softly she touched her pleasure bud, and the exquisite sensations built up and exploded shatteringly over and over as his huge penis continued to slide juicily inside her quivering, convulsing flesh. She cried aloud, throwing back her head as the orgasm engulfed her and her inner muscles spasmed around his iron-hard shaft.

Leofwin himself was driven over the brink by her ecstasy. Moaning her name, he jerked powerfully within her, crashing over the edge of rapture. They both collapsed, still damply entwined in the straw.

And in that moment Elena, physically replete, felt a dark shadow pass over her. Her mind was suddenly filled with the memory of a scarred, handsome face, softened by love, and a huskily accented voice that seemed to haunt her every moment.

The torch gave a final glimmer and died. Elena knew, in that moment, that Aimery le Sabrenn had made her his slave for ever.

Chapter Eleven

With an exclamation of impatience, Isobel rolled away from the spyhole and crouched, panting with desire, on the rush matting of her little secret room. What she had seen – the big chained Saxon so thoroughly pleasuring Aimery's virginal little convent bitch – had aroused her unbelievably; she was so wet, so quivering with juices that she had to have somebody, and quickly.

She heard a low, muffled cough outside the door. Her brow darkened. A spy – someone spying on her! Swiftly, she moved across the room to fling open the door, and Pierre almost fell into the room.

Isobel chuckled softly. Of course. Pierre, who followed her everywhere like a faithful big dog. She had neglected him a little lately – remiss of her, especially as he was so young and handsome . . .

She relocked the door carefully; Pierre gazed at her eagerly, with hope flaring in his faithful brown eyes.

Isobel moved deliberately across to the low bed and lay back on it luxuriantly. Then, very slowly, she lifted her silk skirts to her waist, and spread her stockinged thighs. She watched Pierre all the time, saw him jump with excitement, imagined the lovely, swelling bulge at his groin. Shuddering with anticipated pleasure, she reached down to touch her moist nether lips. Her pleasure bud was already hot and throbbing. She slid one finger around it, lovingly, raising her knees higher and letting them fall apart so Pierre could see all her crinkled, hairy lushness; the serf's eyes were wide with longing.

'You see how I need you, Pierre?' Isobel whispered softly. 'You see how I need a good, stout man like you to pleasure me? But I've not quite decided yet, Pierre. Show me – show me what you can do, and then I'll decide . . .'

And lasciviously she continued to stroke her deliciously-engorged clitoris, safe in the knowledge that the dumb serf would never be able to tell anyone of the lady of Morency's crude preferences.

Nodding eagerly at her invitation, Pierre unlaced his leggings and pulled out his already-rampant phallus. Isobel eyed it with mock severity, pursing her lips. 'Not bad,' she said critically, 'but I'm a little disappointed in you, Pierre.'

Crestfallen, the youth gripped his engagingly curved penis with his hand and started working it quickly, hissing between his teeth, his eyes fastened on Isobel. The swollen purple knob glistened and throbbed angrily; he watched her in an agony of desire, as the red tide of frustration built up inside.

Lazily, Isobel, still reclining on the bed, reached to undo the lacing of her fine gown, lifting her full breasts from the confines of her chemise and squeezing them together, played lazily with her hardened pink nipples, as though Pierre did not exist.

It was too much. The sweat stood out in beads on Pierre's broad forehead; his balls were tight and aching. His hand suddenly dropped to his side; his huge shaft reared upwards with a life of its own, jerking hungrily towards the woman on the bed.

'Come on, Pierre. You can do better than that – '

172

With a gasp, Pierre rushed across the room, his penis rearing threateningly. Violently, he flung himself between Isobel's parted legs, trapping her hands above her head, knocking the breath from her. Then, nudging her open thighs still further apart, he thrust his throbbing manhood desperately into her wet glistening flesh. Isobel made a sharp cry of protest; but her words quickly became soft moans as Pierre's thick, pulsing shaft slid so deliciously into her aching love passage and began to ravish her.

'Pierre,' she gasped aloud. 'How dare you, you wicked boy . . .'

For answer, he shuddered and leaned into her still further, driving himself into her juicy moistness with all his power, relishing every moment as his engorged penis filled her wildly clutching vagina. She locked her ankles around his back, and came almost immediately, bucking with ecstasy as his wild thrusts continued. Then, as she spasmed and relaxed, Pierre, muttering wordlessly to himself in his extremity, withdrew his long, slippery shaft and began to rub it excitedly across Isobel's flushed, pouting breasts.

Isobel moaned aloud, shuddering in renewed orgasm as his swollen, silky glans caressed her incredibly sensitised nipples. Gripping and caressing the proud stem of his manhood, Pierre crouched over her greedily, rubbing his penis first against one breast, then against the other, his eyes closed in ecstasy. At last, with swift, jerking movements of his strong hand, he drove himself to the brink; and Isobel watched, wide-eyed, as his proud member quivered in ecstasy and his seed spurted out in milky jets all over her white breasts.

With a sigh of contentment, he bent to lick it off greedily, guzzling like a child at her nipples, his subsiding manhood still deliciously hot against her smooth belly.

Isobel lay back, utterly sated as his strong, rough tongue trailed across her flesh, the afterwash of pleasure still trickling gently through her. She closed her eyes, smiling contentedly.

Then she jerked upright, almost throwing Pierre to the ground.

Someone was knocking, lightly but insistently, on the door. A voice – Alys' voice – could be heard, low and urgent. 'My lady. My lady Isobel. Messengers have arrived! They say that the lord Aimery won't be returning to Thoresfield till tomorrow at the earliest. I thought you ought to know.'

Isobel got up, hurriedly rearranging her rumpled gown, tying up her laces with trembling fingers. She flung open the door.

'Damn you, Alys,' she muttered viciously, 'must you follow me everywhere? Go, and prepare my bath – and a fresh gown. And not a word of this to anyone, you understand? Or I'll beat you with my own hands . . .'

Alys, who had not failed to see the bemused Pierre sprawled on the bed, swung round and marched off, her face red and angry. One of these days, her ladyship would go too far. One of these days, she, Alys, would cease to act as Isobel's faithful spy – and then, it would be interesting to see what happened at Thoresfield, she told herself grimly.

Elena sat on the edge of the bed in the upper chamber of the castle – the very room where she had spent her first night in the Breton's arms. It was almost dark, but wax candles had been lit against the soft dusk; a flagon of sweet wine, together with spiced chicken, soft manchet bread and honeyed grapes had been set out carefully on the little table.

She clasped her hands anxiously in her lap, feeling utterly bewildered.

She'd spent another night in the cell, with Leofwin sleeping beside her, and during all the long day that followed, they'd talked quietly of the past.

She'd been resigned to yet another night of imprisonment when two guards had come down to her dark cell, about an hour ago, and dragged her up here. She'd had no time to bid a proper farewell to her fellow-prisoner, Leofwin, but he'd managed to whisper to her in their own tongue as the guards waited impatiently for her by the open cell door. 'Soon, I'll escape from here. And you shall come with me!'

For one last moment, she lifted her wistful face towards him. Oh, if only she could escape! But she was a true prisoner here, a prisoner of her heart. She couldn't tell him that, though she thought he had guessed. Since that first wild coupling, he hadn't attemped to make love to her again.

She gave him a swift, brave smile and followed the guards, wondering fearfully what lay in store for her now.

In her wildest dreams, she wouldn't have guessed aright. What lay in store was luxury, just as she had experienced on her first night here. Isobel's attendant, Alys, waited quietly on her; here, in this now-familiar room, she was bathed and anointed with scented oils, and clothed in stockings and a chemise of finest cream silk. Her gown too was silk, in palest blue; it had a long, closely-fitting sleeves and a flowing skirt that clung to her waist and then flared out around her slender hips. Her tiny waist was further emphasised by an exquisite silver girdle that trailed almost to the floor; and as a finishing touch Alys helped her into a pair of dainty red leather shoes that fastened at the side with little buttons. Then, with the utmost care, Alys brushed out her newly-washed hair, gleaming softly gold, and braided it loosely, coiling it with ribbon at the nape of her slender neck.

Elena, dazed and bewildered, gazed unseeing at her own reflection in the silver mirror Alys had silently handed to her. 'Why, Alys?' she whispered. 'Why all this finery?'

'I only do as I'm bid,' said Alys shortly, turning to leave.

She was interrupted by a sudden cacophony of noise from the courtyard outside the window. Men were shouting, running, barking out orders; there was the unmistakable sound of horses' iron-shod hooves on the cobbles.

Elena, her breath stopped short in her throat, faltered out, 'What is it, Alys? What's happening?'

Alys paused by the door. 'The lord Aimery and his men have returned.'

'Has he – has he defeated the rebels?'

'Doesn't he always?' Alys started to open the door, and hesitated. 'Best get out of here, my lady, while you can. You're too good and beautiful for this evil place . . .' She looked as if she would say more, then pressed her lips together suddenly and hurried out, slamming the door behind her.

Elena's heart was hammering. She flew to the window, and looked out.

Far beyond the estate, the great forest that surrounded Aimery's lands was in ominous darkness. But the castle and its courtyard were a blaze of light and activity. The night air was cool on Elena's flushed cheek as she gazed down. Mounted knights, still on horseback, milled around, pushing back their stern helmets, while eager squires carrying wavering lanterns rushed to do their bidding. The cold, silvery moonlight glimmered on harsh Norman faces, on chain-mail hauberks and the glinting steel of swords. Grooms hung to the big destriers' reins as the victorious knights dismounted, and Elena leaned from the window, longing for just a glimpse of Aimery le Sabrenn. Perhaps her captivity in the cells had been a mistake. Perhaps . . .

The door opened slowly, and Isobel de Morency walked in, and Elena knew that all her stupid hopes were in vain.

Isobel, her enemy, shut the door behind her, and

176

smiled. It was not a friendly smile. She was exquisitely dressed, in an opulent silk gown of madder-red, embroidered with gold thread. Her raven black hair was concealed by a thin white veil, secured by a delicate golden circlet on the crown of her head; and her slanting green eyes glittered with suppressed excitement.

Elena knew now that this woman hated her. She stood very still, her back to the window, and waited.

Isobel said, 'Well, my little convent girl. So you know now that the lord Aimery has returned.'

Elena bowed her head briefly in acknowledgement and resumed her quietly defiant stance, her hands clenched at her sides.

'So,' went on Isobel, walking further into the room, 'the game begins afresh. A word of warning, however. I would rather – *much* rather – that the lord Aimery did not know about the time you spent below, in the cells. It was, you see, purely for your own safety. As a Saxon, you might otherwise have suffered reprisals from the other inhabitants of the castle.'

Elena's heart thudded slowly in understanding, her eyes meeting Isobel's malevolent gaze in renewed scorn. So, her imprisonment was not Aimery's order! He knew nothing of it! A sudden wild hope blazed through her.

Isobel paused by the table where the food had been set out. Picking up a honeyed grape, she placed it delicately on her tongue, licking her dainty fingers one by one. 'But,' she went on silkily, 'if, my dear Elena, you should take it into your silly head to complain, why, then, I shall have to tell Aimery about your ardent coupling with the prisoner Leofwin. Rather – bestial, my dear, wouldn't you say? And you did appear to enjoy it so much . . .'

Renewed despair washed over Elena in numbing waves. How did Isobel know so much? The cruel Frenchwoman was toying with her, manipulating her, and Elena felt suddenly quite helpless again in her evil toils. As steadily as she could, she said in a low voice, 'You know very well, my lady, that I did what I did in order to save the man Leofwin from the punishment you threatened.'

Isobel laughed and took another grape, savouring its plump, juicy sweetness. 'Whose word do we have for that, my dear? Yours? Rather a feeble excuse, I would have thought, for such enthusiastic copulation! Do you really expect Aimery to believe you?'

Elena sagged back against the stone window ledge, her eyes wide and dark in her white face. Isobel laughed softly, lapping up her distress.

'Tonight, Elena, we will play the game more subtly than ever, you and I. And remember, there can only be one winner.'

She turned to go, and shut the door softly behind her.

Outside, on the landing, the smile vanished from Isobel's face. She was, for the first time since Madelin, seriously worried.

The girl was breathtakingly beautiful, and quietly brave. Isobel would gladly have left her for yet another night in that dark cell, but she feared Aimery's anger too much. Better play safe for the moment. Have her bathed, fed and clothed in luxurious garments while Isobel made her next decision – the best time to tell Aimery how the innocent convent girl, with whom he had become so besotted, had been rutting on the soiled straw of the prison cell with a virile Saxon rebel.

Isobel knew from experience that Aimery was always grimly ready for sexual release when he got back from the tension of battle. He would be on edge, covered in sweat and dust, physically honed, wanting plenty of activity. She, Isobel, would be waiting for him.

Aimery le Sabrenn strode into the hall at the head of his men, his armour glinting in the spurting light from the cressets, his hair streaked with sweat where he had removed his helmet.

The floor had been freshly strewn with herb-scented rushes. The serfs, busy setting up the trestle tables for the evening meal, stood back in deference and gazed in awe at their Breton lord. Tales of the recent battle against the Saxon rebels were already flying round the castle; the bravery and strength of Aimery le Sabrenn needed no embroidery.

Hamet, at his master's side as always, said in his soft, rich voice, 'My lord. Shall I order wine to be brought to the high table?'

Aimery hesitated. 'In a while – though see that the men are served with everything they want. First, I shall go and change.'

Hamet nodded. 'My lord.' He watched thoughtfully as Aimery le Sabrenn, showing no outward signs of the tiredness that must grip him after two days and nights in the saddle and some of the bloodiest skirmishing the Saracen had yet seen against these native rebels, made purposefully for the stairs that led to the sleeping chambers.

For two days and nights, as he swept through the forest with his men, Aimery had thought of the girl. The scent of her hair, the caress of her silken skin, had stayed with him. The way she had sunk to her knees and whispered, 'You are all I ever dreamed of, my lord.' Words that were followed, so sweetly, by her little cries of love. She was innocent, yet so instinctively, wildly sensual – all that a man dreamed of.

If Isobel had obeyed his instructions, the girl would have been well taken care of in his absence. Already he felt the hard ache at his loins, the tightening of desire at the pit of his belly. Later, he promised himself. Later . . .

His face set, he headed for his own room, fully intending to summon his squire to remove his armour, and then to go down and feast with his men. But on his

179

way along the gallery, he saw a soft line of light beneath the door of the small chamber that the Saxon girl used. He stopped, and pushed open the door, quietly.

Elena, lying curled on her bed in silent despair after Isobel's visit, spun round. The Breton stood in the shadowy doorway; his harsh, gaunt face was unreadable.

Elena's thoughts whirled giddily. What had Isobel told him? Had she told him about Leofwin? And, whatever happened, she must remember what they'd all told her about him. That he was using her, intent on destroying her because of his poisonous hatred for all Saxon women. She crouched on her narrow bed, trembling.

He said, simply, '*Caran*,' and held out his arms, drawing her to him.

He kissed her deeply, hungrily; his hands roving over her face, her breasts, her slender hips. Elena, in disbelief, wrapped her hands round his wide shoulders, shuddering at the kiss of steel, running her fingers through his mane of tawny hair. He still loved her. Nothing had changed – everyone was wrong.

With a soft murmur of impatience, the Breton unlaced her gown and chemise, barely allowing the filmy silk to slip to the floor before bending to kiss her small white breasts. Then he unbraided her hair, combing it sensually with his fingers so that it glittered around her face and shoulders. Elena shuddered with desire, her soft, naked body clamped against the cold chain-mail of his hauberk. Aimery gave an oath of impatience at his own hampered body; lifting her up and swinging her gently onto the bed, he quickly unbuckled his armour, and threw off the long linen undershirt that he wore beneath it.

Elena watched him from the shadows, her heart hammering passionately as his muscled torso gleamed in the golden candlelight. He was so strong, so beautiful. He sat on the edge of the bed, swiftly pulling off his dusty boots and leggings; she leaned towards him, and caressed his shoulder gently.

A laugh rasped in his dry throat. 'Ah *caran*. See what you do to me . . .' He took her small hand within his own sword-calloused palm and ran it slowly up the rough silk of his steel-muscled thigh to close over the hot, throbbing bulge of his genitals.

Elena gasped, the spasms of pleasure running through her, as she felt his powerful penis quiver and surge beneath her trembling fingers. Catching her lower lip between her teeth, she stroked again experimentally, loving the soft, silken feel of his inner thigh, the rough coarseness of his heavy testicles, and then the pulsing, almost frightening strength of that mysterious phallus, the very core of him, rearing up massively now against his flat, darkly-fleeced abdomen. Already, she felt a burning need to feel that magnificent male strength within her. Instinctively she bent her head to lick at the swollen purple glans, to catch its velvety rim between her soft lips while her hand cupped his testicles.

Aimery groaned aloud, his fingers kneading her hardening nipples. 'Little one, how quickly you learn. Your mouth is so sweet. And now, it is my turn . . .'

With swift, powerful movements, he lifted her unresisting body across the bed and crouched between her tender, outspread thighs. Then he bent his head and started to lap at the soft, moist folds of her secret flesh.

Elena drew up her knees in ecstasy, stroking and clutching at his thick hair as his strong tongue darted fiercely at her quivering bud of pleasure then slid down tantalisingly to probe at her honeyed entrance, thrusting and caressing until she moaned aloud, almost at the very brink. Her eyes opened wide in momentary disappointment when he suddenly pulled himself up beside her, enfolded her in his arms, and rolled onto his back.

'Ride me now,' he whispered. 'Take me into yourself, Elena. Make me your prisoner.'

As he guided her astride his hips, she shuddered in delirious excitement at her sudden sense of power over him. She saw his soft, lazy smile as her eyes widened in surprise at this new, blissful sensation. Gently, experimentally, she wriggled above him, feeling his hugely thrusting penis desperately trying to gain entry; then, as she poised carefully above it and felt the swollen glans just start to slide between her hungry flesh lips, she gasped aloud in pleasure.

Carefully, she lowered herself inch by inch. Surely – surely, it was too much! Surely this hot pillar of flesh would never fit inside her own tight, aching entrance!

Aimery reached up slowly with his strong brown hands, his silvery-grey eyes strangely intent. Gently he began to roll and twist her jutting rosy nipples. The pleasure shot darkly through to her abdomen, like hot tongues of flame; she rose with a soft cry, and sank down again onto his beautifully engorged shaft, gripping tightly with her silken sheath as waves of almost unbearable pleasure washed through her.

He filled her now. Her whole being was nothing but glorious sensation. Languidly, teasingly, he continued to play with her aching breasts, driving her to delirium as she slid herself up and down on his magnificently solid penis, feeling it fill her, posess her, as she gripped tighter and tighter, driving herself relentlessly to glorious ecstasy.

Smiling softly into her dazed eyes, Aimery reached deliberately to stroke her engorged, exposed clitoris with the pad of his thumb. 'Oh . . .' Elena threw her head back with a wild cry, tossing back her mass of golden hair in abandon as the molten pleasure seared her; the Breton's face tautened as he clutched fiercely at her juicy buttocks and pumped himself into her, spending himself within her just as her own fierce, rapturous orgasm racked her quivering body.

She collapsed onto his chest, her breasts and hair

caressing him, the waves of delight still washing over her as he gently kissed her face, her hands, her hair.

A candle guttered and went out. She was suddenly aware of the raucous sound of men feasting in the great hall below. Another world; the world where Aimery belonged. A dark shadow passed over her heart. Her face suddenly troubled, she raised her head to gaze down at him, pushing back his tousled hair with her fingers and gently caressing his lean, scarred cheek.

'I want to remember you like this,' she said quietly.

He took her finger and nibbled it gently between his lips, sending little pleasure messages through her still-heated body. 'You talk, *caran*, as if we are to be separated,' he said softly. 'Another premonition? Have you so little confidence in me?'

He cradled her gently in his arms. Elena felt his solid warmth, and tried desperately to fight away her fear, telling herself that all her doubts were a nightmare and this was the reality. She pressed her cheek against his warm chest and listened to the sound of his slow, steady heartbeat.

Exhausted after two nights without sleep, Aimery's breathing grew slow, and he fell asleep, still holding her tightly.

Chapter Twelve

*I*t was Alys who accidentally let slip to the lady Isobel that Aimery le Sabrenn had not joined his men for the evening meal. Isobel, pacing her room in an agony of tension, whirled round on her unfortunate maid. 'Then where is he, you fool?'

Alys, her pocked face stricken with sudden fear as she realised her mistake, backed instinctively towards the door. 'He – he is with the Saxon girl, my lady! He went to her room immediately on his return, more than an hour ago. Nobody dares disturb them . . .'

Isobel strode across the chamber and struck her servant hard on the cheek. 'You're lying! Stupid slut, you're making this up.'

Alys back whimpering to the door. 'No, my lady! I swear! They all know about it, down below in the hall. Hamet has told them to begin the feast without him.'

'Get out,' said Isobel dangerously. 'You've already said too much. Get out of my sight. No – wait! One thing you can do for me – find out where Morwith is. And send her to me immediately!'

Shaking with almost uncontrollable anger, Isobel waited for Alys' footsteps to die away down the corridor. So, Aimery, instead of celebrating his victory over the Saxons with his men, was in the chamber of the little Saxon slut, pleasuring her, making her gasp and writhe in sluttish ecstasy!

Like molten iron ready to be forged, Isobel's anger cooled and hardened. Quietly, she tiptoed down the back stairs, the stairs used by the house serfs to bring hot water and food to the upper storey of the stronghold. She had her ring of keys fastened to her girdle. Purposefully she went down the dark, echoing stone steps that led to the dungeon where the Saxon rebel Leofwin was still imprisoned.

She didn't realise that Alys, still burning from the blow to her cheek, was watching her every move.

Hamet, though he'd given the order for the feasting to begin, was also missing from the high table, like his master. He'd removed his armour, to wash and change. Then he'd gone outside in the darkness to the stables, to check that the horses were all right. He lingered for a while enjoying the dark peace out there, the scented smell of the hay and the horses' contented whickering.

He knew without being told that his master had gone straight to the beautiful Saxon girl's room. In his fierce loyalty to his master, he was instinctively worried, because he knew that the lady Isobel hated Elena and would stop at nothing to destroy her.

He went back out into the courtyard, checking that the guards were alert and in position inside the palisade. Then, a muffled giggle from the shadows caught his attention, and he whirled round, his sword drawn.

It was the Saxon redhead Morwith, watching him from the darkness behind the stable wall.

'It's not your sword I'm after, my lord Hamet,' she murmured huskily. Hamet grinned, his teeth white in the darkness, and strode towards her, catching her up in his burly arms.

* * *

It was there that Alys found them, her attention caught by the soft rasp of indrawn breath and the rustling of clothes as she edged round the corner of the stables. She caught her breath as the cold moonlight shone on the two figures coupled together, oblivious of everything.

Hamet had caught Morwith up in his big arms, supporting her so that her shoulders rested gently back against the stable wall. While she, her skirts rucked up shamefully around her waist, had wrapped her legs tightly round the Saracen's hips, locking her ankles together; he was thrusting into her eagerly, his face nuzzling at her generous breasts, while she flung her head back and groaned in delight.

The Saracen's loose-fitting hose gaped at the crotch; Alys gasped and felt the blood burn hotly in her cheeks as she glimpsed the base of his powerful, thick shaft, ramming so eagerly up into the lady Morwith's lascivious flesh, while his heavy balls bounced up and down with exertion. Oh, Morwith was so lucky! If only she, Alys, could feel that huge, dusky penis driving into her own love-starved flesh, ravishing her so sweetly!

Biting her lip in anguish, Alys pressed herself into the shadows. Avidly, her hand slipped down to her own heated love mound; it was juicy, desperate. Pulling up her full skirts impatiently, she pressed with her busy fingers, working away hotly at her swollen nether lips. Oh, to feel the Saracen inside her, pumping fiercely away, his mouth guzzling greedily at her own aching breasts . . .

Then the Saracen drew his penis slowly out of Morwith, so that the tormented Alys could see almost all of its slippery black length. Alys bit her lip in an agony of desire as he drove it back in with a hoarse cry of triumph and proceeded to jerk quickly to his climax, his muscular hips thrusting madly, while Morwith bucked and spasmed in his arms, her heels drumming excitedly against his waist. It was too much for Alys. Groaning aloud, squeezing her hard nipples tightly with her free hand, she rubbed fiercely at her clitoris with her fingers, spasming in solitary delight, her secret flesh pulsing and twitching hungrily as she reached her lonely orgasm.

The inevitable disappointment coursed through her. She wanted a man inside her; a man's hard, strong flesh, so she could clutch at him with her churning love passage and savour every delicious moment until the last spasm died away.

Her mouth thinning in disappointment, she let her skirts drop, and waited for the two of them to recover from the violence of their copulation and make themselves decent.

That Morwith was nothing but a slut. Alys had heard, indeed the whole castle had heard how she'd spent the whole night with three of the guards. But because she had a bonny, unmarked face and a plump figure, the men were round her like flies to a honeypot.

Her feet dragging, Alys stepped forward out of the dark shadows. 'You, Morwith! The lady Isobel wants you,' she called out sullenly.

Morwith spun round. 'Spying again?' she taunted. 'I suppose it's the nearest you'll ever get to the real thing, Alys!'

Her mouth pressed tight, Alys headed back to the hall, not waiting to see whether or not the redhead followed.

Her plans complete, Isobel de Morency glided along the gallery and gazed down into the great candlelit hall below.

The feast to celebrate the return of Aimery's soldiers and the rout of the Saxon rebels was in full swing. Serfs rushed from the hot kitchens carrying platter after platter of hot, spicily-scented food: boars head with chervil, venison, roast heron and haunches of pork in cinnamon, accompanied by jugs of strong wine and ale for the jubilant men lining the trestle tables in the body of the hall.

With a pang of bitterness, Isobel observed that Aimery le Sabrenn had condescended to join his men at last. Seated there at the high table in a fine grey woollen mantle, surrounded by his loyal knights, he looked magnificent, a natural leader of men as he rose to his feet and drank to the health of King William of England. A man to worship with his proudly handsome face and his beautiful, battle-hardened body.

And he'd just come from the little Saxon's slut's bed . . .

Isobel's long fingernails dug into her smooth palms as she watched and waited in the shadows. Her patience was stretched almost to breaking point as the feasting and drinking went on interminably and Aimery, though finished with the food, went on talking and drinking with his soldiers. Hadn't she known him when he was an impoverished, land-hungry mercenary? Hadn't she helped him rise this high? And yet he'd not bothered to come and see her, his lady.

The poison gathered in her blood, festering. Stepping at last out of the darkness, she walked along the gallery and glided down the stairs into the great hall, her red silk skirts rustling. There was a satisfying silence as men turned and gaped. They at least knew how beautiful, how desirable she was even if the Breton didn't!

Swallowing down her icy anger, she walked proudly up to the high table, her head held high. 'My lord,' she said in clear, melodious tones, 'I crave a moment of your time.'

Silence fell at the high table. Aimery said, 'Now? Here?'

Isobel held herself steady. 'In private, if you please.'

Aimery hesitated, his face unreadable. Then with a slight bow of his head, he said, 'My time is all yours, my lady Isobel.'

Liar, burned Isobel. *Liar!* But she kept a smooth, calm

188

smile on her face as she turned to go back upstairs, with Aimery behind her.

To Aimery, Isobel's chamber seemed dark and oppressively hot after the space and airiness of the great hall. He suddenly became aware that he'd drunk a lot of wine – too much. As he followed Isobel inside, it took him some moments to adjust to the shadowy darkness, relieved only by a single tall candle in a silver holder. Isobel's hand lay lightly on his sinewed brown forearm; his nostrils were assailed by a musky eastern perfume. He was aware suddenly of impending danger, of some obscure evil.

Then he saw them. In the dark corner. The redhead, the Saxon serf called Morwith, crouched on all fours; her bottom cheeks pouting obscenely from beneath her ragged tunic. And kneeling behind her, shafting her vigorously, was a big blond Saxon, clad only in ragged breeches, with his hands shackled behind his back. Morwith the redhead was writhing in pleasure, eagerly thrusting her buttocks at the grunting, sweating man as he thrust his penis deep within her.

Aimery, his mouth set tight, swung round towards the door, suddenly realising that he was in no mood for Isobel's tricks tonight. But Isobel barred his way, her back to the door, a strange, excited gleam in her dangerous green eyes. 'Wait, my lord! There is more . . .'

'Of that,' said Aimery acidly, 'I've no doubt. But you'll excuse me, lady, from your entertainments this evening.'

Isobel's eyes darkened almost to points of blackness. 'Even if I tell you,' she hissed, 'that the scene in the corner was enacted only yesterday by your little convent slut, Elena, and a Saxon prisoner?'

Aimery felt the blood drain from his hard-boned face. 'God's blood, but you jest, lady. Let me pass. Your games no longer amuse me.'

Isobel's eyes spat venom. 'It's the truth! Are you so

unwilling to hear it? I saw them myself – saw the Saxon scum, pleasuring one another – just like these two! It's the truth, my lord – ask her! Bring your little slut in, and ask her!'

Aimery felt the bile rising in his throat. Madelin. Just like Madelin.

'Ask her,' went on Isobel softly in his ear. 'Force her to watch this pair in their open lust, and see if she can deny it. One thing more, my lord. The man with whom she copulated so eagerly was a Saxon rebel – a traitor. She is a danger to you and your men, conspiring wickedly against you.'

Madelin and Elena. Elena and Madelin. The past churned up in the dark, wine-soaked recesses of Aimery's agonised brain. He had been making wild, abandoned love to Madelin when the Saxons came and captured him, just as she had planned. The witch had stood over him, still naked and moist from his love as her Saxon compatriots struck him to the ground, tied him with ropes, kicked him. She'd stood over him, with a smile on her beautiful face, and a long sword in her hand . . .

'You really thought I loved you, didn't you, Breton?' she had taunted him softly. 'Such pride, such self-delusion.' It was then that she had slashed at his face. 'Take him away.'

Now, the fierce, devouring anger burned white-hot in his brain. 'Very well, then,' he grated out to the waiting Isobel. 'Fetch her.'

He sat blindly in the carved chair, gripping at its arms for support, while she was gone. The couple on the floor were bucking wildly towards climax; he felt his own phallus rearing hot and hard in cynical desire, pushing against his leather belt. He knew he had already drunk too much wine; but he reached out to fill Isobel's goblet from the half-full jug at his side, and drank it all down, hoping for numbing release.

* * *

Elena was asleep, dreaming of Aimery when Isobel came in. The soft smile died on her lips when she saw who was shaking her awake.

'The lord Aimery wishes to see you – slut,' breathed Isobel, with a fierce triumph burning in her eyes. 'Go, he is waiting in my room.' Trembling with a nameless fear, Elena clothed herself and left the room. Isobel watched her go, then moved back to the girl's still warm bed, slipping something quickly between the sheets.

As soon as Elena entered Isobel's room, the room that she hated, she saw Aimery, and as he looked at her the expression in his cold, slate-grey eyes was enough to fill her with despair. Isobel followed behind her, and shut the door; it was then that she became aware of the couple on the floor, entwined around one another, damply exhausted; Morwith the redhead, and a big blond serf, clad only in ragged breeches, with his hands chained behind his back.

'Leofwin!' she gasped out, her hand to her mouth.

Isobel's chuckle warned her what she had done. The Saxon on the floor turned round to look at her, grinning. He looked like Leofwin, but he wasn't. The sick dread rose through her limbs, numbing her. Aimery said nothing, but watched her from his chair with cold, fathomless eyes. She started to tremble.

Isobel said, rapturously, 'So you recognised the little scene they have just enacted for my lord's entertainment! You thought he was Leofwin, didn't you, this fine Saxon who has just serviced Morwith so delightfully? With his mane of blond hair, and the shackles on his wrists, I can quite understand your mistake. Because, only yesterday, you were lying on the floor, pleasurably sated, just like Morwith here . . .'

Elena took a step forward, her hands clenched to whiteness, 'No – no!'

Isobel hissed, 'Do you dare to deny it? That you coupled, like those two in the corner, with the Saxon rebel Leofwin, while my lord Aimery was away?'

Elena hung her head in bitter despair, her long golden hair sweeping her pale cheeks. Defeat. Isobel had defeated her.

At last, Aimery spoke, and his voice was like the slither of steel through her naked heart. 'Your only hope,' he said expressionlessly, 'is to convince me that you were forced against you will.'

Brokenly, Elena shook her head. No, she was not forced. At least, not physically. She had been told that Leofwin would be beaten if she refused to comply – but how could she prove it? And at the time, she had felt so alone, so bereft. But all the time that Leofwin was making love to her, it was Aimery – Aimery, with his dark, bitter soul and his wonderful prowess – that she was dreaming of . . .

She swallowed down the searing ache that threatened to choke her and said, in quiet despair, 'No, my lord. I – I was not forced.'

The silence hung ominously heavy in the airless room. Even Morwith and her partner, whom Isobel had summoned because he looked so like Leofwin, had subsided into stillness, watching and waiting.

Isobel, scenting success within her grasp, said smoothly, 'One more thing, my lord Aimery – bad news, I fear. I learned a short while ago that the prisoner we talk of, the Saxon rebel Leofwin, escaped a short while ago from his cell. While you were feasting just now with your men, someone stole down to the dungeons and released him.' She shook her head in mock concern. 'You will, I think, find the key hidden in the convent girl's room.'

Aimery was on his feet; Elena whirled to face Isobel, her dark blue eyes shadowed with despairing denial. 'No! That is a lie!'

Aimery gripped Elena's shoulders and twisted her round to face him, hurting her. His white-ridged scar made his expression dark and menacing. 'Be very careful, Elena. That man, Leofwin, is a dangerous ringleader. If what Isobel says is true – '

'It isn't!' she whispered, gazing up into his wintry face. 'She's lying, I swear it! How can you believe her?'

'Why don't you come with me, my lord?' said Isobel silkily, turning to leave the room.

Aimery followed her, dragging Elena behind him, his fingers bruising her wrist.

Glancing behind to make sure he could see, Isobel entered Elena's small room and triumphantly drew back the sheet of her narrow bed. There, starkly black against the white linen, lay a big iron key.

'Look – the key to the dungeons,' said Isobel, shaking her head sadly. 'Do you need any more proof, my lord?'

With casual, biter strength, Aimery flung Elena across the bed. She lay there stunned, the breath knocked from her body.

'Do what you will with her, Isobel,' said Aimery le Sabrenn curtly. 'She's all yours.'

The moonlight gleamed softly on the deserted court-yard, on the dark granaries and low-roofed stables where the horses whinnied restlessly.

Elena, taking a deep breath, forced herself to watch a tiny wisp of straw that fluttered uncertainly across the cobbles, lifted now and then by the warm night breeze. Perhaps, if she watched it very carefully, if she concentrated on its light, delicate dance with every fibre of her being, then she might forget the overwhelming horror of what was happening to her.

About an hour ago, two of Isobel's guards had tied her up here with her back against the palisade. They'd stripped her first, at Isobel's orders; Isobel had looked on, her face so full of savage triumph that Elena hoped she would choke on it.

It was Isobel who ordered the men to lift their trembling prisoner's arms, so that her breasts were raised high, her rosy nipples hardening already in the soft kiss of the night air; Isobel who told them to plant her feet widely apart before securing her ankles with leather straps, so Elena knew, with burning shame, that all her pale golden fleece was exposed; even the tender pink flesh that peeped from between her thighs.

She's all yours, Aimery had said with cold scorn to Isobel. His words of utter contempt still rang in her ears. At first she'd tried to struggle, but the guards had tightened the straps that bound her wrists and ankles, dragging her feet yet further apart. One of the men had surreptitiously brushed his big, calloused hand high between her legs, drawing in his breath in appreciation; Elena felt the shame flood through her body, and leaned back against the palisade in numb despair.

Isobel watched her enemy's degradation in silent joy. 'Beg,' she said softly. 'Beg for forgiveness, Saxon girl; promise me that you'll crawl to me on your knees, and then I might – just – consider releasing you!'

Elena shook her head wildly, her long hair sweeping her naked shoulders. 'Never!' she whispered. 'You know I didn't free the Saxon! I would rather see you in hell, than apologise for something I've not done!'

Isobel's face tightened, her features sculpted to ivory by the moolight. She turned to the guards. 'See that the girl is not actually harmed,' she said curtly. 'Otherwise – ' She shrugged her shoulders expressively and moved to go back into the hall. To Aimery.

Elena watched her depart and hated her with a wild, bitter passion, because it was better to feel this hatred than to feel the aching void which overwhelmed her when she thought of Aimery.

She whirled round suddenly in alarm, her bonds tugging at her wrists and ankles. In the pools of darkness that lay between the outbuildings, she could see men coming, sidling up in the shadows. Word had got round, and the scum of the estate was gathering, like a den of rats, to gaze on her punishment.

Her naked flesh burned. Her exposed breasts

194

throbbed, her rosy nipples tingled as the soft night air caressed them. And between her legs, at the pit of her abdomen, she was aware of a pulsing ache of shame, the dark pain of utter degradation.

She held her head high and proud, trying her best not to see them, but their appreciative mutters drifted across the hushed courtyard. Her guards stood on either side of her, grinning broadly in anticipation.

'See what we have here, lads!' one of them called encouragingly to the silent furtive onlookers. 'What'll you give us for a closer peek at this fine slave, eh?' He reached out with his rough hands and cupped her breast in his palm; Elena shuddered and wrenched her head to one side. 'Just look at these proud beauties,' he went on, rubbing her nipple with his thumb, 'good enough for the lord Aimery himself!'

Someone lurched forward out of the shadows, but the other guard pounced on him and drove him back.

'No touching, now! But you can have your fill of watching. See, if I spread these lovely legs a little further for you, you can see that sweet pink flesh, all parted and melting . . .'

Dazed with shame, Elena tried not to listen any more. Their hot, greedy looks; their casually filthy comments as they gazed lecherously at her vulnerable body and pawed secretly at their swelling erections. It was all far worse than any physical abuse.

She was squeezing her eyes shut in desperation, trying to block out their leering faces, when suddenly, silence fell. The men in the shadows melted away, like the vermin they were, as a tall, familiar figure brushed them aside.

'What is the meaning of this outrage?'

Elena's head jerked upwards, her heart beating. That deep, velvety voice was so familiar. Hamet, the Saracen – Aimery's servant. *Aimery had sent for her.*

Even as the thought flashed through her mind, she knew she was wrong.

But nevertheless Hamet pushed the remaining stragglers aside scornfully and walked up to her, his dark face full of concern. 'Elena – what is happening?'

'The – the lady Isobel's orders, sire!' stuttered the guard at her side, quailing beneath Hamet's icy anger. 'This lass here, she helped a Saxon rebel to escape, and the lord Aimery himself commanded her to be punished. She's not actually been harmed, sire!'

'Then see,' said Hamet, 'that she is not.' In a swift, sinuous movement, he pulled his woollen cloak from his shoulders and wrapped it gently round Elena's trembling, bound figure. She lifted her dazed blue eyes to him in mute appeal, but he frowned and shook his head sadly.

'I have no power to countermand my master's orders,' he said quietly. 'Or the lady Isobel's, for that matter. But,' and he turned once more to the guards, 'if you let any of that – that scum out there come near her again, or touch her yourselves, then you will answer to me, personally. Do you understand?'

'Sire!' The guards stood rigidly to attention as Hamet turned, reluctantly, and headed back towards the hall.

Elena sagged in her bonds, half-sleeping, half-waking, throughout the short midsummer hours of darkness. Thoughts of Aimery came to her like a nightmare now, not a dream. How could he? How could he let this happen to her?

Dawn broke early, revealing itself in pink and golden streaks above the dark line of the forest. Alys hovered warily outside the kitchens, on the pretext of fetching hot water for her mistress. She'd heard and seen everything, and ranted silently against them all. It was too much! They way the lady Isobel had treated her, Alys; the way that slut Morwith had laughed at her so openly for her plainness! And now, they were making that sweet girl, Elena, suffer unbearably.

Alys looked across the courtyard and shivered. It was

cold in this early grey light. The girl was pinioned there still, her head bowed, the Saracen's big cloak wrapped tightly round her slender figure. The watch had changed twice during the night; two young, yawning men-at-arms were with her now, plainly bored and weary since Hamet had warned them all against any sport with their prisoner. That Hamet might be a heathen, but he was the only decent one amongst them all.

Alys shifted the bundle in her arms, lifted her chin resolutely, and set off across the deserted courtyard towards them. Now was the time. As she'd calculated, the big gates were just about to be dragged open, in readiness for the dawn patrol to ride out.

The guards watched warily when they saw Alys coming. She was well known as a troublemaker, only too ready to carry spiteful tales back to her mistress.

'You're to set her free,' said Alys briefly. 'And then you can go.'

'But – '

'Quickly, damn you! You want me to tell the lady Isobel that you dispute her commands? Be off with you!'

Worried, they did as she said. The girl almost fell when her limbs were freed, but she struggled to lean against the palisade. Her small face was white and drawn. The guards hesitated still; Alys snapped, 'Go on, you great brutes!' and watched until they were out of sight. Then she turned urgently back to Elena.

'Now's your chance to escape!' she hissed, thrusting the bundle towards her. 'Here are some clothes, and a little food. Head for the forest – get away from this evil place while you can. Quickly, they'll be closing the gate again soon!'

The girl took the bundle, but she looked dazed and uncertain, her eyes wandering longingly towards the great hall. God help her, thought Alys, but the sweet maid is still in love with the Breton. After what he's done to her . . .

197

'Go, for pity's sake!' she pleaded. 'Don't you realise that Isobel will never, ever let you have him? That between them, they'll destroy you?'

As if waking from a long dream, the girl tightened her grip on the little bundle and took a deep, shuddering breath. Then she hurried towards the beckoning gates, not looking back.

Alys watched her go as the first pale rays of dawn spread tentatively across the castle courtyard. She should have done more. She should have told the lord Aimery about the key, and told him who it really was who set the dangerous Saxon rebel free.

But she didn't dare. Not yet. She was too frightened of Isobel.

Chapter Thirteen

*I*t was the shrill birds of the forest that woke her as they clamoured in alarm above her head, their wings beating in panic against the suffocating canopy of the high trees. Someone was coming!

Elena leaped to her feet in alarm, her throat dry. It was late afternoon and the sun was still hot as it slanted through the dusty branches. She'd not meant to fall asleep, but this soft, grassy bank beside the trickling stream had been so tempting, the sun so warm, that she'd lain down on the mossy turf and slept in utter exhaustion.

All day, she'd wandered deeper into the trackless forest, driven by nothing other than the wild, instinctive urge to get as far away as she could from the domain of Aimery le Sabrenn. Now, she was alone, and frightened, and completely lost. And she could hear the echoing sound of voices, male voices, and heavy footsteps crackling through the undergrowth nearby.

She cowered behind the trunk of a great gnarled oak, her heart hammering wildly. Outlaws. Brigands! Or perhaps Isobel de Morency had ordered the soldiers to follow her, to kill her.

Holding her breath in panic, she pressed herself into

the shadows as three young men came into sight, laughing and talking to each other. They paused to drink at the stream; she thought for one wild moment that they'd pass by without seeing her. But suddenly one of them, getting to his feet, spotted her and called out, 'Look – over there! A girl!'

She tried to run, but in her state of exhaustion she was no match for their nimble feet. They caught her easily, gripping her wrists, staring curiously down at her and asking questions all at once. 'Who are you? Where are you going? Why are you all on your own in the forest?'

The knowledge swept over her that they were Saxons – men of her own race. In sudden blind inspiration, Elena stammered out, 'I'm looking for Leofwin. Please, do you know him?'

The name was like a magic talisman. Smiling in wonder, the young men stepped back, releasing her.

'Leofwin?' said one, his grin wide and friendly in his sunburned face. 'Know him? Lass, if you're a friend of his, then you're a friend of ours! Come with us!'

Considerately adjusting their energetic pace to her weary limbs, the three young Saxons led her along the winding paths of the forest, until at last they came to a sun-dappled clearing set between stately oaks. The same stream ran more deeply here between rocky boulders, emptying itself just beyond the clearing into a deep, limpid pool fringed with ferns. The stream's banks were edged by soft, rabbit-nibbled turf that was like velvet to Elena's bruised and aching feet.

In the shade of the trees were some low turf shelters, built carefully to merge into the undergrowth. In front of them a young woman was tending a simmering cauldron over an open fire; she looked up questioningly as the men led Elena into the clearing.

'This is our home,' said the young, suntanned man who'd first spoken to her. He gestured proudly round the clearing, as if it were some nobleman's estate. 'My

200

name is Gyrth – I'll introduce you to the others later. But first things first. You must eat, and rest!'

The young woman, who was plumply pretty with thick blonde curls, brought her over a wooden bowl full of hot, delicious rabbit stew, and smiled at her shyly. Elena ate hungrily, suddenly realising how long it was since she'd had a proper meal. The sun was starting to set behind the tops of the great trees, but its rays still warmed the clearing, mottling the mossy turf with soft shadows.

She felt safe, and at peace, as long as she tried not to remember about Aimery.

What was he doing now? Was he thinking of her?

She put her bowl to one side, suddenly no longer hungry. By now the others had gathered round her companionably; the woman and the young men, with their own bowls of food.

'You have come far?' The pretty woman, Freya, handed her a beaker of clear water from the stream. 'Forgive me for prying, but you look so gently-born, and so tired. No lady should wander on her own through the forest!'

Elena hesitated, knowing she could never tell them everything. 'I – I was captured from a convent, and held as a serf at Thoresfield.' She clasped her fingers tightly round the wooden beaker. 'Leofwin was kind to me there. I thought perhaps he might help me again'.

'So you too escaped from Thoresfield!' breathed Freya, leaning forward. 'When Leofwin reached us last night, he said that the place is full of evil; that he wants to go back there and raze it to the ground, and kill its Breton lord! Oh, did you suffer greatly there?'

'Leave her alone, woman!' said Gyrth sharply, seeing the tears that sparkled suddenly in Elena's blue eyes. 'Isn't it enough that she was the Breton's prisoner?'

Elena bowed her head. 'If you and Leofwin will but shelter me for a while,' she whispered, 'until I find somewhere elsc to go – '

'How do we know she's not a spy?' broke in a venomous voice. 'Sent by the Breton to track down Leofwin and bring the soldiers down on us?'

Elena looked up, startled. A girl had just joined them, standing with her hands on her hips at the edge of the circle. Vividly pretty, with a suntanned, elfin face, she wore her silver-blonde hair cropped short like a soldiers', and wore a boy's tunic that only emphasized the soft curves of her slender figure. A murmur of protest ran through the rest of them at her challenging words.

'Leave her be, Sahild!' said Gyrth shortly. 'Leofwin himself will be here to identify her soon enough.'

'Don't be so sure of that, Gyrth! I still think she's a spy!'

Elena shrank instinctively from the venom in the girl, Sahild's, blue eyes. Freya meanwhile, seized Elena's hands and held them up angrily. 'Look! Look at these rope marks on the poor girl's wrists! She's been bound, Sahild, bound and punished! Would the Breton really do that to his spy?'

Sahild glared. 'Just don't blame me if the soldiers do follow her here!' And she flounced off into the trees.

Quickly Freya put her arm round Elena's trembling shoulder. 'Take no notice of Sahild – she's always wary of newcomers. You see, we've all suffered at the hands of the Normans, and we value our refuge here so highly.' She touched Elena's wrists gently. 'You poor thing. How you must have suffered. Leofwin will be so pleased that you've found us.'

'Will Leofwin be here soon?' Was it her imagination, or did a strange, expectant hush fall over them all at her question?

'Soon,' said Freya softly. 'Very soon.'

After their meal, Elena helped Freya to clear away. Sahild seemed to have disappeared, for which she was glad. With Freya, she took the wooden platters down to the stream to wash them; Freya chatted companionably, soothing her secret fears. When they got back to the clearing the men, taking advantage of the evening sunshine, had got out their bows for archery practice; and Elena, sinking down onto a mossy stone, watched them entranced, her chin clasped in her hands.

They were good, she could see. Even though they laughed and joked as they waited their turn, their concentration was intense. Two of the men looked so alike that she kept confusing them; they must be brothers, she decided, both bronzed and handsome in their soft leather tunics and boots, with long, wayward blond hair bleached by the sun.

Just then, one of the brothers glanced across the clearing towards her. Catching her eye, he grinned and winked; she smiled back shyly.

'Hands off, convent girl,' hissed a voice at her shoulder. Elena whirled round to see Sahild standing behind her; the beautiful outlaw girl dropped to her knees to face her, her eyes malicious. 'If you're looking for a man, you should have stayed with Aimery le Sabrenn. They say he's incomparable as a lover. What a pity you didn't wait to find out!'

Elena took a deep breath as Aimery's name jolted through her. Then she said, steadily, 'You don't like me being here. I'm sorry, for I mean you no harm. Leofwin is my friend.'

The girl's mouth twisted in a slow smile. 'Then you can help us kill the Breton,' she said softly. 'You'll enjoy that, won't you, seeing as you hate him so much?' And, without waiting for a reply, she went quickly across the clearing to join the men in their archery practice.

Elena watched her, dazed by her venom. Just then Gyrth, who had been watching from a distance, sauntered over to sit beside her, his bow across his knees.

'I'm out of the contest,' he said ruefully. 'Mind if I join you?'

Still shaky from Sahild's hissed words, Elena forced a smile. 'Of course not! I don't know how you can decide on a winner – you all look so good to me. Especially those two, the ones who look so like each other.'

The twins, you mean? Wulf and Osric. Yes, they're the best we've got. And Sahild is as good as any man with her bow.' Gyrth frowned a little into the setting sun, his hands clasped loosely on his knees. 'But we need to be even better. You know, some say that it was because of William's archers – the Bretons, the Flemings, the men of Maine and Poitou – that we lost the day at Hastings. They fired high above our shield wall, and killed King Harold. But some day soon, we'll drive the Frenchmen out!'

Elena suddenly remembered that night when a band of mail-clad knights, with Aimery le Sabrenn at their head, had ridden out menacingly into the blackness of the night to hunt down rebels such as these. How could Leofwin, Gyrth and these men, however brave, hope to defy the might of King William's armies? She shivered suddenly; Gyrth laid his hand gently on her shoulder.

'Why don't you rest for a while? You look exhausted. And Elena, take no notice of Sahild! She doesn't speak for the rest of us, you know!'

Elena nodded, trying to smile. 'Where are the rest of your womenfolk?'

He shrugged wryly. 'You've met them. Freya and Sahild, that's it.'

'And Leofwin? When will he be back?'

He hesitated, just like Freya did when she asked the same question. Again, the air of mystery. 'You'll see him soon enough,' he said finally. 'Now, you must rest. I'll fetch Freya to attend to you.'

Suddenly, Elena realised how very tired she was. Freya took her to an empty hut; she longed to curl up on the straw pallet in the corner, but first she decided to go down to the stream to wash the dust of her journey away.

The sun was setting at last behind the trees as she scrambled down the bank towards the water's edge.

Then she stopped, frozen. Further downstream, where the water eddied into the deep, limpid pool fringed by overhanging alders, two people were already bathing. A girl and a young man. And the girl was Sahild.

As they rose gasping and laughing from the clear water, the droplets streaming from their naked bodies, Elena saw that the man was one of the twins she'd admired earlier. She wondered if he was the one who'd grinned at her. Then he emerged further from the water; and she saw, with a shock that brought the blood coursing to her cheeks, that he was already hugely erect, and the suntanned, crop-headed girl was fondling his penis happily, whispering endearments in his ear and rubbing her small, pointed breasts against his muscled chest.

With a husky laugh, the man lifted the girl in his arms and carried her to the soft, grassy bank on the other side of the stream, laying her down eagerly. Then he cupped her slim, boyish buttocks with his hands and eased his pulsing erection deep within her, groaning aloud in ecstasy as Sahild clasped him to her.

Elena gasped aloud as she saw the second brother move out of the shadows, smiling. He, too, was naked; he crouched lazily beside them, fondling his own ravening penis, waiting patiently.

Elena tore her eyes away and hurried back upstream to wash herself, splashing her burning cheeks with the cool water. Thoroughly shaken by the shameless pleasuring she'd seen, she walked quickly back to the hut Freya had shown her and curled up on the straw pallet, closing her eyes and shutting her mind to everything except sleep.

With sleep came her dreams. She saw a faceless figure, a knight, lying bound and helpless in the centre of the clearing. Instead of the sunlit, friendly forest scene she'd been part of today, everything was dark and sinister; the trees reached out gnarled black fingers in silent threat, and the bound man was surrounded by a ring of fierce, menacing figures, who gathered round him with knives in their hands, ready to plunge them into his helpless body. Elena tried to cry out, to stop them, but her throat was closed up with fear. She ran to the man and threw herself across him, to protect him from the knives; he turned to look at her, and his strange, silver-grey eyes were filled with hatred. *'Aimery,'* she whispered, agonised. *'Oh, Aimery. No . . .'*

She woke up. It was pitch black in the little hut. Her heart raced wildly, and her eyes were still wet with tears from her dream. She pulled herself up, and buried her burning face in her hands.

Just then, the door to the hut opened softly, and Freya stepped inside. 'So you're awake. Good.' There was a hint of suppressed excitement in her carefully controlled voice.

Elena jumped to her feet. 'Leofwin – he's here?'

'Yes – ' Again, Elena noticed the slight hesitation. 'You must follow me.'

The clearing was deserted. It was a warm, sultry night and to Elena the air seemed almost oppressive as Freya led the way deeper through the trees into the blackness of the forest. High above them, an owl hooted softly and Elena jumped, her heart hammering.

She saw the ring of lights first. Small fires, flickering eerily like will o' the wisps through the tangled trunks of the forest. Then she saw the people, sitting cross-legged in a circle round the fires, their heads bowed as if in prayer. Only they weren't praying but murmuring, chanting low, mysterious words to themselves as if they were in another world.

Elena felt the shock juddering through her at the unreality of the scene. Were these really the same people who inhabited that sunlit, peaceful clearing? Yes, there they were. Garth, Freya, Sahild and the twins, the other men.

But tonight, here in this mysterious moonlit glade,

hemmed in by ancient, gnarled oak trees, everyone seemed different – frighteningly so. And in the centre of the ring, dully illuminated by the low, flickering fires, was a huge, flat slab of stone, cold and grey and ominous.

Elena whirled round to flee, her throat dry with fear. She realised now. The nuns had spoken in hushed whispers about the old religion, the gods of ancient Britain, surviving still in the darkly remote forests and the wild northern hills. Sickened, she remembered morbid rumours of rites and magic, of stern, cruel priests and human sacrifices. *This was a sacred grove* . . .

Freya's hand closed round her wrist, preventing her escape. Her voice was low and hypnotic. 'Sit here, Elena, beside me,' she whispered. 'And don't be afraid. Remember, Leofwin will be here soon.'

Helplessly, Elena sank to her knees in the circle. Where else could she go? The soft droning of muttered voices throbbed in her head. Someone leaned forward, breaking the tight circle to throw a scattering of dried herbs on the tiny fires. The pungent smoke assailed her nostrils like incense, sweet and heady. She was aware of the girl Sahild watching her coldly and felt another pang of fear; but Freya's fingers stroked her wrist soothingly, and as she breathed deeply she felt strangely calmed.

Someone was passing her a brimming bowl. She drank obediently, finding it to be rich, honey-sweet mead. The potent liquid hit her stomach almost instantly, making her limbs warm and melting. She held the big bowl wonderingly. It seemed to be made of silver and was carved with strange inscriptions: bulls' heads, birds, spoked circles, and a single crude engraving of a tiny, ithyphallic man, his lewd penis rising to his shoulders.

Her eyes widened at the startling obscenity, yet she was unable to draw her eyes from it, until at last someone gently prised the bowl out of her hands and she let it go, reluctantly. From across the circle, one of the twins smiled at her mysteriously; she smiled shakily back, dazzled by the sudden warmth of his smile, feeling dizzy and unreal.

Something was about to happen in the forest that night, and she felt wildly, terribly excited. The image of the tiny silver man and his enormous member seemed to dance mockingly before her eyes in the darkness; she suddenly realised that she was hot and moist, and her pleasure bud was pulsing hungrily.

A tall man stepped silently out from behind the dense, shadowy oaks. An intense hush fell suddenly over the kneeling circle. The man wore a long, dark cloak and Elena saw with a shock that a mask covered his face; a strange, sinister mask made of bronze with black, staring eyeholes. Elena shuddered in nameless fear as the man started to speak in low, vibrant tones. 'The time has come,' he said softly. Surely his voice was familiar? Yet it was so muffled by the mouthless mask and her senses were swimming, from the scented smoke fumes and the mead.

A murmur of excitement ran through the circle at his words, and he held out his hand commandingly for silence. 'Which of you is the chosen one?'

There was a deathly silence. Shivers of fear ran up and down Elena's spine. Then Freya stood up slowly. Her face looked strange, and her eyes glittered unnaturally. 'Here, master,' she whispered. 'It is I. I am to be first.'

'And who have you chosen as your menfolk?'

'The brothers, my lord – Wulf and Osric!'

The two young men, the twins with their lithe, muscled bodies and long, sun-streaked hair, got to their feet, their heads high and proud. They looked as if they were in a trance; Elena gazed and gazed at them, hypnotised by their youthful, masculine beauty. This could not be real.

A soft breeze moaned through the trees, wafting the sweet smoke from the fires all around the clearing.

'Summon your men, Freya,' said the tall masked man in a low voice. 'And prepare for the final sacrifice.'

Sacrifice! Sweet Jesus . . . Half-forgotten tales of grim rituals, of live burial and hideous impalement, tore through Elena's subconscious mind. She leaped to her feet.

'I – I must go!' she stammered out in confusion. 'I should not be here.'

Sahild laughed unpleasantly. 'The little convent girl doesn't approve of our ceremony. I told you she wouldn't!'

But the men on either side of Elena pulled her gently down. 'Stay,' they whispered soothingly in her ear.'There is nothing to fear. All you will witness is pleasure. Stay, and watch!'

They gave her more mead to drink; the little ithyphallic man grinned up at her, mocking her, and she felt the languorous warmth of the potent honey drink seep meltingly through her veins. When she looked up again, the two men, Wulf and Osric, were standing on either side of Freya, undressing her with deliberate care. When she was completely naked they bowed in silent homage before her. Elena watched, her throat dry. But she had thought that Freya was Gyrth's woman! And Wulf and Osric, she'd seen them earlier, with Sahild! Yet Gyrth was smiling, and Sahild too looked spellbound.

Slowly the twins caressed the naked woman, kissing and licking every inch of her plump, golden flesh. One of the brothers reached for the half-empty bowl of mead and trickled some of it over her full breasts; then they each took a brown nipple in their mouths, licking and sucking the sweet, sticky liquid over her breasts, while caressing and stroking her with their hands.

Freya stood very still, her eyes half-shut in rapture, for as long as she could bear it. Then she sank to her knees with a sigh, and her eyes closed. Raptly, the men slipped their own clothes to the ground, while everyone in the circle gazed in silence. Elena could hardly breathe. The two men stood there in blond, muscular beauty, their magnificent twin phalluses rearing proudly over the kneeling Freya's fair curls. Then, with tender care, they lifted her in their strong arms and laid her on the cold, waiting stone.

Elena felt the low, aching pressure building up relentlessly in her loins. Her breasts swelled and throbbed; little tongues of desire arrowed to her abdomen, setting her flesh on fire. She moistened her lips at the powerful eroticism of the moonlit scene unfolding before her as Freya writhed voluptuously on the grey stone slab, the secret flesh between her thighs already plump and glistening.

The two men stood at her head and feet, naked, muscular, beautiful. Wulf bent to kiss her, thrusting his tongue deep within her swollen mouth. Then, with a soft smile that turned Elena's heart over, he started to rub his engorged phallus against her nipples, and Freya groaned aloud, her legs threshing with desire.

Gently, Osric grasped her thighs, parting them widely so that everyone could see the wet, shiny folds that emerged from her golden fleece. 'Please,' she was murmuring hotly. 'Oh, please . . .'

Osric grasped his thick, solid penis with his right hand and dipped it purposefully towards her throbbing vulva. But instead of entering her, and giving her what she craved so much, he rubbed the velvety glans gently round her entrance, just brushing against her hungry pleasure bud. The touch of his swollen, massive member drove her to distraction; she gasped aloud, her breath coming short and fast, and began thrusting her hips wildly against him.

The masked man stepped forward. 'Enough. She is ready.'

And, with a nod to the twins, who stood obediently

210

aside, he took his place at the edge of the raised stone dais. He lifted Freya's legs gently, bending her knees and pulling her towards him so that her quivering plump buttocks rested almost on the edge of the stone. Then he parted his long cloak slightly, so that his enormous phallus reared forth, dark and mysterious, as if it had a pulsing life of its own.

Meanwhile, Wulf and Osric stood at Freya's shoulders. Matching each other's movements, smiling conspiratorially at one another, they began to gently rub one another's pulsing shafts, pushing them downwards to brush against Freya's hard brown nipples. Freya moaned and arched her hips desperately, making little animal sounds of pleasure in the back of her throat.

The masked man gripped his penis, stroked gently with it at her hot vulva, and thrust himself in up to the hilt.

Elena felt her own hot, wild excitement racing through her body. Her own secret parts were wet and slick as the mysterious masked man slowly withdrew his magnificent length, now shining wet with Freya's juices, and drove himself in, again and again, while the twins masturbated one another with loving care over Freya's plump breasts.

Freya was beside herself with rapture, gripping and writhing at the masked man's deliciously satisfying penis. She came quickly, racked by an intense, voracious orgasm, as the faceless man thrust firmly into her, his hands resting on either side of her on the big stone slab. With wicked grins of delight, the twins pumped each other to a state of frenzy, shooting their milky sperm in ecstatic spasms across the girl's breasts, rubbing their shafts lasciviously in the pooling liquid and letting their heavy balls drag along her silky flesh until all of her upper body gleamed with their deliciously mingled seed.

Freya lay sprawled on the stone, sated and flushed,

her blonde hair spread out in thick curls around her shoulders.

The masked man let the cloak fall over himself, and drew back into the shadows.

'The first sacrifice,' he said softly. 'Who is next?'

Elena was so aroused that she ached. Her blood coursed through her veins like fire; her breasts burned to be touched, while the flesh between her thighs was swollen and damp. The mead pulsed through her in dizzying waves.

'Next?' repeated the masked man. She couldn't see his eyes through the black holes of the mask, but she knew he was looking straight at her.

Sahild stood up eagerly; the masked man shook his head, still watching Elena. Wulf and Osric, at a nod from the man, walked slowly towards her; Elena stood up shakily.

'Yes,' she breathed. 'Oh, yes! *I* am next . . .'

Chapter Fourteen

With gentle fingers, the twin brothers divested Elena of her clothes and lifted her carefully onto the stone slab, stroking her, soothing her. They turned her over, face down, so that her throbbing breasts kissed the cold stone. Catching her breath in delight, Elena rubbed her hardening nipples against its flat surface.

The brothers were moving down her body, kissing her with delicious feathery strokes, but it was the faceless man she was thinking of, waiting there in the shadows, ready to thrust his hugely powerful shaft into the aching void at the pit of her belly.

'Raise yourself.' One of them – Wulf, or was it Osric – was muttering in her ear. She twisted her head and saw that he had a tiny, arrow-shaped scar at the base of his tanned throat. 'Raise your hips, beautiful Elena – yes, that's right . . .'

Blindly she did as she was told, thrusting her quivering buttocks into the air, not caring about her shame, about the watching silent circle drinking in her white, firm flesh, the dark bottom cleft, the pink, glistening lips that twitched and trembled hungrily. Oh, please, she begged silently, let it be soon!

Wulf – or was it Osric – was pouring scented oil into his palms from a phial. Then he began to stroke and pull at her dangling nipples, lengthening the dark teats, sending exquisite shafts of pleasure through her sensitised body. And the other twin was softly parting her buttocks, and licking slowly; starting at the top of her crease and sliding down with his wicked tongue.

'No!' gasped Elena. 'No – '

'Hush,' murmured a twin in her ear. 'Nothing but pleasure, little one, I promise you.'

Someone in the circle began the low, murmuring chant again; rhythmic, throbbing, exciting. And a darting tongue had found her tight, secret hole. Even while the twin's fingers played with her hot, juicy nether lips, sliding lightly past the little bud that quivered and strained for more, his tongue plunged into that shameful rear entrance, swirling, licking, thrusting. Elena moaned aloud as the dark pleasure swept through her, feeling the moisture gather and slip over the twin's big hand as he rubbed his knuckles up and down her churning vulva and pressed his tongue so deliciously deep within her hidden passage.

Elena caught her breath and went very still as the unfamiliar sensations gathered in her womb and she hovered on the very brink of ecstasy, ready to crash over the edge.

'Stop,' muttered one of the brothers thickly, abondoning the small breasts he was teasing so deliciously with his oil-softened hands. 'Stop, damn you, Osric. Can't you see she's almost there?'

Elena wanted to cry out in loss as their hands abandoned her. She couldn't bear it, for these two beautiful men to leave her, when she was on the brink of such wickedly ecstatic pleasure . . . 'Please!' she moaned, biting on her lip in her anguish.

Then cool hands stroked her buttocks, parting them, soothing them. Elena sighed, burying her head in her arms, and felt the trickle of warm oil running down her crease. The gentle but persistent nudging began again at her tight rear entrance; thinking it was Osric's tongue, she smiled rapturously and thrust towards him.

With a shock, she realised it wasn't his tongue, but the velvety head of an engorged penis that was trying to enter her there. Like a blind animal; stubborn, persistent, prodding. No, she protested silently. It was too big!

Then a hand stroked her softly between her flesh lips, finding the hard bud of pleasure and caressing it, very lightly. Elena shuddered, and gasped aloud as fresh waves of desire racked her body. At the same moment, she felt the engorged phallus slipping through her dark rear hole, sliding deep within her, filling her to bursting and sending a heavy, aching pleasure throbbing through her taut abdomen.

She went very still with the shock of it, almost afraid to move with this huge, pulsing shaft so deep inside her. The crowd was still murmuring its insistent, almost demonic chant; she felt the watchers' rising excitement, breathed in the heavy scent of the aromatic flames, like incense numbing her brain, heightening every sensation to a level of wild eroticism.

The beautiful brothers, Wulf and Osric, were standing by her shoulders. Opening her pleasure-hazed eyes, she saw that they were fully erect again, their penises pulsing with glorious life, their testicles tight and hard. They smiled down at her kindly in the shadows and bent to kiss her shoulders, reaching underneath her crouching body to caress and tease her dangling breasts with sweetly pinching fingers.

And, behind her, the masked man who had so shamefully, so lewdly taken her secret entrance was starting to move.

Elena cried out as she felt the huge, hard shaft slide relentlessly between her silken walls. A twin bent to kiss her, smothering her cry; she responded wildly as he thrust his tongue deep within her mouth. The masked man's penis was fully in her now; she realised with a numbing shock that she could feel the rough, hairy skin of his balls dangling against her tender bottom cheeks. And his hand was still sliding up and down her juicy vulva, teasing and stroking that aching cleft.

The dark waves of pleasure built up relentlessly. Lifting her head, Elena let out a long, low moan. The man behind her, responding to her needs, began to drive his shaft in and out in long, pulsing strokes that penetrated deeply; at the same time he lightly stroked the shaft of her straining pleasure bud, while the two brothers cupped and fondled her oiled, tingling breasts. Clutching blindly at the wonderful phallus that pleasured her so dispassionately, Elena felt her whole body come to a trembling standstill; felt the huge, cataclysmic orgasm rack her quivering flesh in wave after wave of rapture mingled with an agonised sense of shame as the mysterious man behind her gripped her buttocks fiercely and drove himself to his own wild climax. She heard him grunt harshly deep in his throat as he jerked and spasmed deep within that forbidden passage.

Melting in the afterglow of forbidden pleasure, Elena collasped limply on the cool stone slab, aware of the hot, hungry eyes from the firelit circle watching her avidly, longing to share in her rapturous release. The twins continued to caress her gently, their own huge erections almost weeping with tormented desire as they stroked her lovely, flushed breasts. Gently, they turned Elena round and lifted her shoulders so that she was sitting up on the stone, blinking dizzily into the firelit shadows.

The masked man stood before her, at the foot of the stone slab. As she'd always known, it was he who'd pleasured her in that wonderful, shameful way. But who was he? His cloak still covered his tall, powerful

216

body, but as she gazed up at him, desperately trying to frame her question, he slowly took off the bronze mask.

She gasped, '*Leofwin!*'

Gently, Leofwin the Saxon wrapped her in his cloak and carried her back to the clearing, laying her gently on a soft straw pallet in his own shelter.

'My Saxon princess,' he said tenderly. 'You're safe now.'

So Elena became one of the outlaws. During the next few days, she learned how to snare rabbits and skin them; how to mend the rough, homespun clothing; and how to make bread for them all, by heating large flat stones in the fire and placing round cakes of unleavened rye dough on the surface until they were cooked. Freya helped her to learn, and was always kind and friendly. But Sahild watched her with narrowed eyes, and hardly ever spoke to her.

At night, Elena slept in Leofwin's arms. He was a strong, tender lover, and there was no hint of the mysterious, almost sinister rites that had marked her first night in the forest. She felt safe, and shut her mind to the past, trying not to think of Aimery the Breton.

Then, early one evening in the soft shadows of dusk, she was going down to the pool to bathe the heat of the day from her limbs when she saw something in the bushes that made her freeze. A man, sprawled on the ground with Sahild.

All the men had gone out hunting for the day, except for Leofwin, who had injured his ankle slightly in an expedition the day before. But – what was Leofwin doing with Sahild?

It soon became obvious.

Leofwin was sprawled back on the mossy turf, his eyes closed in ecstasy, his legs spread wide. Sahild was crouched over his hips, her back to Elena. She shifted slightly, giving Elena a clearer vision; and what she saw made her senses swim. Because Leofwin's huge penis, darkly, erect, was rearing up from his disarrayed clothes, and Sahild was sucking and licking him enthusiastically, diving her lips over his flesh, gripping the base of his thick shaft and making strange little moaning noises in the back of her throat. Leofwin, who had made passionate love to her only last night.

Feeling sick with betrayal, Elena whirled round to go, and almost fell into the arms of Wulf, who stood behind her. His strong hands fastened round her shoulders. 'Wait,' he said.

Elena's hands pummelled frantically at his broad chest. 'Let me go!' she whispered blindly. 'Damn you, Wulf – let me go!'

He held on to her, ignoring her wild struggles. 'Listen, Elena,' he said, in a low, urgent voice. 'Leofwin loves you. We all love you. This is the way we live in the forest. Didn't you realise, after that first night?'

She stopped struggling, and stared blankly up at him.

That dark, erotic ceremony on her first night here. She'd tried to push it to the back of her mind. Pretended it had never happened, would never happen again. *This is the way we live in the forest.*

Her heart thudded as she gazed up at him. He was so young, only about her age – so handsome and carefree and kind. That first night, she'd seen him and his brother making love to Sahild down by the stream, and then they'd both caressed her, so beautifully, while the masked Leofwin stood waiting in the shadows.

Already aroused by the sight of Leofwin's depravity, Elena felt moist and hot; her stomach churned. With his sun-streaked blond hair and his laughing blue eyes set wide apart in his suntanned face, he set her pulse racing in a way he shouldn't.

His hands had slipped now from her shoulders to her breasts. Lightly, still gazing into her eyes, he caressed her tender nipples until they peaked and thrust beneath her tunic. She trembled suddenly with wanting him.

He was smiling down at her, his palms rubbing flatly

along her breasts, sending whirling, fiery sensations through her body. 'You called me Wulf,' he said softly. 'How did you know it was me, and not my brother?'

Hypnotised by his gaze, she whispered, 'The little mark – the white scar at the base of your throat, shaped like an arrowhead. I noticed it on the first night, when – when –'

'When Osric and I made love to you?' His hands had slipped round the back of her waist; he held her very close, so she could feel the hot, hard arousal at his loins.

'Yes.'

'And did you enjoy it? I wonder, which one of us did you want the most?' He put his head teasingly on one side, lifting his eyebrows so engagingly that Elena found herself smiling breathlessly in response.

'Both of you,' she whispered, her heart racing. 'Oh, both of you.'

He laughed in response, his teeth gleaming whitely in his suntanned face. 'You should have said – you. You, Wulf! Just you! – For that, I fear, I shall have to punish you, sweet Elena. When the time comes . . .' He smiled, a smile full of secret promise. Suddenly she realised that she didn't mind now about Leofwin and Sahild. *This is the way we live.*

Her body tingled with excitement; Wulf drew her closer, his breath warm on her cheek.

Then they jumped apart as the mingled sound of heavy footsteps and raised, excited voices came crashing through the forest towards them. Gyrth and his men were back from their expedition. Reluctantly Wulf led Elena towards them. 'Good hunting?' he enquired laconically.

'Good hunting indeed!' Gyrth clapped him on the back, scarcely able to restrain his excitement. 'A Norman baggage train, no less! Wine, wheat, even some gold. All on its way to York, where they'll miss it sorely!' He gestured proudly towards the two laden pack ponies that the other men were starting to unload. 'We've brought back as much as we could. This calls for a feast! Where's Leofwin?'

'I'll fetch him,' said Wulf diplomatically, flashing a reassuring smile at Elena.

That night they sat down to a feast of roasted venison and fine wheat cakes that Freya had baked. The men were drinking the heady French wine they'd captured; Elena only sipped at it, but already she could feel it pulsing warmly through her blood. The outlaws were quaffing it down as if it were ale, recounting again and again how they'd ambushed the Norman supply wagons on their way north from Lincoln.

The shadows lengthened, and tiny bats swooped in the trees overhead. The fire crackled hypnotically, and the smell of the venison filled the air with its savoury perfume.

Sahild too was drinking like a man. Her eyes gleamed jealously in the light of the fire as she listened to their stories; she leaned forward intently and said, 'I should have been with you, Gyrth! Why didn't you take me? I'd have killed them all!' She licked her lips. 'After I'd made them suffer, of course.'

Elena shivered at the girl's quiet venom. Leofwin, who had pulled her down beside him as if the episode with Sahild had never existed, put his arm round her, and she was glad to lean into his quiet strength. But Elena knew that Leofwin too was under the influence of the wine, and inflamed by his men's success. As if a kind of subtle blood lust gripped them all, they sat in their shadowy circle round the fire, watching Sahild with baited breath.

Wulf said softly, 'How? How would you make them suffer, Sahild?'

Kneeling upright, conscious that she had everyone's attention, Sahild drew out the dagger she always carried at her belt. The moon sparkled down on her cropped silver hair and her beautiful elfin face. Her wide blue eyes seemed dazed by her own dark imagination. Slowly, she inverted the dagger and began to stroke its thick, ribbed pommel between her thighs. Elena gasped aloud; everyone else had gone very still.

Sahild rolled over luxuriously onto her back, and raised her knees. She wore a soft leather tunic, and deerskin boots that clung to her calves; her lithe, suntanned legs were bare. As her tunic fell back over her hips, they saw that she wore nothing beneath her tunic; her pink secret flesh glistened damply between her slim thighs. Her eyes closing in rapture, she gently positioned the rounded hilt of the dagger between her silken flesh lips, and slid the metal slowly in, her face flushing with pleasure.

Osric leaned over her, watching raptly. 'Is that how you'd torment the Normans, Sahild? Don't you think they might – enjoy it?'

She slanted a wicked grin up at him. Her breathing was short and shallow. 'I'd say – can you do as well as this soldier? Can you fill me with a shaft as solid as this steel? Can you – oh!'

Suddenly she broke off as Freya, who'd been watching avidly in the shadows, jumped up and moved swiftly to crouch over her friend. With nimble fingers, Freya took the dagger's hilt in her own hand and started to pleasure Sahild gently, rubbing the hilt between Sahild's parted legs, while Sahild moaned and writhed on the soft grass. She pulled her tunic high above her head; greedily Freya dipped her head and began to suck and lick at the girl's suntanned, pointed little breasts. She circled the nipples lasciviously with her tongue, while still sliding the rounded metal pommel sleekly in and out of her pink, juicy love channel. Sahild began to moan and whimper, on the verge of explosion; while the men sat round silently in a circle, their hungry expressions lit up by the flickering fire as they waited.

Elena, overwhelmed by the erotic tension, jumped

up suddenly, freeing herself from Leofwin's imprison-
ing arm, and ran blindly away from the lewd scene. She
found herself down by the little stream; breathing hard
in the gathering darkness, she crouched down to bathe
her burning face in the cool water.

She heard soft footsteps coming up behind her. She
felt strong hands on her shoulders, firm fingers that
crept round from behind to stroke her breasts, caressing
her stiffening nipples. She whirled round, the blood hot
in her face. 'Wulf!'

He smiled softly in the darkness, and she melted. His
hands slid round her waist, pulling her up to his hard,
muscular body; he bent his head and kissed her deeply,
languorously, his sensitive tongue stroking and probing
round the soft silken flesh of her mouth.

Elena pushed at his chest, gasping for breath. 'No –
we shouldn't – Leofwin . . .'

Wulf smiled again. 'Leofwin sent me,' he said.

'And me,' added Osric, emerging out of the shadows.

She glanced wildly from one to the other. Already
they were lifting their tunics over their heads, unfasten-
ing their hose from around their slim, muscular hips,
so that she could glimpse their dark, erect phalluses.
She backed away, trembling with excitement. 'No!
Someone might see us!'

'The others,' said Osric calmly, 'will be totally occupied with Freya and Sahild by now.'

'But we,' said Wulf softly, stepping forward to
remove Elena's clothes, 'are for you, sweet Elena.'

She gasped and shuddered as her gown slipped to
the floor and she felt Wulf's hot, silken penis rubbing
against her belly. He bent to kiss her again, and she
clung to him weakly, feeling the hard, rippling strength
of his beautiful, suntanned body, the long strength of
his heavy, shapely legs. And now Osric was behind
her, lifting her long hair and kissing her shoulders,
while his own engorged shaft rubbed tenderly at her
bottom cheeks, nuzzling between her thighs.

Already she was pulsing wet, aching with excitement, her clitoris quivering. Gently they laid her on the soft turf, and kneeled, one on either side of her, their faces amused and tender. With both hands, she grasped their twin penises in delight, caressing and stroking those two magnificent pillars of flesh that waited to do her homage, reaching up to take each one's tip in her mouth, swallowing and licking greedily while the hot hunger churned in her loins.

It was almost dark. She could see the wicked gleam in their dancing blue eyes as they looked at one another and nodded. Then one of them – she thought it was Wulf, but she couldn't be sure – kneeled between her legs, facing her, and lifted her hips gently. He licked his finger and ran it moistly down her slippery cleft, up and down, sliding teasingly past her twitching pleasure bud; she moaned aloud, and he gave a secret smile as he gripped his massively erect shaft and slid it slowly into her. She shouted aloud at the pleasure, gripping hungrily at the hot flesh that nudged its way in, possessing her so beautifully.

Then the other twin – Osric? – crouched astride her head, facing his brother, so that the musky, masculine scent of him excited her nostrils, and her whole vision was filled by the coarse, velvety flesh of his balls and the veined underside of his throbbing penis. Gently, he lowered himself over her, caressing and pinching her breasts with his fingers; until, with a little gasp, she felt his hairy sac kiss her soft lips, and instinctively she began to lick and caress him there with her tongue.

All her flesh, all her senses quivered in reaction to the two men pleasuring her. Wulf's fine penis drove deeply into her; Osric's fingers tugged and tweaked at her nipples, his balls exciting her soft lips. When Wulf's finger slid once more across her hungry clitoris, she moaned aloud, and heard her high, delirious cry of ecstasy echoing round the trees as he slowly, deliberately pumped himself into her and wickedly teased that tight, hard little bud, while Osric squeezed her nipples, tenderly.

She threw herself into the air, spasming wildly, as the pleasure exploded in white-hot shafts through her tense, yearning body. Wulf drove himself into her fiercely, his taut hips jerking, until at last, with a husky groan, he shuddered to his own delicious release, his penis pulsing wetly within her.

'Now me,' said Osric softly, his ravening member jutting hungrily into the empty air.

He was still crouching astride Elena, though careful not to lean his full weight on her. Now, he lowered himself again, rubbing his thick, hairy sac against her lips; she opened her moist mouth as wide as she could, to suck and caress at the coarse skin. He gasped with dark pleasure, throwing his head back; Wulf leaned forward with a wicked grin and took his twin's engorged phallus in his mouth. He swept his lips down hard over the silken, throbbing flesh, licking fiercely at the sensitive glans; then, just at Elena felt Osric's balls tighten and quiver in pre-orgasmic tension, Wulf lifted his head away.

Osric groaned aloud as his hot semen began to spurt into the air; he pushed his testicles hard against Elena's soft mouth, and she shivered with renewed pleasure as she felt the milky liquid surge through him and spatter on her heated nipples.

Then the twins knelt gently on either side of her and began to lick up Osric's sticky seed from her flushed breasts. She lay back dazed with pleasure as the two brothers, their faces exquisitely tender and handsome in the moonlight, caressed and stroked her sated flesh, murmuring her name in adoration as they did so.

They bathed themselves in the moonlit stream, giggling and whispering. Then they headed back towards the clearing, Elena still light-headed with wine and lovemaking.

The fire was burning low. The others reclined in a

circle around it, murmuring in low, hazy voices. From the disarray of their clothing, Elena guessed, blushing, that they too had all been busy pleasuring one another; Gyrth and Freya were still together, kissing languorously. Elena wondered hazily who Leofwin had been with. Did it matter? It certainly didn't seem to when he saw her at the edge of the clearing, and reached out his hand to her with a gentle smile. She went to sit with him, settling contentedly in the crook of his shoulder.

They were talking, telling stories about battles and the old times, before the Normans came. Elena listened, fascinated.

Then Sahild sat up. The twins had settled on either side of her. She was still drinking wine, and her eyes were unnaturally bright. Her tunic had slipped over one shoulder, exposing one high, small breast; she leaned forward, her hands clasping her knees. 'When I first came to the forest,' she began huskily, 'before I met up with you all, something strange happened to me.'

Wulf laughed easily, fondling her bare, suntanned shoulder. 'Is this another figment of your over-vivid imagination, sweetheart?'

She shrugged him off. 'No! Listen, and I'll tell you! It happened in high summer, around the time of the feast of Lughnasad. I'd been wandering through the forest for days, living off what I could find. I was tired and hungry. Then I found the stone – our stone! It was past midnight . . .'

Elena felt the prickles of unease racing up and down her spine. The sacrificial stone, in the sacred grove.

'It was hot,' continued Sahild. She spoke in a low, breathless whisper; she had everyone's rapt attention now. 'I was restless, uneasy. I laid on the cold stone, letting it cool my burning skin. Then, suddenly, I knew that someone else was in the grove with me!

'I jumped up, and a man stepped forward. A big man, wearing a bronze mask of a bull, with dark slits for eyes and great, protruding horns. He wore a crude leather tunic, and was very powerful, with wide shoulders and a great, muscular chest. I shivered as I gazed up at him. He was so strong, so incredibly virile, so mysterious. I wanted to run but I found I couldn't move.

"Who are you?" I whispered.

'He said nothing. But he lifted me, and turned me, forcing me to crouch on all fours on the cold stone slab. My heart was thudding so fiercely I thought it would burst.

'Then, my bull-man kneeled up on the slab behind me and, tearing off my clothing, began to ravish me. And, oh – ' Sahild shuddered deliciously at the memory – 'never, never have I known anything like it! Up and up his wonderful shaft slid into me, never-ending. I thought I would die of pleasure! With his weapon as magnificent as any bull's pizzle, he filled me to bursting, and then began to take me wildly, riding up and down, gripping and pawing at my quivering buttocks.'

'Did he say anything?' asked Freya enviously.

'No, but I could hear him grunting, panting deeply, like some big animal in the shadows behind me. I was so filled with dark excitement that I cried out, over and over again, as he drove himself into ecstasy and spent himself deep, deep within me.' She sighed wistfully.

'I tell you, he drained every last drop of pleasure from my body with his magnificent penis. Short, juicy caresses that made me melt; long, satisfying thrusts that made me cry out in delight – oh, if only I could have seen him properly as he serviced me! I still dream of it now – how his shaft must have looked, so thick, so angry, so wet with my love juices as he pumped himself between my cheeks.

'When at last he slid himself slowly out of me, I slumped face down on the slab, exhausted. And when I turned round, he'd gone! Vanished, into the blackness of the forest . . .' Her voice trailed reluctantly away.

Everyone hung onto the echo of her words, rapt and aroused again.

Only Elena shivered, disturbed by Sahild's strange tale.

In the silence, the dark presence of the forest pressed in around them. She was only too aware again of the mysterious, supernatural forces, the old magic, that underlaid the lives of all these people.

Freya was listening open-mouthed, her eyes glazed with excitement and longing.

'It sounds,' she said, laughing a little shakily, 'like one of the stories they tell about Aimery le Sabrenn! I've heard that the Breton is a truly magnificent lover.'

Elena felt the shock jar through her at Aimery's name. Leofwin's arm tightened protectively around her. 'It's all right, princess,' he murmured soothingly. 'You're safe from him here.' Aloud, to the others, he said, 'Who knows? You might have the chance to find out for yourselves soon.'

Freya turned on him, her eyes wide with excitement. 'What do you mean?'

Gyrth said, with a grin of triumph: 'He means, my sweet, that we found out today from one of our Norman prisoners that the Breton will be travelling to Lincoln shortly, for a meeting with the king's justiciars. If we can get him away from his men, he'll be ours. To do with as we wish.'

A hush fell over the ring of faces. Sahild fondled her dagger. 'How will he die?' she whispered.

'We'll take pleasure in deciding that when the time comes,' said Leofwin chillingly. 'And in letting him know a long time in advance, so he can dwell on the prospect.'

Elena went tense in his arms, her face drained of blood. Leofwin looked anxiously down at her.

'Something is wrong. Elena?'

'No! No, I'm just so tired. Will you all forgive me if I go to bed?'

Leofwin touched her hand affectionately. 'Of course. It's late. I'll join you shortly.'

Sahild watched her go, narrow-eyed.

Elena was asleep by the time Leofwin joined her. She tossed and muttered, dreaming again of the ring of dark, malicious faces around the captive knight in the clearing. 'Aimery,' she groaned aloud. 'Oh, Aimery.'

Leofwin turned restlessly in his sleep and held her close, not hearing what she said.

But Sahild, wandering restlessly outside in the darkness, heard the convent girl cry out the Breton's name and froze outside the hut, her breath an indrawn hiss of discovery.

Elena was down by the stream one evening, fetching water, when she heard the men get back. They'd been gone all day – hunting, Leofwin had told her. She was glad they'd returned before nightfall, because the wild forest still frightened her without Leofwin's arms around her.

It was late summer, and the nights were drawing in. Already, the gibbous moon hung palely overhead, and a nightjar let out its eerie cry, making her jump. She picked up her heavy wooden pail and hurried back to the clearing.

It seemed the hunting had gone well, because the men were in high spirits as they stood in a circle gazing down at their prize. Leofwin saw her coming through the trees; his face lit up as he reached out for her, but his eyes were strangely cold, cruel, almost.

'See what we have here, princess,' he said softly. 'A fine day's hunting.'

Elena, bewildered by his mysterious air, stepped forward into the circle of men and looked down.

An unconscious man lay bound on the mossy turf. A soldier. Stripped of his chain-mail and helmet, he lay limp and defenceless in his linen tunic, his arms trussed behind his back, his legs tightly bound. She couldn't see his face, but his hair was thick and tawny, and streaked with blood.

She let out a low cry.

'Recognise him?' said Leofwin with grim satisfaction. 'Aimery the Breton – ours at last! We got him away from his companions on the road to Lincoln, though he still put up a damned stubborn fight.'

Elena whispered, 'Is – is he dead?'

Leofwin laughed shortly. 'Not yet. I promised the others we'd have some fun with him before he breathes his last.' He pushed at Aimery's shoulder with his booted foot, turning him onto his side; Elena's heart lurched sickly as she saw the familiar, strong-boned face, the silvery scar, the dried blood on his forehead. His eyes were closed, with shadows under them like bruises; and she saw that his leg was gashed, the blood seeping through his woollen hose. She dug her fingernails into her palms to stop herself crying out loud and said, as steadily as she could,

'The King would give a fine ransom for him. Lord Aimery saved his life once, in battle.'

Gyrth smiled chillingly. 'Don't worry, they'll give us gold for his body. When we've finished with him.'

'That's right.' Sahild stepped forward, her face a cold mask of triumph. 'And Elena will want to join in with his punishment. She'll want to see him beg aloud, and plead for death, won't you, Elena? Won't you?'

Elena felt the bile rise in her throat. Blindly, she stammered out, 'I must go. I've left things down by the stream – '

She got to the water's edge just in time. She leaned over the bank and retched helplessly. They were going to kill Aimery, and she realised that she couldn't bear it.

When she got back, her pale face outwardly composed and calm, the outlaws were drinking and celebrating. Their laughter was wine-soaked and coarse; they talked determinedly of vengeance. Suddenly to

229

Elena her summer idyll seemed a summer lie. Even the twins, of whom she'd grown so fond, had a hard, cruel light in their eyes. They all hated Aimery so much.

She forced herself to take her usual place in their circle beside Leofwin, and said quietly, 'Where is he?'

Sahild said scornfully, 'Where he should be. Bound to the old oak by the stone – ready for us. Though we hardly needed to bother to tie him up. With that leg injury he won't get far.'

Leofwin said, 'It's nothing serious. Tonight he'll stay where he is, and tomorrow we'll feed him, restore him to some semblance of strength. Then – we'll begin.'

His calm words chilled Elena to the bone. She bowed her head, her eyes dark with distress, and pretended to drink the mead they offered her in celebration.

The injured, helpless Aimery le Sabrenn was to be their next sacrifice.

Sahild watched the convent girl with cold scorn. How she despised her. She'd come amongst them uninvited, with her innocent blue eyes and soft feminine ways, and cast her spell over the menfolk until they were all besotted with her.

No-one had listened to Sahild when she warned them that the convent girl was a spy. They wouldn't listen to her now – she knew better than to try. But she, Sahild, had heard the girl moan out the Breton's name in her sleep; she'd watched her face go pale every time he was mentioned, and had followed her secretly as she went down to the stream to be sick.

Sahild thought she knew how to deal with her. She caught Freya's hand quietly in the darkness. 'Freya. You know those stories you mentioned about the Breton?'

Freya nodded avidly. 'Yes. Oh, yes!'

'Then let's,' said Sahild, 'find out if they are true.'

Chapter Fifteen

*A*imery stirred and groaned as consciousness returned. His head hammered painfully from the blow that had finally felled him. He remembered, with a brief grimace at his own stupidity, how the Saxons who waited in ambush on the road to Lincoln, had lured him away from his men, yelling to him that they had Hamet and were about to kill him.

A trick, of course. He realised it the instant before the blow that felled him, when he saw the Saracen galloping wildly towards him – too late.

He shifted his limbs experimentally; his leg throbbed damnably where a sword had caught him a glancing blow. Fortunately the wound was superficial, but it was enough to slow him down. Not that he'd get away tonight, with these leather thongs round his wrists and ankles, strapping him to the tree.

Judging by the position of the moon and stars, it was well past midnight. There was a curious raised stone slab in the middle of the shadowy clearing; he thought wryly of pagan ceremonies, of tales of human sacrifice. Then he shut his eyes and tried to empty his mind, as he'd taught himself to do during the long night before a battle. Waiting for dawn, possibly for death.

He was brought back to reality by the sound of whispered giggles. He opened his eyes, startled, and saw two women approaching him stealthily in the darkness. One was plumply pretty, with curling blonde hair; while the other was slender and boyish, with her silver hair cropped short like a soldier's around her elfin face.

'There!' whispered the plump one. 'I told you he'd be awake!'

They stood in front of him, assessing him. 'Greetings, Breton,' said the short-haired one softly. 'My name is Sahild. And this is Freya. We've come to get better acquainted with you.'

Saxon witches, thought Aimery to himself.

Freya was saying, nervously, 'What if Leofwin finds out we're here? Won't he be angry?'

'He won't even know.' Sahild laughed chillingly.

Aimery listened grimly, his face expressionless. They talked of Leofwin – the Saxon leader Elena had helped to escape. Her beautiful face still haunted him, damn her.

Then he braced himself, expecting death, because the Saxon elf-witch Sahild had drawn a wicked knife from her belt, and was holding the point at his throat.

She smiled, chillingly. Then to his surprise she started to cut at his tunic, ripping the linen away from his chest, slashing at the lacings of his hose so that they fell in tatters round his leather boots, fragments of fabric clinging to the dried blood on his leg.

Then she went very still, the knife still poised in her hand, while Freya edged up close to his other side, her eyes wide.

'Oh,' Freya sighed happily, 'It's true, what they say! He's so beautiful!'

And with eager fingers she began to stroke his pinioned shoulders, running her palms over the ridged muscle of his bronzed chest, sliding down to the flat plane of his stomach where the dark, silky mat of hair

232

arrowed down to his groin. His phallus hung long and thick between his iron-hard thighs.

Aimery's eyes glittered. 'I suppose,' he said calmly, 'that it's a long time since you've seen a real man.'

The girl Sahild whipped the point of her blade to his neck, nicking his throat. 'So you speak Saxon, do you? Arrogant scum!' She turned to the other girl, who was stroking the rough silk of his heavily muscled legs with rapt attention. 'Time to teach the Breton some manners, Freya!'

Freya whispered keenly, 'What are we going to do?'

'We're going to humiliate him,' said Sahild. She smiled, and Aimery felt a shiver of unease ripple down his spine. Already his phallus was stirring though he fought hard for control.

Then the two blonde Saxon witches began to undress in front of him, and he groaned inwardly.

'See here, Breton,' Sahild was whispering. She was slim-ipped and boyish, apart from her pointed breasts. 'Wouldn't you like a taste of this?' And she stood in front of him with her hands on her hips, dressed only in her soft deerskin boots, her body firm and lithe in the moonlight.

His lip curled. 'Saxon slut,' he said. 'You think you can interest me?'

Sahild gasped, then she reached out to grip his heavy testicles, laughing softly. She twisted hard. 'I know I can interest you,' she said. 'Animal. Animal.'

Freya gave a little cry of delight, wriggling her plump breasts. 'Look at him, Sahild! Oh, look!' She was gasping in pleasure as the Breton's heavy phallus stirred into life. The blood pulsed along the thick, veined shaft that prodded hungrily against Sahild's cool hands as she caressed and squeezed his big, velvety sac.

Aimery shut his eyes, trying to fight his helpless arousal with all his iron strength; but the girl's cool hands were too much. He clenched his fists tightly in their bonds and waited, resigned, knowing that he was fully erect.

Freya's eyes widened as she gazed on the massive shaft that reared so powerfully from the pinioned Breton's loins. 'Oh, Sahild,' she whispered, licking her lips. 'Please – can I?' And she reached to touch.

'One moment,' said Sahild sternly. 'We're going to make the most of this, you and I.'

It was then that Aimery saw that she'd brought ropes with her. She was clever and resourceful, this elf-witch – he'd give her that. With nimble fingers, she retied him at the wrists with a long loop of rope, which she secured to the tree. Then she cut his old bonds, and forced him to slide down and kneel on the ground with his back against the tree trunk, his arms stretched taut above his head. He resisted, every inch of the way; but she held the knife to his throat menacingly.

'Fight any more, Breton, and you're dead. Now for the real test. You think you can defy us. We know you can't.' She moistened her lips salaciously, running her narrowed eyes over his bronzed, naked flesh. 'We're going to pleasure you, Freya and I. And every time you give in to us – every time you climax – we shall punish you.'

The kneeling prisoner laughed bitterly. 'You'll be disappointed then.' His erection had subsided during his struggles; he felt coldly unaroused.

'Oh,' said Sahild, 'I don't think so. Freya – he's yours.'

With a little sigh of pleasure Freya sank to her knees beside the Breton and rubbed her palms against his hardening nipples; then she thrust out her ripe breasts, grinding their soft flesh against him. She then bent to touch his long, lazy phallus where it lay along his bent thigh; Aimery fought silently for control, and won.

Sahild broke in. 'It seems you have a certain amount of restraint, my fine lord Aimery. Either that, or you've got a problem. Let's find out what really excites you, shall we?'

'Not you,' drawled Aimery, 'that's for sure.'

She hissed in anger. Turning her back on him, she went over to her discarded clothes, and came back with her leather belt and another, unfamiliar object that gleamed in the moonlight. She handed the belt to the crestfallen Freya. Then she held out her hands, to show him what she carried.

It was a thick bone, he realised with a shock; sun-bleached and pale, from some animal in the forest. At least, he hoped it was an animal, he thought wryly. As long as his arm from wrist to elbow, it had been carved and polished into the familiar, obscene shape of a man's phallus, the knob at either end ground down and rounded smoothly.

Sahild stood in front of him, her booted feet planted firmly apart, so he was looking up at her slender brown thighs. Gazing down at her captive defiantly, she gripped the thick bone phallus and slowly, licking her lips, began to slide the smooth, rounded head up between the pink, glistening lips that peeped from between her golden fleece. 'Oh,' she murmured lasciviously, 'that's good. So good.'

Aimery said, 'Is that what you use when your man can't get it up?'

She stopped, her face frozen with malice. Then she said, 'Hit him, Freya – with the belt. Hit him hard.'

Obediently Freya unfolded the belt and drew it down hard across his bent thighs, inches from his somnolent penis. Aimery jerked in his bonds and bit his lip; she hit him again, her face intent. Sahild drew the obscene bone phallus from her damp vulva and rubbed its glistening tip across her small pointed breasts, her lips parted in pleasure as she drank in the Breton's humiliation.

'Watch,' she said, 'watch and enjoy. You want me really, don't you? You wish it was you, ramming up me like this . . .' She stood almost astride him now, her vulva inches from his face; he could smell the musky, animal scent of her. She slid the bone phallus up inside herself again, her face glazed with ecstasy, and drove herself swiftly to orgasm, shuddering and heaving as the sweet pleasure racked her body.

Aimery's penis jerked hungrily, rearing up towards her, and he shut his eyes. Sahild gazed with pleasure at his darkly massive erection. 'Do you still want to tell me, Breton, that you don't find me exciting?'

He forced a cold smile. 'Is that the best you can do? I've seen old whores on the streets of Rouen that put up a better show.'

Sahild's eyes went very pale, and her eyes glittered. 'Oh, you'll be sorry for that, you bastard. Very sorry. Freya, do what you want with him. Afterwards, we'll punish him properly.'

With a rapturous sigh, the plump girl positioned her legs on either side of the kneeling prisoner, and squatted astride his lips. Her eyes half-closed already in rapture, she parted her swollen sex lips with loving care and rubbed her cleft juicily along the velvety tip of his hungry phallus, moaning softly to herself.

Aimery clenched his teeth.

Shuddering, Freya slid down on the full length of his penis, gasping with delight, caressing her bouncing breasts with fevered fingers. 'Oh, Sahild,' she whispered. 'I don't think I can last very long! He's so deep inside me, so strong and cool. I've never known anything like it – '

'Ride him, then,' said Sahild sharply. 'Take him with you to the brink. Make him spend himself inside you! I want to see him groan.'

And Freya did as she was told, bouncing up and down in delirious ecstasy, her love passage tight and juicy around the Breton's massive shaft.

Aimery fought his own climax dispassionately. The girl would climax very soon; he could tell by the wild twitching of her hungry inner flesh; and he was nowhere near. He watched with narrowed eyes as she trembled on the brink and ground herself wildly against him, gasping and muttering in the delicious throes of orgasm.

She collapsed against his chest, dazed with pleasure. Her weight hurt his leg, and he closed his eyes. At last she eased herself off him, still flushed and trembling. He was ramrod straight, his mouth set in a thin, hard line.

'Is that it?' he enquired with quiet scorn.

Sahild was still fingering her thick bone phallus, stroking her lips with it. 'No, it isn't,' she said softly.

They rearranged his bonds roughly so that he was forced to turn around on his knees and face the tree; his arms clasped round its trunk, his cheek rasped by the rough bark. His naked hips were forced into exposure. Sahild knelt behind him and slowly ran her hand over his tight, muscular buttocks. Then she licked her forefinger and slid it down the dark, hairy crease between his cheeks. She felt the little puckered hole tighten in shame; heard the hiss of the Breton's indrawn breath as he pressed his face against the tree.

'So,' she said. 'That's what you like, is it, Breton?' She lifted the bone phallus and gripped its cool length lovingly.

Elena couldn't sleep, for thinking about Aimery. Tomorrow the Saxons were going to kill him – slowly. Her dark longing for him burned in her blood, as it had from the first moment she met him. She couldn't bear to think of his suffering.

Holding her breath, she eased herself from the sleeping Leofwin's arms. He snored gently and turned over in his sleep, still sodden with wine. Silently she slipped into her tunic and crept out of the hut.

Sahild whirled round, hearing light footsteps coming through the trees. Quick as a flash, she slipped into the blackness at the edge of the clearing, dragging Freya with her.

As the covent girl drew near, Sahild pounced on her, smothering her cries by putting her hand over her mouth and holding the knife to her throat.

'One word, convent girl, and you're dead! What are you doing here?'

'I couldn't sleep.'

'You'll never sleep again, if you breathe a word of this to the others. Worried about your Breton, were you?'

Elena tried to fight down her panic. 'I – I don't know what you mean, Sahild!'

'I may not know everything,' said Sahild grimly. 'But I've been watching you, and I'd hazard a guess that you and the Breton were lovers! And I still think you're a spy. Coming to set him free, were you?'

Elena tried desperately to order her thoughts as the knife pricked at her throat. If Sahild ever guessed how she felt about Aimery . . .

'What are you two doing here, then?' she challenged, trying to sound cool and calm. 'Perhaps *you've* come to set him free!'

Sahild chuckled, relaxing her grip. 'Oh, no. You can see what we've been doing. Look!'

And she thrust Elena forward to the edge of the clearing, where she could see Aimery, bound and naked, his face pressed to the tree so he could see nothing.

Elena's heart pounded painfully as Sahild dragged her across to the prisoner. 'Now's your chance to prove that you're really one of us, convent girl. Otherwise I'll tell Leofwin that you're a spy! Here – take this, and use it on him!'

And she thrust the long bone phallus into Elena's trembling hand. 'What do you want me to do?' Elena whispered between white lips.

'What do you think?' hissed Sahild scornfully. She pushed Elena onto her knees behind the Breton. 'Shove it up his arse, of course – go on. Go on. Slide it behind

238

his tight cheeks – push – that's it! Go on, make him whine for mercy!'

And Elena, quivering with shame yet wildly excited at what she was being forced to do, gripped the thick phallus in her palm. She slid its rounded end tentatively up and down the tight crease between the Breton's cheeks; then, finding the brown, puckered little hole, she pushed blindly.

Aimery swore aloud in Breton, struggling to twist his head to see who was inflicting this new torment; but the ropes caught him, restraining him. Freya kneeled low by his hips, excitedly watching his straining phallus as it pulsed into erection again. 'Oh, he likes it, he likes it!'

Elena slid it in deeply, surprised at how easily it went in, feeling him clutch instinctively at its cool length with his rectal muscles. The pleasure and shame swept over her at his proud helplessness.

'Again!' hissed Sahild. 'Drive it in and out now – quickly – that's it! See how he quivers and throbs!' She leaned against the tree, next to the Breton's head, and whispered viciously in his ear. 'You like it really, don't you, my fine lord Aimery? You're nothing but a base-born mercenary, aren't you? And it shows!'

'You like feeling that cool shaft sliding deep inside your tight arse – filling you – fucking you. That's what you're used to, a slim young soldier's eager cock shoved up inside you! I can see your balls twitching and tightening. Any moment now, you'll be grovelling, pleading for more, before your hot seed shoots out. Then, if you're very lucky, we'll start again.'

Aimery gritted his teeth, his eyes closed. 'Anything you say. Just as long as I don't have to do it with you, Saxon whore.'

Sahild spat on him. It landed on his scarred cheek. She spat again; then she reached for her belt, and struck him across his broad, sweat-streaked brown shoulders so that he shook in his bonds.

Elena, hotly aroused herself, saw how his proud penis reared and jerked against his smooth belly; saw how his heavy balls tightened against his body. Oh, how she longed to soothe him in his extremity, to bring him the wild comfort of pleasure in the midst of his degradation! With frenzied fingers, she drove the bone phallus swiftly in and out of that pulsing rear entrance; Aimery let out a great groan, and strained against his bonds until she thought they would break.

His climax shook them all with its ferocity. His buttocks clenched tightly round the slippery bone phallus, almost dragging it from her grasp; his whole body shuddered, and the sperm jetted from his penis in great spurts, time and time again, until the soft earth beneath the tree was pooled with the milky fluid. Elena felt her own pleasure bud quiver hotly, wishing desperately that he was driving himself into her, instead. She leaned forward, greedily rubbing her hot breasts against his hard buttocks; her nipples hardened and peaked, and she felt the moisture gathering between her legs, longing for him.

Gently, so as not to hurt his still pulsing rectum, Elena withdrew the phallus, and pressed its length against her cleft, rolling it gently between her legs. It was enough. She climaxed silently but ferociously, the hot pleasure waves crashing over her as the shaft of hard bone soothed her throbbing little bud of flesh.

Sahild rolled up her belt, and nodded at her approvingly. 'You did well there, Elena. You earned your pleasure.'

Still dazed from orgasm, Elena nodded blindly, not realising what had happened.

Then, she heard the hiss of Aimery's indrawn breath, and she realised what Sahild had done. Aimery knew, now, who it was who had degraded him. He'd heard her name.

She froze in anguish. He knew. What could she do? If he let them know, let Sahild know what had existed between them, then she was lost, and all her plans were in vain. Sahild would drag her back, and denounce her to the others.

He was straining to turn his head, to see his tormentor, but his bonds stopped him. But she heard his voice, and it was dark with scorn. '*Saxon scum.*'

Then he sagged in his bonds, lapsing into semi-consciousness.

Sahild and Freya got dressed, chattering companionably as if nothing much had happened. Then they linked arms with Elena, not seeming to notice how pale and quiet she was, and wandered slowly back.

'What a wonderful evening,' sighed Freya rapturously. 'But what will they do with him tomorrow?'

Sahild shrugged. 'Whatever happens, they'll make sure that it's good sport for us.' She turned companionably to Elena. 'You did well tonight – really humiliated him. Maybe they'll let you help tomorrow.'

Elena, feeling sick and dazed, tried to smile. 'Maybe,' she acknowledged shakily.

They left Elena outside Leofwin's hut. She pushed the hide door aside and tiptoed in. She had already decided what she must do.

Leofwin was still asleep. Thank goodness he had drunk so much wine. Taking a deep breath, she went over to where his discarded clothes lay in a heap, and picked up his tunic and his knife. Then she crept out again; dawn was starting to break coldly in the east. After checking that Sahild and Freya were nowhere in sight, she plunged back towards the sinister grove, her heart beating wildly.

Aimery le Sabrenn was still slumped against the broad oak to which he was bound, his eyes closed, his face stubbled and shadowed with utter exhaustion.

Swallowing hard, Elena drew close to him, the knife gleaming in her hand. 'Aimery,' she whispered.

He looked up tiredly and saw the knife. 'So you've come to kill me now, have you?'

241

She flinched. 'No! I've come to set you free!'

His steely grey eyes narrowed in scorn. He grated out, 'What game is this?'

'No game, I swear!' Her small face grimly determined, she started to saw through the rope that bound his wrists. 'Aimery – I didn't want to hurt you, earlier. But I thought that if I didn't join in, the others would suspect!'

The knife sliced through the thick rope; one of his hands was free. She started on another cord; Sahild had been thorough.

Aimery said, his voice hard with scorn; 'You expect me to believe all this? What does your lover, Leofwin, think of your nocturnal wanderings?'

She caught her breath. 'He doesn't know. Quickly – oh, quickly! They'll be awake soon.'

Her knife severed the last strand of rope. He got slowly to his feet, testing his injured leg; he seemed big and naked and muscular in the grey light of sunrise. Elena shivered and pushed the clothing she'd brought towards his hands. 'Here – put these on! And go, please go. Don't you realise that they're going to kill you?'

'The thought had crossed my mind.'

Swiftly he pulled on Leofwin's tunic. He buckled the belt and looked at her suddenly, his familiar grey eyes burning into her. 'I thought you would be glad at my death.'

She gazed up at him, drinking in those strong, proud features; the cynically curved, beautiful mouth; the lean, stubborn jaw darkened now by stubble. Her small fists clenched round the knife; she burned for him, remembering the dark, glorious pleasure he'd revealed to her with his powerful body. 'Would I be here now if I wanted you dead?' she whispered in a low voice. He hesitated, suddenly uncertain.

'Please, please go, Aimery!' Daylight was spreading its cold light across the forest – someone might come, any moment now.

Too late! She moaned aloud at the sound of crashing footsteps plunging through the forest towards them. She whirled round. There – at the other side of the clearing: Gyrth, Leofwin, and Sahild! All heavily armed.

'There she is!' shouted Sahild triumphantly. 'See, she's cut him free – she's a spy – I knew it!' She raised her bow and took aim.

Before she could even cry out, Elena felt Aimery grab her. He held her in front of his body like a shield; then he snatched the knife from her nerveless hands and held the blade tight against her throat.

'Move any closer,' he called out ominously to the outlaws, 'and I'll kill her. Shoot, and *you'll* kill her.'

Sahild pulled her bowstring taut. 'Then I'll kill her, Breton, never fear! She's a spy, a traitor to her kind! After that, I'll kill you – you won't get far, with that leg!'

Elena, trapped tightly against Aimery's powerful body, saw Sahild's arrow aimed straight at her heart.

Then Leofwin moved. Before Sahild could release her bowstring, he swung his arm fiercely, knocking her over; then he turned to glare in helpless impotence at his enemy. 'Let her go, Breton!'

Aimery smiled chillingly, the white scar pulling at his mouth. 'Oh, no. I'm taking her with me, Leofwin. If you try to follow me, I'll kill her – slowly.'

Leofwin lurched forward blindly; Gyrth grabbed him and used all his strength to hold him back. 'Let her go, Leofwin – she's not worth it.'

Sahild, lying winded on the ground, gasped out, 'Fools! You should have let me kill them both!'

Swinging Elena round, Aimery pinioned her arms behind her back, gripping both her slender wrists in one strong hand. Then, the knife gripped ready in his other palm, he pushed her into the darkness of the forest, away from the clearing, away from the helpless outlaws. 'Move,' he hissed. 'Move, damn you!'

Chapter Seventeen

*T*he serfs toiled in the fields, wearily gathering in the last gleanings of the wheat harvest. Hard-faced reeves moved amongst them with whips. 'Faster. faster!' All eyes were on the heavy rain clouds piling up above the bleak moors to the west.

Elena worked blindly, beyond weariness. Last night, when they got back to Thoresfield, she'd been herded in with the other serfs, and at dawn she was sent to the fields with them. At least she'd not been thrown in the dungeons and flogged, as other runaways were. Or handed over to Isobel.

She shivered as the cold wind blew across the field and the first heavy raindrops started to fall from the leaden sky. Her back ached with stooping, and her fingers were raw from the stubble, but she scarcely noticed.

It all seemed like a dream now, yesterday's flight through the forest with Aimery. They'd sped breathlessly along the secret, grassy tracks beneath the trees, further and further from Leofwin and the outlaws. Aimery's injured leg dragged slightly, but otherwise his lean, hard body seemed untouched by his ordeal. He never once let go of her arm.

As the day wore on, the canopy of trees grew less dense, and the huge, mossy oaks started to give way to birch and bracken. It was then that Aimery stopped at last, breathing hard. Elena swayed for support against a tree, almost sobbing with fatigue.

He said, 'We're almost at the boundary of the forest. You can go back now. I don't need a hostage any more.'

'You know I can never go back.' Elena forced her voice to be steady. 'You know they'd kill me. For helping you to escape.'

His mouth thinned, pulling at his scar. 'I'm sure you can find some way to redeem yourself. Why did you do it?'

Her dark, fathomless blue eyes met his cold grey ones. 'Because I didn't want you to die,' she said in a low voice.

His lips curled in scorn. He gripped her chin, forcing her to look up at him again as she trembled at the touch of his lean brown fingers. 'You're full of tricks, little Elena, aren't you? Such fine excuses. How you enjoyed humiliating me with your friends!'

She shuddered, remembering the bone phallus and her own fierce, shameful excitement at this proud man's degradation. 'I had to do it – don't you see? Or they'd have suspected me, and then I wouldn't have been able to free you!'

'So clever,' he murmured coldly. 'So subtle, so ingenious . . .'

Slowly he ran his fingertips through her hair, lifting it and letting it fall like golden silk. Then he took her face in his hands and kissed her fiercely, the stubble of his jaw rasping at her soft cheek. The tears burned in her eyes.

He let her go, so suddenly that she almost fell. 'Someone's coming,' he said.

It was the soldiers, led by Hamet, who'd been scouring the forest ever since Aimery's capture.

Now she was back at Thoresfield, a forgotten serf. And she'd just heard from the other serfs that Aimery was leaving for the south, to join his king.

Isobel was in the hall, attending to a visitor – Godric, a Saxon thane who lived on a small neighbouring estate. He'd managed to hold on to his property by feigning illness when King Harold's summons to battle arrived, and then by vowing immediate allegiance to the victorious William. He was well aware that the lord Aimery utterly despised him, and he was glad to have audience with the lady Isobel instead.

'I need more workers, my lady,' he was explaining. 'The summer fever took so many of my serfs, and I've still half the harvest to get in and the threshing to be done. I heard that the lord Aimery was leaving shortly, and I thought maybe you'd be wanting rid of a few workers, before the winter sets in.'

Isobel was thinking hard. Aimery was out riding, inspecting his lands for a final inventory before he left. Now – now was her chance.

She hadn't been able to conceal her dismay when the little Saxon slut was brought back to Thoresfield on the back of Hamet's horse. And Aimery hadn't even punished her for running away! When Isobel had suggested that the girl be flogged, he told her curtly to mind her own business. The girl was still at large, even if she was out in the fields; still a threat to her, until she and Aimery were safely away from Thoresfield.

'Do you want women as well?' she asked Godric thoughtfully.

He grinned. 'If they're willing wenches, yes. If they're pretty, and will satisfy a few of the male slaves, then that's even better.'

'I know one who's just right for you,' said Isobel, her eyes gleaming. 'She's young, and extremely pretty – and she knows a lot of tricks. You'll probably want to try her out yourself before you hand her over to your men for their sport. You can have her for five pieces of gold.'

The man licked his fleshy lips. 'My lady. How can I thank you?'

'Just take her. Quickly.' Before Aimery gets back, she added silently to herself.

When Aimery and Hamet finally rode into the courtyard, the rain was falling steadily from an overcast sky. They'd been talking of the long journey to London, then perhaps to Normandy where William was again involved in defending his lands against the troublesome Fulk of Anjou. When they got to the stables, Aimery dismounted quickly and led his big black horse inside, dismissing the groom and starting to unfasten the girth himself, as the rain pounded on the rye straw thatch overhead. Hamet followed him into the hay-scented warmth, checked that they were alone, and said hesitantly,

'About the girl, my lord. Be careful that you don't judge her too harshly.'

Aimery carried on unbuckling the saddle, his expression forbidding. 'Of whom, friend Hamet, are you talking?'

Hamet stood his ground. 'Elena, my lord.'

Aimery turned round to face him. 'She came here as a rebel spy. She set the rebel leader free, then ran off to join him and lived with him in the forest. And you think I judged her harshly? She's alive, isn't she?'

'You told me that it was the girl who freed you.'

Aimery turned to stroke his horse's thick black mane. He remembered the forest, remembered the three Saxon witches who'd degraded him until he broke. He remembered how he'd felt when he realised that one of them was Elena. He said, 'There are other things I've not told you, Hamet. Believe me, the girl's escaped lightly.'

Hamet bowed his dark head and said no more.

Aimery pushed past him into the wet courtyard. 'I've decided I'm leaving tonight. Prepare an escort, will you?'

Alys crouched in the shadows by the steps that led up to the hall. The heavy rain streamed down from the eaves, turning her mousy hair into straggling rats' tails and soaking her clothes. But she didn't care. She had to see the lord Aimery! She had to!

This afternoon, while he was out, they'd made sport of her again – the lady Isobel, with her minions, Morwith and Pierre. Isobel had called her up to her room, and told her that she had a new beauty salve that would make a woman wildly desirable to any man if she rubbed it into her most private parts. She'd given Alys a phial of it; Alys had rushed away and smeared it carefully where Isobel had suggested, on her nipples, between her legs.

Then, the ointment had started to tingle and burn, driving her into a frenzy of desire. The lady Isobel had called Alys back into her room, and made her watch while Morwith was serviced crudely on the floor by the virile Pierre. Alys was driven mad by lust as she watched, longing to feel Pierre's great thick penis cooling her own burning flesh; while Isobel had laughed at her. Laughed at her!

Alys had rushed off to wash away the tormenting salve in icy cold water, her heart burning with rage. And then, she'd seen the girl, Elena, roped and driven away with some other serfs by that brute Godric. She'd heard Isobel tell him to take them quickly, before Aimery returned.

Now, Alys waited in the pouring rain, her heart pounding, as Aimery's tall, familiar figure emerged from the stables and came towards the steps. If Isobel knew what Alys was about to tell him, that it was the lady de Morency who had freed the dangerous Saxon rebel, then hidden the key to the dungeons under the girl's pillow, then Isobel would kill her.

'My lord Aimery.'

'Yes?' He stopped mid-stride, his scarred face dangerous as the bedraggled woman stepped in front of him. 'My lord – I have something that I must tell you! Please – can we go somewhere private?'

Godric cursed as the rain poured down and turned the track to muddy sludge. Damn it, he'd be lucky to get home before nightfall with these sullen slaves. And the girl that Isobel had been so anxious for him to take – the pretty blonde one with the big blue eyes – she was giving him more trouble than the rest put together! While his surly reeve kept an eye on the rest of his purchases, he'd roped the blonde girl to his saddle, so she had to almost run to keep up, and he could keep an eye on her just by turning his head. But she was still a damned nuisance, arguing and complaining.

He reined in his horse, swearing vividly, and turned round in the saddle. She'd stopped yet again, her feet planted firmly in the mud, her head raised proudly even though he could see that she was white with tiredness.

'I won't go any further! You can't make me!'

'Can't I indeed!' He unfurled the vicious plaited whip he carried. 'We'll soon see about that, you stubborn wench.'

He broke off in surprise as he heard the thunder of a galloping horse's hooves pounding down the muddy track towards them. He squinted through the rain impatiently, and gasped in surprise.

Aimery. Aimery the Breton. Looking as black as thunder . . .

Godric watched stupefied as the big Breton soldier, his cloak dripping wet, pulled up his huge black horse beside the girl. Then he drew a knife from his belt, and started to cut her free.

249

'Hey!' Godric called out. 'My lord, I paid good money for that girl! Gave it to the lady Isobel, before witnesses. Ten pieces of gold.'

'Five,' replied the Breton curtly, and flung the money towards him so that it landed in the mud. Then he carried on slicing through the rope. The girl, Godric noted, looked dazed.

'My lord!' said Godric fussily. 'I don't, as it happens, choose to sell her back to you! I particularly singled her out – after all, she'll be no use to you once you've left Thoresfield! The lady Isobel told me she was very skilled, with lots of tricks. A clever little whore, she said – '

Aimery stopped then. He came up to the man, Godric, in three powerful strides; pulled him off his horse, and hit him so hard on the chin that he landed on his back in the squelching mud.

Then he picked up the girl in his arms and set her on his big horse. Swinging up in the saddle behind her, he held her tightly in his arms and swung his horse back towards Thoresfield.

Aimery the Breton carried her through the courtyard, where his men, preparing for the imminent journey south, looked on in silent amazement; then through the hall and up to his room, where he slammed the door shut.

He laid his burden carefully on the thick wolfskin pelts that covered his big bed, then went to put more logs on the fire, kicking at the embers with his booted foot to get the flames leaping higher.

Elena struggled to sit up, her soaking tunic clinging to her skin. Her teeth were chattering with the cold. 'W – why did you come after me?' she whispered.

'Because I didn't damn well know you'd gone!' He stood with his back to the flames, towering over her, his face dangerously angry. But, she realised with a little thud of her heart, *not with her* . . . When he looked down at her, his grey eyes burned not with anger, but with tenderness.

She swallowed hard, fighting down the painful hope, and pushed the soaked tendril of hair from her pale cheeks. Then she began to shiver, uncontrollably.

Aimery le Sabrenn cursed under his breath, and strode towards her. Swiftly he peeled her soaked garments from her chilled skin; then he fetched a warm woollen cloak from the coffer by the bed and wrapped her in it. He pulled the luxurious wolfskin cover from the bed and laid it on the floor before the fire. Then he picked her up in his arms as if she weighed no more than a feather, and laid her down on it.

Elena shivered more than ever, but not just with the cold. It was the way he looked at her – the way those hard, steely grey eyes burned into her.

She lay curled on the thick fur, wrapped in his cloak, the flames leaping and dancing in the darkening room, the rain pounding down outside the window. The cloak he'd wrapped her in slid apart; he bent to kiss her exposed breasts, his mouth burning hot against her cold skin. The fierce pleasure knifed through her.

He stood up, his face darkly intent, and started to remove his own clothes. She gazed up at him silently, drinking in his wide-shouldered, masculine beauty; his long, heavily-muscled legs covered with silky dark hair; his proud, mysterious phallus, which stirred already with life against his inner thigh.

He knelt to lie beside her, naked, and took her in his arms. His body was gloriously strong and warm against her own cold, trembling flesh. He pressed her close to him, silently covering her face with kisses; she wondered if she was dreaming. This must be a dream. And he was leaving tonight.

His hands roved across her back and her hips, warming her, melting her. When he knelt to kiss her secret flesh, she shuddered with desire, tangling her fingers wantonly in his thick damp hair; his tongue was hot and wonderful as it slid languorously between her lips, driving her into a frenzy of molten desire. She reached out to clutch at his massively erect penis, stroking its silken length with silent rapture, tenderly caressing the velvety sac of his scrotum, feeling him pulse and quicken beneath her fingers.

He entered her quickly, his own desire burning hard at his loins; but then he pleasured her slowly, withdrawing almost to the brink and then sliding in again, filling her, caressing her, until she writhed her hips deliriously against the fur-covered floor and wrapped her ankles tightly around his strong thighs. He held her wrists to the ground on either side of her head, pinioning her gently, and bent to kiss her breasts, teasing and drawing out her rosy teats until she gasped with longing, her hips thrusting blindly towards him, her face flushed.

He smiled softly, and began to plunge his massive shaft deep within her, faster and faster, every powerful stroke driving her quivering bud of pleasure into a rapturous orgy of need, until she exploded in a shimmering frenzy, clutching blindly with her moist inner flesh at the wonderful phallus that filled her so exquisitely. Then he drove himself to his own powerful climax, jerking strongly within her still-pulsing flesh. and collapsed beside her, damp with perspiration.

Elena lay sated in his arms, her eyes closed. She didn't want this moment, this languorous, perfect peace, ever to end.

But reality pressed in. Outside the window, below in the great hall, she could hear the sounds of Aimery's knights, preparing to leave.

The pain sliced through her. He was leaving, and taking Isobel with him. Oh, why hadn't he just let her go with that man Godric, instead of bringing her back to remind her that there could never, ever be another man to compare with him?

She twisted her head away; he leaned up on one

elbow, the firelight warm on his face, and touched her eyelashes gently. 'Elena. Why are you crying, Elena?'

His voice was husky and tender, and it twisted her heart. She fought back her tears furiously and sat up, clutching his warm cloak around her naked shoulders and staring blindly into the fire. 'Why did you bring me back, Aimery?'

'Isn't that obvious, *caran*?'

Caran. Beloved . . . Her heart thumped wildly, making her dizzy. She whispered, 'No, it isn't obvious. I don't understand.'

He sat up beside her and clasped her in his arms so that her cheek was against his shoulder. 'I've been wrong, Elena – about a lot of things. Chiefly, I failed to realise just how much Isobel hated you.'

Elena, hardly daring to breathe, whispered, 'I thought it was *you* who hated me.'

'Never. Oh, never.' He drew her towards him, and tenderly kissed her hair. 'Elena – if the rebels had caught you, they would have killed you for helping me to escape. Why did you do it?'

'I – I couldn't bear it. They were going to kill you, Aimery.'

'I'm a soldier. I've faced death – and worse – many times.'

Her voice was low. 'I've told you – I couldn't bear it.'

He was silent; she read it as coldness. Someone, one of his men, thumped on the door outside and called out, 'My lord! The men are ready, and your horse is saddled up!'

'I'll be with you shortly.' But still, he didn't move.

He was leaving her – any minute, he was leaving her. Elena swallowed down the agonising ache in her throat and forced her voice to be clear and cool. 'What will happen to me when you go to join the king?'

His hands tightened round her shoulders. '*Caran*. You're going to join me, of course.'

The blood pounded dizzily in her head. 'But – Isobel?'

'Isobel,' he said softly, 'leaves at dawn tomorrow – by herself. Where she goes, I don't particularly care.'

He stood up slowly, still holding her, and she clung to him, unable to stop trembling now.

'I'll send for you, *caran*. Hamet is staying here for a while – he'll take care of you. As soon as I know where the king is posting me, I'll send for you.'

'Are you going to fight? In France?'

'Most likely. The king has need of me there.'

'But you might be killed.'

'It's my occupation, Elena. My life.' He smiled down at her anxious face. There was another, harsher knock on the door. 'My lord Aimery! Your men await you!'

Aimery said, 'I must go.' She lifted her face to him proudly, her eyes shining for him. 'At least, now,' she said softly, 'I know what love is.'

He kissed her with infinite tenderness, a promise of future passion; then he left the room.

She went to the window, in a trance, and gazed out into the sullen grey drizzle of the courtyard. She watched him mount his black horse, pull its strong head round towards the open gates, and set off at the head of his men.

He turned round once and looked up at the window where she stood. He raised his hand in silent salute, and rode out of the gates, heading south to fight for his king.

BLACK
lace

NO LADY
Saskia Hope
30-year-old Kate dumps her boyfriend, walks out of her job and sets off in search of sexual adventure. Set against the rugged terrain of the Pyrenees, the love-making is as rough as the landscape. Only a sense of danger can satisfy her longing for erotic encounters beyond the boundaries of ordinary experience.

ISBN 0 352 32857 6

WEB OF DESIRE
Sophie Danson
High-flying executive Marcie is gradually drawn away from the normality of her married life. Strange messages begin to appear on her computer, summoning her to sinister and fetishistic sexual liaisons with strangers whose identity remains secret. She's given glimpses of the world of The Omega Network, where her every desire is known and fulfilled.

ISBN 0 352 32856 8

BLUE HOTEL
Cherri Pickford
Hotelier Ramon can't understand why best-selling author Floy Pennington has come to stay at his quiet hotel in the rural idyll of the English countryside. Her exhibitionist tendencies are driving him crazy, as are her increasingly wanton encounters with the hotel's other guests.

ISBN 0 352 32858 4

CASSANDRA'S CONFLICT
Fredrica Alleyn
Behind the respectable facade of a house in present-day Hampstead lies a world of decadent indulgence and darkly bizarre eroticism. The sternly attractive Baron and his beautiful but cruel wife are playing games with the young Cassandra, employed as a nanny in their sumptuous household. Games where only the Baron knows the rules, and where there can only be one winner.

ISBN 0 352 32859 2

THE CAPTIVE FLESH
Cleo Cordell

Marietta and Claudine, French aristocrats saved from pirates, learn their invitation to stay at the opulent Algerian mansion of their rescuer, Kasim, requires something in return; their complete surrender to the ecstasy of pleasure in pain. Kasim's decadent orgies also require the services of the handsome blond slave, Gabriel – perfect in his male beauty. Together in their slavery, they savour delights at the depths of shame.

ISBN 0 352 32872 X

PLEASURE HUNT
Sophie Danson

Sexual adventurer Olympia Deschamps is determined to become a member of the Légion D'Amour – the most exclusive society of French libertines who pride themselves on their capacity for limitless erotic pleasure. Set in Paris – Europe's most romantic city – Olympia's sense of unbridled hedonism finds release in an extraordinary variety of libidinous challenges.

ISBN 0 352 32880 0

BLACK ORCHID
Roxanne Carr

The Black Orchid is a women's health club which provides a specialised service for its high-powered clients; women who don't have the time to spend building complex relationships, but who enjoy the pleasures of the flesh. One woman, having savoured the erotic delights on offer at this spa of sensuality, embarks on a quest for the ultimate voyage of self-discovery through her sexuality. A quest which will test the unique talents of the exquisitely proportioned male staff.

ISBN 0 352 32888 6

ODALISQUE
Fleur Reynolds

A tale of family intrigue and depravity set against the glittering backdrop of the designer set. Auralie and Jeanine are cousins, both young, glamorous and wealthy. Catering to the business classes with their design consultancy and exclusive hotel, this facade of respectability conceals a reality of bitter rivalry and unnatural love.

ISBN 0 352 32887 8

OUTLAW LOVER
Saskia Hope

Fee Cambridge lives in an upper level deluxe pleasuredome of technologically advanced comfort. The pirates live in the harsh outer reaches of the decaying 21st century city where lawlessness abounds in a sexual underworld. Bored with her predictable husband and pampered lifestyle, Fee ventures into the wild side of town, finding an an outlaw who becomes her lover. Leading a double life of piracy and privilege, will her taste for adventure get her too deep into danger?

ISBN 0 352 32909 2

THE SENSES BEJEWELLED
Cleo Cordell

Willing captives Marietta and Claudine are settling into an opulent life at Kasim's harem. But 18th century Algeria can be a hostile place. When the women are kidnapped by Kasim's sworn enemy, they face indignities that will test the boundaries of erotic experience. Marietta is reunited with her slave lover Gabriel, whose heart she previously broke. Will Kasim win back his cherished concubines? This is the sequel to *The Captive Flesh*.

ISBN 0 352 32904 1

GEMINI HEAT
Portia Da Costa

As the metropolis sizzles in freak early summer temperatures, twin sisters Deana and Delia find themselves cooking up a heatwave of their own. Jackson de Guile, master of power dynamics and wealthy connoisseur of fine things, draws them both into a web of luxuriously decadent debauchery. Sooner or later, one of them has to make a life-changing decision.

ISBN 0 352 32912 2

VIRTUOSO
Katrina Vincenzi

Mika and Serena, darlings of classical music's jet-set, inhabit a world of secluded passion. The reason? Since Mika's tragic accident which put a stop to his meteoric rise to fame as a solo violinist, he cannot face the world, and together they lead a decadent, reclusive existence. But Serena is determined to change things. The potent force of her ravenous sensuality cannot be ignored, as she rekindles Mika's zest for love and life through unexpected means. But together they share a dark secret.

ISBN 0 352 32907 6

MOON OF DESIRE
Sophie Danson

When Soraya Chilton is posted to the ancient and mysterious city of Ragzburg on a mission for the Foreign Office, strange things begin to happen to her. Wild, sexual urges overwhelm her at the coming of each full moon. Will her boyfriend, Anton, be her saviour – or her victim? What price will she have to pay to lift the curse of unquenchable lust that courses through her veins?

ISBN 0 352 32911 4

FIONA'S FATE
Fredrica Alleyn

When Fiona Sheldon is kidnapped by the infamous Trimarchi brothers, along with her friend Bethany, she finds herself acting in ways her husband Duncan would be shocked by. For it is he who owes the brothers money and is more concerned to free his voluptuous mistress than his shy and quiet wife. Alessandro Trimarchi makes full use of this opportunity to discover the true extent of Fiona's suppressed, but powerful, sexuality.

ISBN 0 352 32913 0

HANDMAIDEN OF PALMYRA
Fleur Reynolds

3rd century Palmyra: a lush oasis in the Syrian desert. The beautiful and fiercely independent Samoya takes her place in the temple of Antioch as an apprentice priestess. Decadent bachelor Prince Alif has other plans for her and sends his scheming sister to bring her to his Bacchanalian wedding feast. Embarking on a journey across the desert, Samoya encounters Marcus, the battle-hardened centurion who will unearth the core of her desires and change the course of her destiny.

ISBN 0 352 32919 X

OUTLAW FANTASY
Saskia Hope

For Fee Cambridge, playing with fire had become a full time job. Helping her pirate lover to escape his lawless lifestyle had its rewards as well as its drawbacks. On the outer reaches of the 21st century metropolis the Amazenes are on the prowl; fierce warrior women who have some unfinished business with Fee's lover. Will she be able to stop him straying back to the wrong side of the tracks? This is the sequel to *Outlaw Lover*.

ISBN 0 352 32920 3

THE SILKEN CAGE
Sophie Danson

When University lecturer Maria Treharne inherits her aunt's mansion in Cornwall, she finds herself the subject of strange and unexpected attention. Her new dwelling resides on much-prized land; sacred, some would say. Anthony Pendorran has waited a long time for the mistress to arrive at Brackwater Tor. Now she's here, his lust can be quenched as their longing for each other has a hunger beyond the realm of the physical. Using the craft of goddess worship and sexual magnetism, Maria finds allies and foes in this savage and beautiful landscape.

ISBN 0 352 32928 9

RIVER OF SECRETS
Saskia Hope & Georgia Angelis

When intrepid female reporter Sydney Johnson takes over someone else's assignment up the Amazon river, the planned exploration seems straightforward enough. But the crew's photographer seems to be keeping some very shady company and the handsome botanist is proving to be a distraction with a difference. Sydney soon realises this mission to find a lost Inca city has a hidden agenda. Everyone is behaving so strangely, so sexually, and the tropical humidity is reaching fever pitch as if a mysterious force is working its magic over the expedition. Echoing with primeval sounds, the jungle holds both dangers and delights for Sydney in this Indiana Jones-esque story of lust and adventure.

ISBN 0 352 32925 4

VELVET CLAWS
Cleo Cordell

It's the 19th century; a time of exploration and discovery and young, spirited Gwendoline Farnshawe is determined not to be left behind in the parlour when the handsome and celebrated anthropologist, Jonathan Kimberton, is planning his latest expedition to Africa. Rebelling against Victorian society's expectation of a young woman and lured by the mystery and exotic climate of this exciting continent, Gwendoline sets sail with her entourage bound for a land of unknown pleasures.

ISBN 0 352 32926 2

THE GIFT OF SHAME
Sarah Hope-Walker

Helen is a woman with extreme fantasies. When she meets Jeffrey – a cultured wealthy stranger – at a party, they soon become partners in obsession. In the debauched opulence of a Parisian retreat, and a deserted island for millionaires, they act out games of master and servant. Now nothing is impossible for her, no fantasy beyond his imagination or their mutual exploration.

ISBN 0 352 32935 1

SUMMER OF ENLIGHTENMENT
Cheryl Mildenhall

Karin's new-found freedom is getting her into all sorts of trouble. The enigmatic Nicolai has been showing interest in her since their chance meeting in a cafe. But he's the husband of a valued friend and is trying to embroil her in the sexual tension he thrives on. She knows she shouldn't succumb to his advances, but he is so charming. With Dominic and Carl – two young racing drivers – also in pursuit of her feminine charms, Karin is caught in an erotic puzzle only she can resolve.

ISBN 0 352 32937 8

A BOUQUET OF BLACK ORCHIDS
Roxanne Carr

The exclusive Black Orchid health spa has provided Maggie with a new social life and a new career, where giving and receiving pleasure of the most sophisticated nature takes top priority. But her loyalty to the club is being tested by the presence of Tourell; a powerful man who makes her an offer she finds difficult to refuse. Captivated by his charm, but eager to maintain her very special relationship with Antony and Alexander, will she be making the right decisions?

ISBN 0 352 32939 4

JULIET RISING
Cleo Cordell

At Madame Nicol's exclusive but strict 18th-century academy for young ladies, the bright and wilful Juliet is learning the art of courting the affections of your noblemen. But her captivating beauty tinged with a hint of cruelty soon has its effects on the menfolk nearer the college. Andreas, the rugged and handsome gardener, and Reynard, a chap who will do anything to win her approval, even be a slave to her tireless demands.

ISBN 0 352 32938 6

DEBORAH'S DISCOVERY
Fredrica Alleyn

Deborah Woods is trying to change her life. Having just ended her long-term relationship and handed in her notice at work, she is ready for a little adventure. Meeting American oil magnate John Pavin III throws her world into even more confusion as he invites her to stay at his luxurious renovated castle in Scotland. Once there, she learns his desires, and those of his friends, are more bizarre and complex than she had realised. What looked like being a romantic holiday soon turns into a test of sexual bravery.

ISBN 0 352 32945 9

THE TUTOR
Portia Da Costa

Like minded libertines reap the rewards of their desire in this story of the sexual initiation of a beautiful young man. Rosalind Howard takes a post as personal librarian to a husband and wife, both unashamed sensualists keen to engage her into their decadent scenarios. Cataloguing their archive of erotica is interesting enough, but Rosalind is also expected to educate the young cousin of her employer. Having led a sheltered life, the young man is simmering with passions he cannot control.

ISBN 0 352 32946 7

THE HOUSE IN NEW ORLEANS
Fleur Reynolds

When she inherits her family home in the fashionable Garden district of New Orleans, Ottilie Duvier has every reason to think that her life will be plain sailing from there on. However, when she arrives to take possession of the mansion, she discovers it has been leased to the notorious Helmut von Straffen; a debauched German Count famous for his decadent Mardi Gras parties. Determined to oust him from the property, and see off the cunning manoeuvres of her scheming half-brother, she soon realises that not all dangerous animals live in the swamp!

ISBN 0 352 32951 3

ELENA'S CONQUEST
Lisette Allen

It's summer – 1070AD – and the gentle Elena is gathering herbs in the garden of the convent where she leads a peaceful, but uneventful, life. When Norman soldiers besiege the convent, they take Elena captive and present her to the dark and masterful Lord Aimery to satisfy his savage desire for Saxon women. Captivated by his powerful masculinity, she is horrified to discover that she is not the only woman in his castle. A battle of wits ensues between her and the decadent Lady Isobel; her cruel and beautiful rival.

ISBN 0 352 32950 5

WE NEED YOUR HELP . . .
to plan the future of women's erotic fiction –

– and no stamp required!

Yours are the only opinions that matter.

Black Lace is the first series of books devoted to erotic fiction by women for women.

We intend to keep providing the best-written, sexiest books you can buy. And we'd appreciate your help and valued opinion of the books so far. Tell us what you want to read.

THE BLACK LACE QUESTIONNAIRE

SECTION ONE: ABOUT YOU

1.1 Sex (*we presume you are female, but so as not to discriminate*)
Are you?
    Male   ☐
    Female   ☐

1.2 Age
    under 21   ☐   21–30   ☐
    31–40   ☐   41–50   ☐
    51–60   ☐   over 60   ☐

1.3 At what age did you leave full-time education?
    still in education   ☐   16 or younger   ☐
    17–19   ☐   20 or older   ☐

1.4 Occupation _____

1.5 Annual household income

      under £10,000 ☐   £10–£20,000 ☐

      £20–£30,000 ☐   £30–£40,000 ☐

      over £40,000 ☐

1.6 We are perfectly happy for you to remain anonymous; but if you would like to receive information on other publications available, please insert your name and address

    _____

    _____

    _____

    _____

SECTION TWO: ABOUT BUYING BLACK LACE BOOKS

2.1 How did you acquire this copy of *Elena's Conquest*?

    I bought it myself ☐   My partner bought it ☐

    I borrowed/found it ☐

2.2 How did you find out about Black Lace books?

    I saw them in a shop ☐

    I saw them advertised in a magazine ☐

    I saw the London Underground posters ☐

    I read about them in _____

    Other _____

2.3 Please tick the following statements you agree with:

    I would be less embarrassed about buying Black Lace books if the cover pictures were less explicit ☐

    I think that in general the pictures on Black Lace books are about right ☐

    I think Black Lace cover pictures should be as explicit as possible ☐

2.4 Would you read a Black Lace book in a public place – on a train for instance?

    Yes ☐   No ☐

SECTION THREE: ABOUT THIS BLACK LACE BOOK

3.1 Do you think the sex content in this book is:
 Too much ☐ About right ☐
 Not enough ☐

3.2 Do you think the writing style in this book is:
 Too unreal/escapist ☐ About right ☐
 Too down to earth ☐

3.3 Do you think the story in this book is:
 Too complicated ☐ About right ☐
 Too boring/simple ☐

3.4 Do you think the cover of this book is:
 Too explicit ☐ About right ☐
 Not explicit enough ☐

Here's a space for any other comments:

SECTION FOUR: ABOUT OTHER BLACK LACE BOOKS

4.1 How many Black Lace books have you read? ☐

4.2 If more than one, which one did you prefer?

4.3 Why?

SECTION FIVE: ABOUT YOUR IDEAL EROTIC NOVEL

We want to publish the books you want to read – so this is your chance to tell us exactly what your ideal erotic novel would be like.

5.1 Using a scale of 1 to 5 (1 = no interest at all, 5 = your ideal), please rate the following possible settings for an erotic novel:

Medieval/barbarian/sword 'n' sorcery ☐
Renaissance/Elizabethan/Restoration ☐
Victorian/Edwardian ☐
1920s & 1930s – the Jazz Age ☐
Present day ☐
Future/Science Fiction ☐

5.2 Using the same scale of 1 to 5, please rate the following themes you may find in an erotic novel:

Submissive male/dominant female ☐
Submissive female/dominant male ☐
Lesbianism ☐
Bondage/fetishism ☐
Romantic love ☐
Experimental sex e.g. anal/watersports/sex toys ☐
Gay male sex ☐
Group sex ☐

Using the same scale of 1 to 5, please rate the following styles in which an erotic novel could be written:

Realistic, down to earth, set in real life ☐
Escapist fantasy, but just about believable ☐
Completely unreal, impressionistic, dreamlike ☐

5.3 Would you prefer your ideal erotic novel to be written from the viewpoint of the main male characters or the main female characters?

Male ☐   Female ☐
Both ☐

5.4 What would your ideal Black Lace heroine be like? Tick as many as you like:

Dominant	☐	Glamorous	☐
Extroverted	☐	Contemporary	☐
Independent	☐	Bisexual	☐
Adventurous	☐	Naive	☐
Intellectual	☐	Introverted	☐
Professional	☐	Kinky	☐
Submissive	☐	Anything else?	☐
Ordinary	☐	_____	

5.5 What would your ideal male lead character be like? Again, tick as many as you like:

Rugged	☐		
Athletic	☐	Caring	☐
Sophisticated	☐	Cruel	☐
Retiring	☐	Debonair	☐
Outdoor-type	☐	Naive	☐
Executive-type	☐	Intellectual	☐
Ordinary	☐	Professional	☐
Kinky	☐	Romantic	☐
Hunky	☐		
Sexually dominant	☐	Anything else?	☐
Sexually submissive	☐	_____	

5.6 Is there one particular setting or subject matter that your ideal erotic novel would contain?

_____

SECTION SIX: LAST WORDS

6.1 What do you like best about Black Lace books?

_____

6.2 What do you most dislike about Black Lace books?

_____

6.3 In what way, if any, would you like to change Black Lace covers?

_____

6.4 Here's a space for any other comments:

_____
_____
_____
_____
_____

Thank you for completing this questionnaire. Now tear it out of the book – carefully! – put it in an envelope and send it to:

Black Lace
FREEPOST
London
W10 5BR

No stamp is required if you are resident in the U.K.